P9-CJJ-000

HOT MAHOGANY

BOOKS BY STUART WOODS

FICTION

Santa Fe Dead§
Beverly Hills Dead
Shoot Him If He Runs†
Fresh Disasters†
Short Straw§
Dark Harbor†
Iron Orchid*
Two-Dollar Bill†
The Prince of Beverly Hills
Reckless Abandon†
Capital Crimes‡
Dirty Work†
Blood Orchid*
The Short Forever†
Orchid Blues*
Cold Paradise†
L.A. Dead†
The Run‡
Worst Fears Realized†
Orchid Beach*
Swimming to Catalina†
Dead in the Water†
Dirt†
Choke
Imperfect Strangers
Heat
Dead Eyes
L.A. Times
Santa Fe Rules§
New York Dead†
Palindrome
Grass Roots‡
White Cargo
Deep Lie‡
Under the Lake
Run Before the Wind‡
Chiefs‡

TRAVEL

A Romantic's Guide to the Country Inns of Britain and Ireland (1979)

MEMOIR

Blue Water, Green Skipper (1977)

*A Holly Barker Book †A Stone Barrington Book ‡A Will Lee Book §An Ed Eagle Book

HOT MAHOGANY

STUART WOODS

G. P. PUTNAM'S SONS NEW YORK

G. P. PUTNAM'S SONS
Publishers Since 1838
Published by the Penguin Group
Penguin Group (USA) Inc., 375 Hudson Street, New York, New York 10014, USA • Penguin Group (Canada), 90 Eglinton Avenue East, Suite 700, Toronto, Ontario M4P 2Y3, Canada (a division of Pearson Canada Inc.) • Penguin Books Ltd, 80 Strand, London WC2R 0RL, England • Penguin Ireland, 25 St Stephen's Green, Dublin 2, Ireland (a division of Penguin Books Ltd) • Penguin Group (Australia), 250 Camberwell Road, Camberwell, Victoria 3124, Australia (a division of Pearson Australia Group Pty Ltd) • Penguin Books India Pvt Ltd, 11 Community Centre, Panchsheel Park, New Delhi–110 017, India • Penguin Group (NZ), 67 Apollo Drive, Rosedale, North Shore 0632, New Zealand (a division of Pearson New Zealand Ltd) • Penguin Books (South Africa) (Pty) Ltd, 24 Sturdee Avenue, Rosebank, Johannesburg 2196, South Africa

Penguin Books Ltd, Registered Offices:
80 Strand, London WC2R 0RL, England

ISBN-13: 978-0-399-15515-4

Printed in the United States of America

Book Design by Stephanie Huntwork

This book is for John Mariani.

HOT MAHOGANY

1

Elaine's, late.

Stone Barrington breezed into the restaurant and found his former NYPD partner, Dino Bacchetti, waiting for him, Scotch in hand.

A waiter set a Knob Creek on the rocks before Stone, and he took a large sip.

"Where have you been?" Dino asked.

"You mean for the past week?"

"You've been gone a week?"

"Dino, remember when I went to Lakeland, Florida, to ground school for the new airplane? For a week?"

"That's where you've been?"

"No. I've been in Vero Beach, Florida, for flight training."

"For a week?"

"For three days."

"You have a new airplane?"

"Not exactly. I had the engine removed from my Piper Malibu Mirage and replaced with a turbine—that's a jet engine, turning a propeller. So now it's called a JetProp, and it's like a new airplane, and because it's like a new airplane, my insurance company insisted

I have flight training in it from a guy named John Mariani, in Vero Beach."

"Whatever you say."

"Dino, why don't you remember any of this? How much have you had to drink?"

"You think I'm drinking too much?"

"You seem to be in a state."

"What sort of state?"

"The word *stupor* leaps to mind."

"Genevieve will be here in a few minutes," Dino said. Genevieve James was Dino's girlfriend, a nurse in the ER at a nearby hospital.

"Good."

"When she gets here, don't leave me."

"Why not?"

"I'm in some sort of trouble."

"What kind of trouble?"

"I don't know, but if you're here, she won't hurt me."

"Well, I'm not getting in the middle of this," Stone said.

"Just sit there in your chair and don't say anything, and it'll be all right."

"Okay. I'll just sit here."

"Stone?" Dino was looking over Stone's shoulder, toward the door.

"Yes?"

"Have you seen Lance Cabot lately?" Cabot was the newly appointed deputy director for operations of the CIA. Both Dino and Stone had done consulting work for him.

"Not lately."

"Well, he looks like shit," Dino said. "He's aged years."

"How do you know this?"

"Because I'm looking at him right now."

Stone turned and looked toward the door. Lance Cabot stood

there, looking, as Dino had said, years older. He was also a bit disheveled, needed a haircut, and had at least a three-day growth of beard. His face was bruised.

"Good God, you're right," Stone said.

Lance was, ordinarily, the most fastidious of men, always perfectly dressed and groomed. Stone watched as Frank, one of the two headwaiters, greeted him and led him to a table at the rear of the restaurant.

"He didn't even look at us," Dino said. "Something's wrong.... Uh-oh," Dino said.

"What now?"

"Genevieve."

Stone turned to see the beautiful Genevieve enter the restaurant and head for their table. They both stood, while Dino held her chair, a sure sign of fear.

"How are you, Genevieve?" Stone said, giving her a kiss.

"I'm very well, Stone," she said, ignoring Dino. "How was your Malibu training?"

Stone shot a glance at Dino, who was looking very uncomfortable. "Hard work and great fun. The new airplane is faster, smoother, and quieter, only it's not a Malibu anymore; it's called a JetProp."

"I remember," she said.

"I'm going nuts," Dino said.

"What?"

"Lance just came in again, and he looks perfectly fine."

Stone turned and looked, and there he was, younger, undisheveled, unbruised, and perfectly groomed. "We're both going nuts," Stone said.

Lance came over to the table and greeted them all, shaking their hands. "Good evening," he said.

"Lance," Dino said, "you should be working as a magician."

"I beg your pardon?"

"Because, in addition to standing here, you're sitting back there." Dino pointed.

"Oh, that's my older brother, Barton Cabot."

"Ahhhhh," Dino and Stone said, simultaneously.

"He came in ahead of me while I finished a phone call in the car. If you'll excuse me, I'm going to join him, but Stone, I'd like to speak with you alone, after we've ordered dinner."

"Sure," Stone said. In his experience, when Lance spoke to him alone, trouble invariably followed.

Lance went to join his brother.

"Eerie resemblance," Genevieve said.

"Yeah," Dino agreed. "It's like Lance can know exactly how he'll look in a few years."

Genevieve spoke to Dino for the first time. "That's how you're going to look when I'm finished with you," she said.

Stone made a point of inspecting a row of photographs of Elaine's regulars on the opposite wall.

Elaine came over and sat down, exchanging kisses with Genevieve. Dino looked relieved to have her there. "So?" she said.

"I just got in," Stone replied.

"From where?"

"From Vero Beach, Florida."

"What for?"

"Dino will explain it to you," Stone said.

Lance came and tapped Stone on the shoulder. "Let's go into the next room for a minute," he said.

Dino looked anxious. "You'll be all right," Stone said. "Elaine is here."

"She'll help Genevieve," Dino said.

Stone got up and followed Lance into the dining room next door, where people occasionally threw parties and which Elaine used for overflow when the main room was full. They sat down at a table.

"I didn't know you had a brother," Stone said.

"I haven't had a brother for many years. Until tonight."

"Does he live in New York?"

"I don't know," Lance said.

"What?"

"I have no idea where he lives. Neither does he. That's the difficult thing."

Stone settled in for a story.

Stone thought Lance looked as though he needed a drink.

"Can I get you a drink, Lance?"

"Thank you, no. We've got a flap on—two agents missing in Afghanistan—and I have a meeting with the director in two hours."

"In the middle of the night?"

"I have to make a recommendation," Lance said. "We think we know where they are: Do we send in more people to get them and risk the lives of a hundred men, or do we call in an air strike and kill everybody."

"Including the two agents?"

"That's the decision. There's a chopper waiting for me at the West Side helipad. That's why I can't deal with this right now."

"Deal with what?"

"My brother, Barton."

"Start at the beginning, Lance."

"My brother is four years older than I. Barton has been a star all his life: In school, in sports, wherever he went, he was always the star. Our mother died in childbirth with me. When I was twelve, our father died, and Barton became a surrogate father. He joined the Marines during the war in Vietnam, right out of Harvard; got a commission, led a platoon. I was at Harvard then. By the time it was over he was a colonel, commanding a regiment. Nobody in the Marines had advanced so quickly since World War Two. He was sent to the War College and told he would be a general before long, perhaps a future chairman of the Joint Chiefs of Staff."

"Sounds like a spectacular career."

"It was, until he abruptly resigned his commission and disappeared."

"Disappeared?"

"Nobody could find him. I tried and failed. When I was giving my commencement speech at my graduation I looked down and saw him in the audience, but when the thing was over, he had disappeared again. I didn't see him again until tonight."

"So he abandoned you when you were in college?"

"Not entirely. My fees were paid, and a generous check arrived every month from a trust he had set up to receive my inheritance, since I was not yet of age. I wrote to him in care of the bank, but my letter was returned."

"But you heard from him tonight?"

"Not exactly. I had a call earlier this evening from a hospital in New York, saying that the police had found him, three days ago, unconscious, on the street. He had been beaten and, apparently, robbed, since he had no money or identification. His wristwatch had been taken, too. He was unconscious for around thirty hours, and when he woke, he didn't know who he was. The police tried to identify him, and today they finally got a match on his fingerprints and got hold of his service record, where I was listed as his next of kin. Somebody at the Pentagon recognized my name and called me."

"Has Barton recovered his memory?"

"Somewhat. He knows his name, he remembers me, but not

much else. No one has been able to find an address for him, since his wallet was stolen. That's why I need your help."

"What do you want me to do?"

"His doctor told me that this sort of amnesia is usually temporary; the memory comes back in bits and pieces. It's a good sign that he has begun to remember. The hospital had to discharge him, since he has recovered from the beating and he has a next of kin. They released him to me tonight. But I can't take him back to Langley with me, not in the middle of this crisis."

"Do you want me to find him a hotel?"

"I don't think that's a good idea just yet; he needs to regain his memory before he can be left alone."

"I suppose I could put him up at my house for a couple of days," Stone said.

"Thank you, Stone. I don't think he'll be any trouble; he's quite docile. I'd also like you, perhaps with Dino's help, to find out where he lives and, when he recovers himself, take him to his home."

"But you don't have any idea at all where he lives?"

Lance shook his head. "None." He looked at his watch. "There's a car waiting to take me to the helipad. Come and meet Barton." He got up and led Stone into the main dining room.

Barton Cabot was sitting at his table, talking in a companionable way with Elaine, who was sitting with him.

"Stone," Lance said, "this is my brother."

Barton rose and extended his hand. "Barton Cabot," he said. "Elaine and I were just catching up."

"You know Elaine?" Lance asked.

"He's an old customer," Elaine said. "Haven't seen him for at least twenty years."

"I remember being here," Barton said, "but not how I got here or why."

"That's good," Lance said. He sat down and turned to his brother. "Barton, I have to return to my office right now, but Stone, here, who is a good friend, is going to put you up at his house for a few days. You'll be very comfortable there." He slipped a card and some money into his jacket pocket. "My number is there, if you need to reach me. We'll catch up in a few days."

Barton nodded. "It's very good of you, Stone, to put me up," he said. "After all, I'm a perfect stranger, even to myself."

Stone shrugged. "Any brother of Lance's."

Lance stood up and motioned for Stone to follow him. "I'm very grateful for this, Stone," he said as they walked toward the door. He took a card from his pocket and scribbled a number on the back. "That's my cell number," he said. "I'll call you tomorrow to see how he is, but if there's any sort of emergency, you can reach me, night or day, at that number. He seems to be about your size; can you loan him some clothes?"

"Sure, but first let him have some dinner, then I'll get him home and to bed." They shook hands, and Lance went outside, got into a black SUV at the curb and was driven away.

Stone turned and went back to Barton Cabot's table. As he passed his own table he heard Genevieve and Dino.

"If you would just tell me what this is about," Dino was pleading.

"You *know* what it's about," Genevieve replied.

Stone kept walking. He sat down with Elaine and Barton and ordered some pasta, and the three of them had a quiet chat for a while. Barton kept up nicely, offered an opinion once in a while, and was charming, even witty. But he said nothing that seemed to require any direct memory of his circumstances.

Stone gave Barton his card, and he tucked it into a jacket pocket. "Thank you, Stone," he said.

Well, Stone thought, at least he can remember my name. He

excused himself to go to the men's room, and when he returned, both Barton and Elaine were no longer at the table. He saw Elaine sitting up front with some customers and walked up to her. "Where's Barton?" he asked.

"He left," she said. "Got into a cab. I put his dinner on your tab."

Stone hurried outside and looked up and down Second Avenue. There was no sign of Barton Cabot.

"Oh, shit," he said aloud to himself.

3

Stone went back into Elaine's and sat down with Dino and Genevieve, both of whom, he was grateful to see, had fallen silent.

"Dino, I need your help," he said.

"I'd better be going," Genevieve said, standing up.

"No, don't go," Stone said.

"I've got a night shift starting in a few minutes," she said. She pecked Stone on the cheek, fetched Dino a sweeping, openhanded blow to the back of the head, mussing his hair, and left.

"Why do I think you got off light?" Stone asked.

"I still don't know what it's about," Dino said, smoothing his hair.

"You may never know," Stone said. "I need your help." He explained about Lance's brother.

"And you let him walk out of here?" Dino asked, incredulous.

"I had to go to the john, all right? And besides, he was sitting, chatting with Elaine."

"You know Elaine spends her evening cruising tables."

"But why would he just walk out? He knew he was supposed to stay at my house tonight."

"You already told me the guy just barely knows who he is."

"But he's remembering more all the time."

"Maybe he remembered he had a late date."

"You're not helping."

"What do you want me to do? Put out an APB on him? He hasn't committed a crime, and there hasn't been a missing persons report filed, has there?"

"Not that I know of," Stone admitted.

"He's a grown man who's a little shaken up. Eventually, he'll remember more and go home."

"Lance asked me to take care of him."

"You're his brother's keeper? Isn't that *Lance's* job?"

"Lance has a flap on at Langley." Stone told Dino about the meeting with the director.

"Well, I don't envy him his problem," Dino admitted.

"There is something you can do."

"What?"

"Call the precinct and get somebody to do a search of driver's licenses in New York State for a Barton Cabot, then New Jersey and Connecticut, if necessary."

"I guess I can do that," Dino said, producing his cell phone. He pressed a speed-dial button and spoke briefly to someone, then snapped the phone shut. "They'll get back to me."

"I just don't understand where the guy could be going," Stone said.

"You said he took a cab?"

"Elaine said she saw him getting into one."

Dino got out his cell phone and made another call. "They'll call the cab companies and have them put out a radio call to their cabs, asking who picked up a fare at Elaine's and where they took him. It won't reach every cab, but we might get lucky. Shouldn't take long."

A waiter came over and said that Elaine would like to buy them an after-dinner drink, the way she always did. They ordered.

Dino's phone rang. "Bacchetti. Yeah. Yeah. You're sure? Thanks." He closed the phone. "A cab picked him up here and took him to Sotheby's."

"The auction house on Madison Avenue?"

"Nah, they moved to Rockefeller Center a few years ago; I'm surprised you didn't know that."

"I knew that; I just forgot. Why Sotheby's? It's the middle of the fucking night; they're not open."

"You're looking for logic from a guy in his shape?"

"You're right, Dino."

"I usually am."

"Well, not *all* the time, just some of the time."

"Too late; you already admitted it."

"Well, there's no point in going over to Sotheby's, is there?"

"Why not? My car is outside."

They tossed down their drinks, left Elaine's and got into Dino's car, driven by a young officer. "Take us to Rockefeller Center," Dino said. "Sotheby's."

"So, what rookie are you torturing these days?" Stone asked, nodding at the driver.

"He's a lucky kid, this one; he could be out there getting shot at, right, Leary?"

"You're not related to Captain Leary, now retired, are you?" Stone asked.

"He's my father," the young man said, driving swiftly down Second Avenue.

"Well," Stone said, "he made our lives hell for a few years at the One-Nine."

"So he says," Leary replied. "Says he enjoyed every minute of it, too."

"Shut up and drive, Leary," Dino said.

They found Sotheby's, and Dino had Leary drive them around

the block a couple of times, while they looked into darkened doorways with a flashlight.

"Your chicken has flown the coop," Dino said. "Leary, take Mr. Barrington to his lovely home in Turtle Bay."

"I know the joint," Leary said.

"It's not a joint," Stone pointed out.

"Whatever." Leary had them there in five minutes.

As they stopped, Dino's cell phone rang. "Bacchetti. Yeah, yeah, I got it." He hung up and turned toward Stone. "There's a Barton Lowell Cabot at 110 North Shore Road, in Warren, Connecticut. The only guy by that name in three states."

Stone made a note of the address.

"Look," Dino said, "if he hasn't turned up by morning, I'll have the watch sergeant spread the word about him at the shift change."

"Thanks, Dino. I'll keep you posted." Stone got out of the car, and it drove away. Stone walked up his front steps, and as he was fumbling for his key, he saw the moving shadow of someone behind him. He spun around, ready to repel a mugger, and found Barton Cabot standing there.

"Holy shit, Barton," Stone said. "You scared me half to death."

"I'm sorry," Cabot replied.

"Why did you leave Elaine's?"

"I'm supposed to sleep here tonight," Cabot replied, with perfect logic.

"Why did you go to Sotheby's?"

Cabot looked puzzled. "I don't know. But then I came here."

Stone looked at the address on his jotter. "Do you recognize 110 North Shore Road, Warren, Connecticut?"

"Sure, I live there."

Stone sighed and unlocked the door. "Come on, let's get you to bed."

4

Stone showed Barton to a guest room. "I'll get you some pajamas and a change of clothes for tomorrow," Stone said, "as soon as I turn off the lights downstairs and set the alarm."

"Okay," Barton said, sitting on the bed.

Stone went downstairs, switched everything off and tapped in the alarm code, then he went back upstairs to his bedroom to get the clothes for Barton. When he walked into the master suite, Barton was there, staring at four paintings grouped on a wall.

"Can I help you, Barton?"

"You've got some nice things in this house," Barton replied. "I'll give you eight hundred thousand dollars for these four pictures."

"They're not for sale," Stone said.

"Do you have any more Matilda Stones?"

"No, just those. She was my mother."

"Oh. She's a wonderful painter," Barton said. "You don't often see her work on the market."

"Barton, why do you think you have eight hundred thousand dollars?"

He shrugged. "I don't know."

"What do you do for a living?"

"I buy, I sell."

"Pictures?"

Barton looked puzzled. "I guess."

Stone went to his dressing room and got Barton the things he needed, then put them in his arms and turned him toward the stairs. "Do you remember where your room is?"

"Down the stairs, first door on the left," Barton replied. "I remember things I just learned."

"And I'm sure you'll remember even more tomorrow morning," Stone said, gently propelling him toward the stairs. He waited at the top until he heard the guest room door close, then he undressed and went to bed.

Stone walked into the kitchen the following morning to find Barton Cabot having breakfast, deep in conversation with Stone's housekeeper, Helene. What surprised him was that the conversation was being conducted in Greek, Helene's native language.

"Good morning, Stone," Barton said.

"Good morning, Barton. I didn't know you spoke Greek."

"Neither did I."

"He speaks my language beautifully," Helene said, "and with an elegant accent."

"Thank you, Helene," Barton said.

Helene put scrambled eggs and bacon before Stone and went about her work.

"Stone," Barton said, "what sort of work does Lance do?"

"Your younger brother is the deputy director of operations for the Central Intelligence Agency."

"No kidding?"

"No kidding. He was only recently appointed."

"That's a pretty important job, isn't it?"

"It is."

"How did he get it?"

"Well, my first cousin, Dick Stone, was supposed to get it, but before he could start, he was murdered, along with his wife and daughter."

"I'm sorry to hear that," Barton said. "Dick Stone," he mused. "I think I knew him."

"Oh? How?"

"I'm not sure; school, maybe."

"Choate or Harvard?"

"Maybe both. He was younger than I."

"Did you know him well?"

"I don't know, but I think I liked him."

"Everybody liked Dick, except his brother."

"Caleb?"

"That's right."

"He was my class, I think. I didn't like him."

"Neither did Dick."

Stone didn't feel like reciting a long explanation about how Dick had died and who had killed him, so he changed the subject. "If you're done, let's get started."

"Started where?"

"To your house."

"Where is that?"

"At 110 North Shore Road in Warren, Connecticut."

"That sounds right."

"Let's go find out," Stone said.

Helene handed Cabot his old clothes, newly washed and pressed, and Stone led him to the garage and put him into the car.

"What is this?" Cabot asked, indicating the car.

"A Mercedes."

"What kind of Mercedes?"

"An E55," Stone said, pressing the remote to open the garage door.

"That's the fast one, isn't it?"

"The fastest Mercedes," Stone said, backing out of the garage and closing the door. "At least it was when I bought it."

"I have a Mercedes, I think." Barton said.

Stone got them to the other side of town and onto the West Side Highway. Soon they were on the Sawmill River Parkway.

"This is the way I go," Barton said. "I like driving on this road."

"So do I."

"Do you get to Connecticut often?"

"Not as often as I'd like. I have a cottage in Washington, not far from your house."

"Ah yes, lovely village."

"I think so. I thought Lake Waramaug was in Washington Township. Why is your address in Warren?" Stone wanted to see if Barton had an answer to that.

"The south shore is in Washington; the northwest shore is in Kent; and North Shore Drive is in Warren."

"Oh."

"It's a lovely lake, isn't it?"

"Yes, it is."

"I think I've lived there for some time. I think I built the house or at least renovated it," Barton said. "There's a barn, too. I work there."

"At what?"

"At a desk."

They drove in silence for a while, until they got off the four-lane highway at New Milford. Stone put his left-turn signal on as they approached a stop sign.

"It's faster if you turn right," Barton said.

"I guess it is, if you're going to Lake Waramaug," Stone said, changing lanes. "I was turning for Washington, as usual."

They passed through New Milford, then New Preston, then the lake came into view.

"Which way?" Stone asked.

"Take the south road and drive around the lake," Barton said. "I like the drive."

"All right."

Barton made a vague motion with his hand. "There's a cave up there somewhere where people lived for twenty thousand years," he said. "At least that's what I read in a book."

They drove around the lake to the north side, and Stone watched for numbers.

"The second driveway on your right," Barton said.

Stone made the turn and discovered that Barton's house was on a peninsula, jutting into the lake.

"This is the second-largest natural lake in Connecticut," Barton said.

"Is it?"

"Yes."

Stone stopped at the house, and Barton got out and stood there, sniffing the air.

Stone got out, too. "I'll take you inside," he said.

Barton shook his head. "Something's wrong," he said.

"What is it?"

"Something."

Barton Cabot was running his hands through his pockets, and after a moment, he came up with a key. "The barn," he said, turning toward the large outbuilding.

Stone followed him, wondering what the hell was going on. Barton ignored the large barn doors and went instead to a large door on the side of the structure facing the house. He inserted the key in the lock and turned it, but before he opened the door he turned toward Stone.

"Very few people have ever been inside my barn," Barton said.

Stone shrugged. "If you don't want me in there, I won't go in."

Barton went inside. "Close the door and lock it behind you," he said.

Stone stepped into an elegant vestibule and reached for the door. To his surprise, it was made of steel and very heavy. He pulled it shut and turned the lock.

Barton opened another door with his key. He passed through it, giving Stone the same instructions.

Stone locked the second door behind him and turned to find himself in nothing resembling a barn, but a large workshop. On one side of the shop was a wall filled with hand tools that seemed to be very old, over a long workbench. He noticed that there didn't appear to be any power tools. The air was cool and damp. "This isn't a barn, is it, Barton?" Stone asked.

"No. There used to be a barn on this site, but I tore it down, constructed this building, then reassembled the old barn around it."

"That's amazing," Stone said, "but why?"

"To make antique reproductions and to preserve the wood with which they are made. It's temperature and humidity controlled." He led the way to the end of the room and pointed to a wall of racks containing pieces of mahogany and walnut, seemingly from deconstructed furniture. "When I get a piece that's beyond restoration I conserve the wood," Barton said. "I've been doing this for more than twenty years. I'm a very good woodworker, myself, and I employ two other men who are more highly skilled than I. My greatest value is my eye."

"Do you sell your pieces as reproductions or as originals?" Stone asked mildly, as if the question were not an insult.

"Depends," Barton said. "The reproductions we make are from woods of the period and are made with tools, glues and stain formulas of the period. If they stood side by side, it would take a very great expert to pick the original. Viewed singly, hardly anyone alive could authoritatively call one of my pieces anything but an original."

"Then your pieces must be very valuable," Stone said.

"You have no idea," Barton replied. He walked the length of the room and opened another door. "My garage," he said, looking through the door. "My van is gone."

"Should it be there?"

"Will you drive me to Danbury? I must buy a new van."

"Has your van been stolen?" Stone asked.

"I can think of no other reason why it would not be locked in the garage," Barton replied.

"Then why don't we report it to the police? Perhaps it will be recovered; then you won't have to buy a new one."

"Two reasons," Barton said. "One: If the van was stolen, I don't want word to get out, particularly not to the police; two: If the van was stolen, it is probably at the bottom of the East River and, thus, useless to me."

"I see," Stone said. "Or I think I see." He threw up his hands. "Or maybe I don't see."

"If the van was stolen, something very valuable was inside," Barton said.

"What was it?" Stone asked.

Barton didn't reply. Instead, he went to a cabinet and opened the double doors, revealing a safe, which he opened. He pulled out an inside drawer, removed a key, then crossed the room to a larger pair of doors. He unlocked them and swung them wide open, revealing a closet perhaps eight feet wide and twelve feet high. Inside, the rear wall was hung with still more antique hand tools. "Give me a hand," Barton said.

"A hand at what?"

"Go to the right side of the wall. There's a handle, see?"

Stone found the handle.

"There's one on my side, too. Take hold of yours and pull with me."

Stone did as he was asked. To his surprise, the rear wall slid out on wheels. Gently, they rolled the wall into the room, a good four feet from the front of the cabinet.

"Now," Barton said. He stepped behind the wall and flipped a switch. Lights came on.

Stone walked behind the wall and found that it hid a large compartment, in which rested what appeared to be a mahogany secretary, perhaps seven feet tall and four feet wide. It was gorgeous. The soft light brought out tones in the wood that made it extraordinary. "That's the most beautiful piece of furniture I've ever seen," he said.

"And well it should be," Barton said. "Help me close it up again."

Barton switched off the lights, and they moved the wall back into the cabinet. He locked the cabinet and returned the key to the safe, then locked that. "Let's go into the house," he said.

Stone followed him out of the barn, and Barton locked the steel doors behind them. He led the way to the house and used the barn key to open a door. They emerged into a modern kitchen, and Barton continued through that room into a handsome study, paneled in old woods, with leather furniture. "I bought this room from a country house in the north of England and reassembled it here," he said.

"It's lovely," Stone said.

"I need a drink." Barton said, opening cabinet doors to reveal a well-stocked bar. "Would you like something?"

"Thank you, no," Stone said. "Too early for me."

Barton poured himself a Scotch, then took a match from a box and lit the fire that had already been laid in the fireplace. "Have a seat," he said, "and I'll tell you a story."

Stone sat down on the leather couch, and Barton took a chair.

"In the mid-eighteenth century a very fine firm of cabinetmakers in Newport, Rhode Island, called Goddard-Townsend, were making some of the finest furniture in colonial America. The traders and sea captains who populated Newport would bring back mahogany logs from the Caribbean and South America that were nothing like those available today. They were dense and fine-grained, not the spongy, forced-growth trees that make up plantations now, and the furniture of which they were made glowed and smiled at the viewer in a way that can no longer be reproduced. All the best of that wood was gone by the end of the eighteenth century.

"Goddard-Townsend, during the seventeen fifties and sixties, made, among other pieces, a series of mahogany secretaries—probably no more than six or seven. One of these pieces was made for the esteemed Brown family of Newport—Brown University, among other things, was named for them. The piece remained in the family from that time until the late nineteen eighties, when the patriarch, John Nicholas Brown, died. They then emptied out their house in Newport, Harbor Court, and sold it to the New York Yacht Club, which turned the house into their Newport headquarters.

"In 1989, the Brown family put the secretary up for auction at Christie's. I think they thought it might bring a few hundred thousand dollars. It brought twelve point one million dollars, becoming the most expensive piece of American furniture ever sold at auction."

Stone blinked at the price. "That's staggering," he said.

"I expect it staggered the Browns, too," Barton said. "Four years ago I came into possession of one of the other Goddard-Townsend secretaries. It had passed through the hands of several families over the centuries, and I bought it privately from a family who were, perhaps, not entirely acquainted with its value. I won't tell you what I paid for it, but I think that its value at auction will have increased greatly since the Brown secretary was sold in 1989. There are more billionaires around now than then, and they all seem to want eighteenth-century American furniture. The secretary you just saw could very well bring double that of the 1989 sale, if I can establish a good provenance, which is problematical."

Stone tried to get his mind around that number.

"I brought the secretary here, and my people and I set out to reproduce it. With considerable effort I located some good mahogany. We matched the grains closely to the original and went to work. The project took us more than a year, and when we were finished we had two virtually identical secretaries."

"Barton," Stone said, "is the secretary I just saw in your barn the original or the reproduction?"

Barton ignored the question. "Stone, there are people out there who would kill for this piece of furniture," he said. "I know, because they nearly killed me. Perhaps they think they did."

"Barton," Stone said, "please answer my question: Is that secretary the original or the reproduction?"

Barton sighed and took a swig of his Scotch. "I don't know," he said.

6

Stone and Barton left Lake Waramaug and drove to Danbury. "Barton," Stone said, "I'm in some doubt as to whether you've completely recovered your memory."

"I'm not entirely certain, myself," Barton said. "I seem to remember the things I try to, but I don't know if I'm just avoiding thinking about the things I think I might not remember."

Stone shook his head. "Let's start with the basics: If I leave you in Danbury, buying a van, will you be able to find your way home?"

"Yes. I found my way home an hour ago, didn't I? From what the doctor in New York told me, once memory starts to return, it continues. Maybe it stops, and some things can't be recovered, but there's no regression."

"That makes sense, I guess. I'm just concerned about leaving you alone in Connecticut with no sense of whether you'll be safe."

"Safety is a different question," Barton said. "My safety is in the possibility that whoever put me in the hospital thought he had put me in the grave."

"You're speaking in the singular. Was it one man?"

"I don't know; *he* was the most convenient pronoun."

"Do you have any memory at all of how you got into difficulties?"

"No."

"But you think it was connected with the secretary?"

Barton looked at Stone as if he were a simple child. "There are two secretaries; one of them is gone, and so is my van. What do you deduce from that?"

"All right, all right. Is there a way to figure out whether the one in the barn is the original or the reproduction?"

"I can get my people in there and, among the three of us, we can probably figure that out. I wouldn't be surprised if one of them made some sort of mark on the reproduction."

"Then I think you should get them in there, so we'll know which one we're dealing with."

"Why? Whoever has the other one won't be able to tell the difference. No auction house will be able to tell the difference, not that they could auction it without getting caught."

"So you think it will be disposed of privately?"

"I think whoever did this already had a buyer. If you were a thief of art you wouldn't bother to steal, say, a Van Gogh, unless you already had a buyer, would you?"

"I guess not, but what about provenance? Won't the buyer demand it?"

"Either the buyer is an expert or fancies himself one, or he'll hire an unscrupulous expert to authenticate it. Provenance can be arranged."

"Is the piece insured?"

"Yes, but only for what I paid for it. That would be unsatisfactory recompense for the effort I've put into this project."

"But you can sell the one you have, can't you?"

"I always meant to keep the reproduction for myself," Barton said. "Of course, merely owning the reproduction, keeping it in my house, would keep the insurance company from paying for the theft, because their experts would think it the original."

"Which it may well be."

"Yes. I could never let anyone in the house again, unless I

represented it as the reproduction, and I couldn't afford to insure the piece for what it would bring at auction."

"This is awfully confusing," Stone said.

"I'm the one who's supposed to be confused," Barton said.

"It seems to be contagious," Stone replied.

Following Barton's directions, they pulled into a car dealership, and Barton pointed across the lot. "There," he said, pointing to a line of new vans, "that's the one I want, the second in line."

Stone drove him to the showroom. "I'll wait until you've actually bought the van," he said.

"Don't worry, I've brought my checkbook," Barton said. "I'll be out of here in the van in half an hour. Go home, Stone, and I thank you for your help. If my brother should ask, tell him I'm just fine." He got out of the car, closing the door behind him, and strode toward the dealer's showroom.

Stone turned around and pointed the car toward I-84 West. He would be home in an hour and a half.

Stone and Dino sat at Elaine's, eating dinner.

"That's a weird story," Dino said. "Can a piece of furniture be worth twenty-five million dollars?"

"Maybe more," Stone said, "according to Barton."

"Did you see the news tonight?" Dino asked.

"No."

"They rescued those people in Afghanistan. Nobody got hurt."

"So Lance made the right call?"

Dino shrugged. "I guess, unless they ignored his advice."

"Was there anything on the news or in the afternoon papers about Barton Cabot?"

"No, not a word," Dino replied.

"That's kind of odd, isn't it? It's a pretty good story."

"I think it's only a good story if the press finds out he's Lance's brother."

"Or if they hear about the secretary," Stone pointed out.

"I'm not talking," Dino said. "Are you?"

"Nope. Barton hopes whoever attacked him thinks he's dead."

"He would be safer if they thought that, I guess," Dino said.

"And if nobody knows about the secretary he still has, which might be the original."

"Well, yes, I suppose he would be in a hell of a lot of danger, if that were public knowledge."

"I'm not talking," Stone said. "Are you?"

"Nope," Dino said. "What do you think Barton intends to do about all this?"

"Do about it?"

"Come on, Stone, if you had lost a piece of furniture that might be worth twenty-five million bucks, wouldn't you do something about it?"

"I'd call the cops and the newspapers and get as much publicity about it as I could. That would make it harder to sell, and if there was already a buyer, it might make him too nervous to complete the sale."

"So why doesn't Barton do that?" Dino asked. "If he could get it back, he'd have furniture worth fifty million."

"Good point."

"And Barton is a hotshot ex-Marine. That kind of military experience molds a man. Why would he accept being beaten up and left on the street for dead?"

"Another good point," Stone admitted. "Do you think I should call Lance and tell him about all this?"

"You won't have to," Dino said, nodding toward the door. "He just walked in."

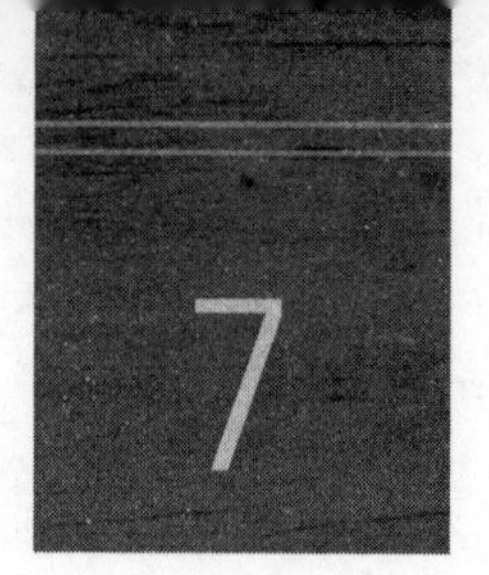

7

Lance pulled up a chair and sat down. He looked uncharacteristically tired and gaunt.

"Congratulations on the extraction of your people," Stone said.

"Thank you. Where is my brother?"

"At home."

"At your home?"

"At his home."

"And where would that be?"

"At 110 North Shore Drive, Warren, Connecticut. I'm sorry, I don't know the zip code."

"You left him alone?"

"As far as I could tell, he lives alone; he's used to it."

"But how is he?"

"Better. He's remembered a lot of things."

"Does he remember what happened to him?"

"Except that."

"Does he recall what he's been doing for the past thirty years?"

"We didn't discuss his history, but from what he did tell me, I think he's spent a lot of it reproducing and selling antique furniture."

Lance seemed struck dumb.

"No kidding," Stone said.

"Reproducing and selling antique furniture," Lance repeated, tonelessly.

"Apparently, he's very good at it. He lives in a beautiful house on a lake and has quite an extraordinary workshop, filled with old hand tools. There were no power tools, come to think of it. In fact, he must have done very well; he offered me eight hundred thousand dollars for four of my mother's paintings. Of course they're probably worth several times that; I suppose that's what makes him successful."

"Are you saying he tried to cheat you?"

"No, I'm just saying he's good at being an antiques dealer."

"Does he have a store?"

"If he does, he didn't mention it, and I didn't see one."

"Do you have his phone number?"

"I'm sorry, I don't."

"When did you leave him?"

"Early this afternoon, in Danbury, buying a new van. His old one disappeared with a valuable piece of furniture in it, around the time he was beaten up."

"I've never heard of anyone being mugged in New York for a piece of antique furniture," Lance said.

"New York is a big market for antiques," Stone said.

"Yeah," Dino chimed in, "people are mugged every day for their cell phones; why not for antique furniture?"

"Right," Stone said, "especially a piece of antique furniture that may be worth twenty-five million dollars."

"Or more," Dino echoed.

Lance looked back and forth at the two, seemingly trying to decide if they were insane. "Are you both insane?" he asked.

"No," Stone said. "If anybody is insane, it's your brother. But he seemed lucid to me."

"And you bought this story about the piece of furniture? How do you know it even exists?"

"Actually, there are two identical pieces of furniture. I saw one of them; I took his word for the other one."

"What kind of piece of furniture?"

"A mahogany secretary, about seven feet tall by four feet wide, built around 1760 by the firm of Goddard-Townsend of Newport, Rhode Island."

"I've heard something about that," Lance said. "Didn't it set some sort of sales record at Sotheby's?"

"Christie's."

"How did Barton get hold of it?"

"Goddard-Townsend built six or seven of them. Barton has two—or rather, one. Maybe. He built the other one himself, with a little help from his friends. Nobody can tell it from the original, maybe even not Barton."

"Because of his amnesia?"

"Because of the quality of the workmanship, according to Barton. One of them was, apparently, in the van when it was stolen."

"Which one? The reproduction or the original?"

"Barton doesn't know. Not that it would matter, since not even an expert can tell the difference."

Lance put his face in his hands. "This is preposterous," he said.

"I know just how you feel," Stone said, "and he's not even my brother."

"Is he still in any sort of danger?"

"Not as long as whoever attacked him thinks he's dead, or doesn't know about the other secretary."

"Why does he think the secretary is worth twenty-five million dollars?"

"Because the last one sold brought twelve million, and that was in 1989. Consult the Department of Labor's consumer price index for the rate of inflation, and ponder on how many crazy billionaires there are running around these days, spending zillions on everything from jet airplanes to New York penthouses. They have to furnish those penthouses with *something,* don't they?"

"Stone, if this is some wild tale you've dreamed up, I'll have you shot; I swear I will. I can do that."

"Lance," Dino said.

"You, too, Dino."

"Don't point that thing at *me,*" Dino said. "This is Stone's story; I don't know any more about it than you do. I have only Stone's word for it, and... well, you know."

"Thanks, Dino," Stone said

"God, I'm tired," Lance said. "I haven't slept since the day before yesterday."

"Lance," Stone said, "go to my house, find a guest room and get some sleep. There's a key under the stone lion on the stoop."

"Maybe," Lance said.

"What's the alternative? Faint in the street? You have a car and driver, don't you?"

"I think so," Lance said.

Stone thought he was fading fast. "Well, with your last remaining strength, go fall into it and give the driver my address. You know it, don't you?"

"I used to. Yes, I know it."

"Quickly, Lance, while your lips will still move."

Lance nodded, got up and, without another word, walked out of the restaurant.

"It will all seem clearer to him tomorrow," Dino said.

"No, it won't," Stone replied.

8

When Stone got out of the cab in front of his house he saw a huge black SUV idling at the curb. He put his key into the front door lock, turned it and walked into the entrance hall to find a man, braced against the living room doorjamb, pointing an evil-looking automatic weapon at him. "Good evening," Stone said. "May I direct you to the silver?"

"Let's see some I.D.," the man said.

"Go fuck yourself," Stone said, brushing past him. "I live here, and I'm going to bed." He got into the elevator and pressed the button. As the door closed, the man was still standing there, pointing the weapon at him, trying to decide whether to fire. Stone didn't care; it had been a long day.

The following morning, as Stone was finishing breakfast, Lance Cabot came into the kitchen, looking refreshed.

"I borrowed one of your shirts and some underwear," he said, taking a stool at the kitchen counter.

Helene, Stone's housekeeper, looked at Lance closely. "You look younger today," she said.

"Thank you, my dear," Lance replied, "but that was my elder brother, yesterday."

"Oh," Helene said, setting eggs, bacon and a buttered English muffin before him.

"Do you eat this way every day?" Lance asked Stone, as he dug into the food. "Why don't you weigh four hundred pounds?"

"Slim genes," Stone said. "Feeling better?"

"Better but not less confused. Give me directions to Barton's house."

Stone complied. "Would your jackbooted thugs like some breakfast?"

"They're very self-sufficient," Lance replied. "I expect they've already eaten."

"One of them pointed a machine gun at me last night. In my own home."

"Sorry about that; my new rank requires a complement of security only slightly less unwieldy than that of the president. There's nothing I can do about it."

"He didn't fire," Stone said. "If I had been after you, you'd be dead now."

"I'm my own last line of defense. Anyway, I told him not to shoot you, or he would have. Believe me."

"If you say so. I don't need a demonstration."

Lance finished his breakfast and turned to his coffee. "That was excellent, my dear," he said to Helene.

Helene turned red and batted her eyelashes.

"Barton spoke Greek to Helene," Stone said. "Did you know he could do that?"

"Latin, too," Lance said, "since prep school. Did Barton say anything about why he left the Marine Corps?" Lance asked.

"I've told you everything he said," Stone replied.

"After I got this job I ordered his service record from the Pentagon, but they said it was sealed."

"Did they say why?"

"They don't know why; the management has changed since then. They just know it's sealed."

"The military mind at work."

"Well, yes, I guess you could call it that. You were inside Barton's house?"

"Yes. It's very impressive."

"Was there any sign of a woman?"

"There was no sign of anyone, but it was very neat, and I doubt that he does his own housework. There must be a woman, even if she's hired."

"Come on, Stone, you're a better observer than that. Tell me something I can use."

"Use for what?"

"For figuring out what's going on with Barton."

"The kitchen has all the latest stainless-steel stuff. He has a study that he imported from a country house in the north of England and reassembled."

"You're not being helpful."

"Those were the only two rooms I was in. For all I know, he has a harem stashed upstairs, or a Boy Scout troop."

"The harem would be more like him. Barton always liked women."

"You make that sound like a bad thing."

"He often made it a bad thing; it was his only weakness."

"I don't know what deductions you expect from me, Lance. He seems to have a lot of money. Did he inherit it?"

"I don't know; I never saw my father's will. The banker who was my trustee wouldn't show it to me. I didn't get control of my inheritance until I was thirty, and by then I hadn't seen Barton for years. I don't know what our father left him."

"Was your father a wealthy man?"

"He seemed to be. God knows, he lived well. There was the house, I suppose, and there must have been some investments. I mean, he left me *something.* He was very clever about how he did it. His instructions to his executor, I was told, were to give me as much as I earned each year, so I was twice as well off as my peers. But you don't earn all that much, working for the government."

"Well, Barton must have had enough capital to get started in the antiques business. He couldn't have made all that much in the military."

"I suppose," Lance sighed. He stood up. "Well, I'm off to Connecticut to confront my errant brother. I should be saving the world, but I'm going to Connecticut."

"Lance, with a cell phone and an Internet connection, you ought to be able to save the world from anywhere, even Connecticut."

Lance left.

Stone's secretary, Joan Robertson, buzzed him in the kitchen.

Stone picked up the phone. "Good morning," he said.

"Bob Cantor is on the phone with you. He wants to have lunch."

"When?"

"Noon, at P. J. Clarke's."

"Okay." Stone hung up. Bob Cantor was a retired cop who did P.I. work, especially the technical kind, for Stone. Bob had never wanted to have lunch before, Stone recalled. Why now?

P. J. Clarke's was already crowded when Stone got there. Cantor waved him over to a table, and they shook hands.

"Drink?"

"I'll have a beer with my bacon cheeseburger, medium," Stone replied.

Cantor ordered for them.

"What's up, Bob?" Stone asked.

"Barton Cabot," Cantor replied.

It took a moment for the penny to drop. "You've talked with Dino."

"Right."

"How much did he tell you?"

"That somebody beat him up."

"What's your interest in Barton Cabot?"

"I served under him in 'Nam," Cantor replied.

"I guess I knew you were in Vietnam."

"I was a squad leader in his company, and later, I got a battlefield commission, after he made colonel and got a regiment, and I led a platoon. When my company commander was killed, the Colonel made me acting C.O. Is Colonel Cabot all right?"

"Far as I know," Stone said. "His brother went up to Connecticut to see him this morning."

"He has a brother?"

"Yep."

"If Colonel Cabot needs anything, will you let me know?"

"Have you kept in touch with him over the years?"

"No. He dropped out of sight after he got home. I heard he'd resigned from the Corps. I just want to know that he's okay. The man saved my life four or five times."

"That's a lot."

"We got shot at a lot."

"Bob, Cabot's brother tells me he was in line to make general. Do you have any idea why he resigned from the Marine Corps?"

Cantor looked away. "Maybe," he said.

9

Stone looked across the table at Cantor, who seemed to be having trouble establishing eye contact. "Bob, what do you mean by *maybe*?"

"You know what *maybe* means, Stone: It means 'maybe so, maybe not.' "

"Is that why you invited me to lunch, Bob? So you could jerk me around?"

"Look, all I want to know is if the Colonel is all right."

"I'll show you mine, if you show me yours."

A rather attractive woman at the next table looked at Stone, shocked.

"Just a figure of speech," Stone said to her. "All zippers remain at high mast."

She looked back at her salad, blushing.

Stone turned back to Cantor. "You first."

"This goes no further?" Cantor asked.

"No further."

"I don't think he would want his brother to know."

"I won't tell him," Stone said.

Their food arrived, and Cantor took the moment to fiddle with his napkin and sip his beer.

"Our food is getting cold, Bob," Stone said.

"All right. Toward the end of our third tour together the Colonel came across something valuable, something that belonged to the South Vietnamese government."

"What was it?" Stone asked, wondering if the South Vietnamese government had possessed an eighteenth-century mahogany secretary from Goddard-Townsend of Newport.

"Let's just say it was a fairly liquid asset."

"Stop being coy, Bob."

"Look, I'm trying to clue you in without causing you any problems, all right?"

"Problems?"

"It would not be conducive to your personal safety to know everything I know."

"Well, I'm very fond of my personal safety, so just tell me what you can without getting me killed."

"Like I said, we came across this fairly liquid asset, and we figured that the South Vietnamese government was about to be overrun by the North Vietnamese government, and we didn't want to see it fall into their hands, so that they could use it against Americans."

"So your motives for... liberating it were entirely patriotic?"

"Not entirely," Cantor admitted, "but we did see that it remained in American hands."

"Whose hands?"

"Our hands."

"How many of you were there?"

"Six," Cantor said, "including the Colonel."

"And you all benefited equally from this item or items remaining in American hands?"

"Not exactly equally, but everybody was pretty much satisfied with the arrangement."

"*Pretty much satisfied?* That means that at least one of you was pretty much dissatisfied, doesn't it?"

"You could look at it that way."

"Bob, how much did you, personally, benefit from this...patriotic act?"

"Let me put it this way, Stone: You've been in my shop."

Stone had indeed been in Cantor's shop, which was filled with exotic electronic equipment. "I have."

"You and I are on pretty much the same pension. Where did you think I got the wherewithal to own, say, two, three hundred grand's worth of gear?"

"I suppose it crossed my mind. I thought maybe you inherited something from somebody."

"My father pressed pants on Seventh Avenue. Inherit?"

"Okay, I get the picture. How much better did the Colonel do than you?"

"It was the Colonel's deal: He took half; the other five of us took equal splits of the other half."

"And how did you transport this windfall back to the States?"

"Safely," Cantor said. "By governmental means, you might say. We didn't do the split until it was on these shores and not on government property any more."

"How wise of you."

"It wasn't us; the Colonel is a very wise man. He found a way to convert the, ah, discovery, to cash, and at something close to its actual value."

"So what went wrong?"

"What makes you think something went wrong?"

"Bob, the Colonel had an outstanding war; he was up for general.

It is what every Marine officer at his level lives and breathes for; but he resigned his commission."

"Well, yeah, there was that."

"Why?"

"He had his reasons."

"Come on, Bob, what were they?"

"Some brass hat got suspicious."

"Was there an investigation?"

"Yes."

"Were you investigated?"

"No, none of us, only the Colonel."

"And what did the investigation determine?"

"Nothing. They couldn't prove a thing. Well, not much of anything."

"What did the investigation prove?"

"It was like this: There was going to be a court martial, but the brass hat running things offered the Colonel a deal. He could cough up the proceeds—all the proceeds—and have the charges dropped and, maybe, get his promotion."

"That sounds like a pretty good offer to me."

"Trouble was, the Colonel no longer had all the proceeds; we had done the split and scattered to the four winds. Three of us were out of the Corps by this time, one was getting out in a matter of days and the other one was dead."

"Did that one get dead because of this... transaction?"

"I don't want to go into that."

"But the rest of you wouldn't give back, so you cost the Colonel his career?"

"No, no, you don't understand."

"Make me understand."

"The Colonel never asked us for our end back; he never even contacted us. The brass hat wanted the money for himself, so the

Colonel turned down the deal and resigned from the Corps. By the time any of us heard about it, the deal was done, and the Colonel was gone."

"Gone where?"

"Nobody knew. He was just gone."

"Did any of you look for him?"

"I did. When I joined the NYPD I did a search every year or so, using department resources, but I always came up dry."

"Are you in touch with the other three guys?"

Cantor shook his head. "We agreed never to make contact again. It was safer that way."

"Did anybody get caught?"

"Nope."

"And you never saw each other again?"

Cantor looked around. "Not until yesterday."

"What happened yesterday?"

"I was having a drink here last night."

"At Clarke's."

"At the bar. I looked up from my glass, and a guy was standing at the end of the bar, looking at me."

"You know his name?"

"Of course, but I'm not telling you. All you need to know is that he was the one who wasn't happy with the cut. In fact, he was so unhappy that a couple of us were going to off him, but he cut and ran before we had the chance."

"Did you talk to him?"

"I looked away for a minute, trying to figure out what to do, and when I turned back, he was gone."

Stone nodded, he hoped sagely.

"Stone?"

"Yes?"

"How is the Colonel?"

Stone told him.

"I'm glad he's all right," Cantor said.

"Bob."

"Yeah?"

"If you see this guy again or hear from him, you should get in touch with me right away."

"Why?"

"To make sure the Colonel stays all right."

10

Stone went back to his office and tried to get some work done, but it took him more than two hours to write a brief that should have taken half an hour. There were times when he wished he had an associate to dump these things on.

Joan buzzed him. "Cabot on line one," she said.

"Which Cabot?"

"There's more than one?"

Stone picked up the phone. "Hello?"

"It's Lance."

"How did it go this morning?"

"We had a very nice lunch together at the Mayflower Inn, in Washington. He seemed not to want me in the house."

"So, did you detect any sign of a woman there?"

"Don't try and be funny, Stone."

"You seemed miffed that I didn't detect that; I just wanted to see if your powers of deduction exceeded mine."

"Barton seems to have mostly recovered his memory."

"What do you mean by *mostly*?"

"He doesn't remember anything about the night he was attacked, but it's common for trauma victims not to remember the trauma."

"Uh-huh."

"You sound skeptical."

"Oh, no, not me."

"Sarcasm doesn't suit you, Stone."

"That was irony."

Lance took a deep breath, obviously trying to remain civil. "I want you to keep an eye on Barton."

"I'm not in the 'keeping an eye on' business, Lance."

"You have a house in Washington; why don't you spend a few days there and drop in on him from time to time?"

"I am not your brother's keeper, to coin a phrase."

"Stone, if you had any idea of the pressures on me at work…"

"That would still not induce the miracle of genetics required to make Barton *my* brother. Here's an idea, Lance: Why don't you instruct Holly to take a little vacation, go up there and keep an eye on him? You said he likes women, and Holly is a very attractive one. She can use my house." Holly Barker was Stone's friend and occasional lover and one of Lance's staff at Langley.

There was a long silence before Lance spoke. "That is actually a very good idea, Stone."

"If she'll do it."

"I think that if I put it as a request for a personal favor she would go up there. You could drop in on her for a visit."

Stone ignored that suggestion, though it had already crossed his mind. He hadn't seen Holly for a while, and the idea of a couple of days in Connecticut with her was appealing. "I hope it all goes well, Lance."

"Thank you. So do I."

"Good-bye, Lance."

"There is just one more thing, Stone."

Stone rolled his eyes. "What is it?"

"There's the matter of the missing mahogany secretary."

Stone said nothing.

"Stone?"

"I'm here."

"There's the matter of..."

"Yes, yes, I got that."

"Barton is very concerned about it, of course, given its value."

"Of course."

"If you can locate and recover it, he is willing to offer you a finder's fee."

"Lance, I'm really very busy with my work, and..."

"A million dollars."

Stone stopped talking. "How's that again?"

"A million dollars in cash. On the barrelhead, I believe the expression is."

"Well, I don't know..."

"Tax free."

Magic words, those. Stone's palms were sweating. The thought of a million bucks at rest in his safe gave him a warm feeling all over.

"I take it, you'll take it."

"I'll see what I can do, Lance."

"Write down these numbers." Lance gave him Barton's home and cell phones. "Cell service is dodgy up there, as I'm sure you know, but you can always leave a message on his machine when you find the secretary."

"Tell Barton to send me any photographs he has of the piece, or pieces, and a list of any identifying marks on the them. I'd also like to know which one I'm looking for."

"He will respond immediately. I'll have one of my people drop off an envelope by nightfall."

"Give my best to Holly," Stone said.

"You may give her your best in person."

Stone wondered what he meant by that.

"And while you're up there, you might just look in on Barton and see how he's doing." Lance hung up.

Stone tried to bring his pulse down. He was going to need Dino's help to find the thing and maybe Bob Cantor's, too, so he would just have to accustom himself to parting with some of Barton's reward.

Stone was sitting in Elaine's, studying the photographs of the mahogany secretary when Dino walked in and sat down. Before he could speak a waiter set a glass of Scotch before him.

"You're still interested in antique furniture?" Dino asked.

"More than ever."

Dino took the photograph and looked it over. "Well, it's certainly a handsome piece of work," he admitted. "I'm not sure I'd fork out twenty-five mil for it, but that's just me."

"You know," Stone said, taking the photo back, "I think if I had a billion, I'd pay twenty-five mil for it, but that's just me."

"Let's call it a purely academic disagreement," Dino said, sipping his Scotch. "Where'd you get the picture?"

"Barton sent it to me."

"Why? Does he think you're a potential buyer?"

"Hardly. He wants me to find it for him."

"You? What are your particular qualifications for finding a missing piece of antique furniture?"

"About the same as yours."

"But I'm not looking for it."

"Yes, you are."

"Stone, why do you think I'm going to help you find this thing?"

"Because, if you help me find it and return it to Barton, you'll be paid the sum of one hundred thousand dollars, cash on the barrelhead, tax free."

"Since I know you don't have that kind of cash in your safe, I assume it's Barton's money we're talking about."

"We are."

Dino regarded him closely. "And how much is Barton paying *you*?"

"You have a suspicious nature, Dino."

"I'm a police officer; I'm paid to be suspicious."

"Well, the NYPD is not offering you a hundred grand to do this particular bit of police work."

"A good point, but you still haven't answered my question: How much is he paying you?"

"More than he's paying you, but I have to do most of the work. And anyway, Barton isn't paying you; I'm paying you out of what Barton pays me."

"I have a feeling that *I'm* going to end up doing most of the work," Dino said.

"All you have to do is quietly circulate a description of the piece among your brother officers, keeping it unofficial, of course."

"And just how do I keep it unofficial?"

"I would suggest that you offer a portion of your reward, say ten percent, to whoever locates it."

Dino stared at Stone. "Barton is paying you *a million dollars* to find it?"

"I didn't say that."

"You're paying me ten percent of what you're getting, and I have to pay ten percent to some street cop?"

"Do you think this is a bad deal, Dino?"

"I think it's an insufficiently good deal."

"All right, what number would make you content enough with your lot, should we find the thing, that you would never feel it necessary to mention it to me again?"

"Two hundred grand."

"And you'll tip your help out of that?"

"Yes."

"And you'll never again mention to me the relative sums earned by the two of us in this endeavor?"

"Probably not."

"Make that certainly not, and you've got a deal."

"Deal. What do you want me to do?"

"Well, find the fucking thing, of course."

"Any suggestions as to how?"

"You're a police officer, remember?"

"I know that."

"Well, use the resources at your command to motivate your subordinates to find it and do so discreetly enough that neither of us will ever get bitten on the ass by your superiors."

"If I get booted off the force for doing this, I'm going to want more money."

"We have a deal," Stone said, "and we're both sticking to it. Anyway, you need motivation for not getting caught using NYPD resources for your personal gain, and the risk of getting the boot might just meet that need."

Dino looked at him narrowly.

"Do I make myself perfectly clear?"

"Okay, okay, but it seems to me I'm taking all the risks."

"Do you remember what happened to Barton Cabot when he last possessed the secretary?"

"Yes."

"Well, that could happen to me, too. *That's* risk."

"All right," Dino said. "Do you have any leads?"

"There is something, but I'm going to have to violate a confidence in order to reveal it."

"Will it make you bleed onto the tablecloth to tell me about it?"

"Metaphorically speaking."

"Eight hundred grand ought to soothe your aching conscience a little."

"It involves Bob Cantor."

"I spoke to him yesterday," Dino said.

"And I had lunch with him today, and you promised not to mention money to me again."

"Tell me."

"Bob served under Barton Cabot in the Marine Corps in Vietnam. Together with four other men, they stole something and got it back to the States, where they divided the proceeds."

"What did they steal?"

"He wouldn't tell me, just that it belonged to the South Vietnamese government."

"Which doesn't exist any more."

"Right."

"And this happened when, in the seventies?"

"Right."

"So the statute of limitations has expired?"

"Right."

"So, what's he worried about?"

"The other three men."

"You said there were four, plus Bob and Barton."

"One of them is dead, probably because he was unhappy with his cut of the deal."

"You're just saying that to make me shut up about *my* cut of this deal."

"I'm just telling you the facts."

"So what does this have to do with anything?"

"One of the other three guys turned up at P. J. Clarke's yesterday; Bob saw him at the bar."

"And?"

"And then he vanished."

"In a puff of smoke?"

"No. Bob looked away, and when he looked back, the guy was gone."

"What does this mean?"

"I think that Bob thinks that this guy was—is *still*—unhappy with his cut."

"And that he stole Barton's secretary to get even?"

"To get more than even. That's my theory, anyway, not Bob's, because he doesn't know about the secretary."

Dino looked uncomfortable.

"Dino, when you mentioned Barton Cabot to Bob Cantor, did you also mention the secretary?"

"At the time, there was no reason why I shouldn't, was there?" Dino asked, defensively.

"I guess not," Stone said.

"And I can't talk to Bob about this, because of your conscience?"

"If it becomes necessary, I'll talk to him."

"So who is this disappearing guy?"

"I don't know," Stone said, "but I may have a way to find out."

12

When Stone got home, he called the cell phone number he had for Lance Cabot and left a message. The following morning, early, Lance called him back. "Good morning, Stone."

Stone tried to wake up fast. "Yeah, good morning." His bedside clock said 5:46 A.M.

"You really should get an earlier start to your day," Lance said. "You'd get more done."

Stone ignored that. "I need your help on something, Lance."

"Is this something to do with Barton's secretary?"

"Yes."

"What, exactly, do you need?"

"At the end of the Vietnam War, Barton was commanding a Marine regiment."

"I suppose that command would be appropriate to his rank."

"Before he made colonel, he had commanded a company, and there was a squad leader, a sergeant named Robert Cantor. Barton got him a battlefield commission, and he became a platoon leader and, later, after Barton got the regiment, an acting company commander."

"I think I've got it."

"I want the names of the men in Sergeant Cantor's squad and Lieutenant Cantor's platoon."

"You realize that those would be two different groups."

"Why?"

"When a sergeant gets a battlefield commission, he's transferred to another platoon, so he won't be commanding the men he served with as an NCO."

"Okay, then I need the names of both the squad and the platoon."

"Why?"

"I can't go into that," Stone said.

"Stone, why are you holding out on me?"

"You're going to have to trust me on this, Lance. In this matter, it's better if I decide what you know and don't know."

"All right. I'll be in the office shortly, and I'll give this to Holly to work on. She'll be in Connecticut by nightfall, and she can give you the records then."

"I'm in New York, Lance."

"I think you should spend at least a night or two in Connecticut, Stone, and while you're there, you can look in on Barton."

Stone sighed. "All right, Lance. And if I need further information can Holly obtain it from Connecticut?"

"She'll have her laptop. Good-bye, Stone."

Stone hung up, turned over and went back to sleep.

Stone arrived in Washington, Connecticut, in the late afternoon. His secretary had called his local housekeeper, and she had freshened up the place with clean linens and bouquets of flowers. She had also laid in food for breakfast.

Holly arrived an hour or so later and seemed happy to be in his arms. She had reddened her hair a few months ago for an assignment and had lost some weight.

Stone thought she looked terrific. "How long did the drive take?" he asked, kissing her.

"A couple of hours. I took a Company light airplane to the Oxford airport and rented a car."

"How about a drink?"

"You talked me into it."

They both drank the same bourbon, so he poured them a Knob Creek.

Holly grabbed her briefcase and led him into the living room to a sofa. "I've got some stuff that Lance said you wanted," she said, opening the briefcase and handing him a folder. "This is the roster of Charlie Company, Second Platoon," she said. "You'll note that Staff Sergeant Robert Cantor is leader of First Squad, and there's a list of the other squad members." She handed him another folder. "When Cantor got his commission, he was transferred to Baker Company and given command of First Platoon. This is that roster. There's a total of thirty or so names on both lists combined, but they had a lot of casualties, so by the end of the war the list was cut in half. Now tell me what this is about."

"All right, but you can't tell Lance about it."

"Why not?"

"It involves something about his brother he'd probably rather not know."

"Okay, but if he orders me, I'll have to tell him."

"I don't think he'll order you to tell him." Stone told everything, beginning with the disappearance of the mahogany secretary and continuing through the story of the theft near the end of the war.

"What did they steal?" Holly asked.

"I don't know, but it must have been fairly easily transported and easy to dispose of after they got it back to the States. And it must have been substantial in value, as it seems to have funded the lives of the participants when they became civilians again."

"Makes sense."

Stone picked up the first folder. "My guess is that the other participants are likely to have come from Sergeant Cantor's squad, since he would have been closer to his men and known them better than he would as a platoon or company commander." He opened the folder.

"He had five men in his squad," she said, "but two of them were fatalities before the end of the war."

"One of them was probably murdered by someone else in the squad," Stone said, "when he was unhappy with the way the loot was divided."

"Both fatalities occurred in 'Nam and are listed as KIA," Holly said.

"I guess it's easier to shoot somebody when your outfit is being shot at."

"Right, and what you've got there are the service records of the remaining three original squad members and Cantor. I didn't think you'd be interested in the replacements."

"Probably not," Stone said, looking through the folders. "He would have trusted the original guys more." He glanced through the records. "Two of these guys were from New York: one from Queens, one from the Bronx. Bob Cantor is from Brooklyn. Would it be unusual for three of a squad to be from the same city?"

"It's the luck of the draw, so it's probably a coincidence," Holly said.

"I think it makes sense to start with the two other New Yorkers," Stone said. "We've got their addresses here."

Holly shook her head. "Those are probably not current; they were the addresses when they enlisted. But there should be next of kin listed with an address. They could still be alive."

"These are guys in their fifties," Stone said.

"Lots of people in their fifties still have living parents."

Stone picked up the phone and dialed a number. "Let's see." He put the phone down again. "Out of service." He tried the other one.

"Hello?" A small child.

"Hi," Stone said, "can I speak with your daddy?"

The kid dropped the phone like a rock, and Stone could hear him screaming for his father.

"Hello?" a male voice said. "Who do you want?" The voice was heavily Spanish-accented.

Stone hung up. "Hispanic. Not our guy. The Pentagon wouldn't have current addresses?"

"Not likely, but the Veterans Administration might, especially if either guy has used his veterans' benefits. I can do a computer search but not now." She leaned over and kissed him hotly.

"I guess it can wait until tomorrow," Stone managed to say.

13

Stone woke the following morning with a warm girl heating his rib cage. He was ravenously hungry, and it occurred to him that they, in their enthusiasm, had never gotten around to dinner.

"I'm not awake," Holly whispered.

"Do you want breakfast?"

"Maybe."

Stone put on some shorts, went downstairs, grilled bacon and scrambled eggs. When he was almost done he whistled as loudly as he could, which was very loud.

A minute and a half later Holly padded down the stairs and walked into the kitchen, very naked.

"Good morning," he said. "Did you forget something?"

She stared at him blankly. "What?"

"Never mind, have a seat. I'm not sure I have a big enough napkin for you, though."

Holly sat down and began eating greedily. "Why am I so hungry?"

"Because we skipped dinner last night."

"Why did . . . ? Oh."

"Yes, oh. It was more fun than dinner, anyway."

"Well, you can take me out to dinner tonight."

"If I'm still here tonight."

"Lance promised me two nights with you to get me to come up here."

"Lance has given me two jobs, and I might not be able to get both of them done if I'm sleeping with you."

"I'm a job?"

"Only in a manner of speaking. He used your presence to lure me up here and check on Barton."

"What's Barton like?"

"A ringer for Lance but older. It's like they're twins who were born a few years apart."

"But is he *like* Lance?"

"Nobody is like Lance. Barton is more talkative, at least with me. He'll like you, though, especially if you go dressed like that."

She giggled.

"Lance says he likes the ladies."

"He didn't mention that to me."

They finished breakfast, then Holly left and returned with her laptop. "Give me the names of the two men from Cantor's squad who interested you."

Stone picked up the files. "Abner Luke Kramer and Charles Larry Crow." He gave her their service numbers.

She went to the V.A. website and through a few pages, typing rapidly. "Here we go," she said. "Private Kramer spent four years at NYU on the GI bill, got a degree in business administration, then went to Wharton for an MBA. Corporal Crow was treated for a couple of months at a V.A. hospital on Long Island, then got himself a V.A. mortgage."

"Any addresses?"

"One for each: Kramer, on West Tenth Street, in Manhattan; Crow, in the Bronx."

Stone wrote down both addresses and phone numbers.

"You going to call?"

"Might be better if I just show up and surprise them."

Holly continued typing. "Google knows about Kramer," she said. "He was an executive vice president at Goldman Sachs in New York until four years ago, but he left to start his own company, A. L. Kramer, which has done very well, apparently. Here's a picture." She turned the laptop so he could see it.

"Distinguished looking," Stone said. "What about Crow?"

Holly tapped more keys. "He started a real estate business, buying dilapidated town houses and reselling them. That's it."

"Well, it's a start, I guess. Want to go meet Barton Cabot?"

"Sure, but I need a shower."

"Me, too."

They showered together and made the most of it.

The touch of early autumn was in the trees along the shore of Lake Waramaug.

"This is beautiful," Holly said.

"Hardly anyplace is more beautiful than Connecticut in the fall. It'll be a little while longer before it's in its glory."

"Maybe I'll stick around for it," she said.

"How's the work with Lance going?"

"I wish I could tell you the details; the information I have in my head these days is mind-boggling."

"What about working with Lance?"

"I'm not the politician Lance is, but it's very interesting to watch him operate. He misses nothing and uses everything to his advantage. He's already cultivating the representatives and senators on the House and Senate intelligence committees. I've no doubt that he'll succeed Kate Rule Lee when she goes."

"He's pretty young for that job."

"He's pretty young for the job he has now," Holly pointed out.

They pulled into Barton's driveway, drove out onto the little peninsula and stopped at the house. Floodlights under the eaves suddenly came on.

"Motion detectors," Stone said. "Those lights didn't come on the last time I was here."

Barton stuck his head out the kitchen door, then came outside, his right hand behind his back.

"You think he's going to shoot us?" Holly asked.

Stone stepped out of the car and raised a hand in greeting. "Remember me?" he asked.

"Of course, I remember you," Barton said. "You think I'm an amnesiac?"

Stone laughed. "I want you to meet Holly Barker," he said.

Holly got out of the car. "How do you do?"

"Well, hello, Holly Barker," Barton replied. He moved his right hand behind his back, then brought it out to shake her hand. He was smiling. "Why don't you two come in for some coffee?"

They followed him into the kitchen, where a housekeeper was at work, then into the study, and by the time they arrived there, Stone noticed that the pistol was no longer tucked into Barton's belt behind his back. It somehow had disappeared on the way in.

The housekeeper came into the study bearing a tray that held coffee and cookies. She set it on the coffee table before the fireplace and left.

Barton poured for them. "So, Holly Barker, are you a Connecticut girl?"

"Nope, army brat, but I live in Virginia these days."

"What brings you up here?"

"A little vacation. Stone offered me his house."

Barton was about to reply when a tiny electronic beeping began. "Excuse me," he said, moving quickly away from the coffee and toward a door. On his way he reached into a drawer and came out with a semiautomatic pistol. He closed the door behind him.

"What should we do?" Holly asked.

"He didn't ask for help," Stone replied.

14

They were still drinking their coffee when two gunshots interrupted them.

"Are you armed?" Holly asked.

"No."

"I am," she said. "Come on."

Stone followed her, wondering how she had concealed a weapon under her tight jeans and close-fitting sweater. She stopped before going out the kitchen door, lifted a leg and removed a tiny semi-automatic pistol from a holster strapped to her right ankle. She looked out the kitchen window for a moment, then stepped outside. "Follow me, and stay behind me," she said.

They were halfway to the barn when Barton Cabot stepped out from behind it, the pistol still in his hand. "Raccoon," he said. "Missed him."

Holly tucked the little pistol back into its ankle holster. "How do the neighbors feel about the gunfire?"

"Oh, they'll think it's a bird hunter in a field nearby," Barton replied.

"Barton," Stone said, "will you show Holly the secretary? Anyway, I'd like to ask you some questions about it."

"All right. Holly, where are you from?"

"Virginia."

"Virginia?" Barton said. "Do you work with my brother?"

"I work *for* your brother," Holly said.

"So you're a spy?"

"Sometimes."

"Did he send you here to spy on me?"

Stone spoke up. "No. Lance sent her here to help me find your lost secretary. And she's working on her own time."

"Oh." Barton looked doubtful.

"Holly has already been very helpful. She knows everything I know about the situation, and I'd like both of us to know more."

Barton nodded, seeming satisfied. He went to his safe, got out the key, opened the large cabinet and, with Stone's help, slid out the rear wall to expose the secretary. Then he switched on the lights in the cabinet.

"Oooh, that's beautiful," Holly said.

"Do you know anything about American furniture?" Barton asked.

"I know how to get to the Ethan Allen store," Holly said.

Barton chuckled. "Well, at least you're honest." He began a lecture on the piece.

Stone had heard it before, so he wandered around the shop, looking at the old hand tools on the walls. They reminded him of things he had seen on the walls of the woodworking shop at Williamsburg, Virginia, where period-style furniture was still made. He returned to Holly and Barton.

"There are only seven of these known to exist, apart from this one, and six of them are in museums or other institutions," Barton was saying. "There are only two of them in private hands, and this is one of them. The other is said to rest in a private home near San Francisco that is built directly over the San Andreas Fault."

"I wonder how the owner's insurance company feels about that?" Holly observed.

"It's probably self-insured."

"How would someone authenticate a piece like this?"

"By being very familiar with other pieces from the same maker." He pointed to the carved scallop shells at the top of the piece. "For instance, the cuts made in these figures can be matched to the work of a maker, by the tools he used and the strokes he made. There are no signatures, numbers or brass plates identifying the maker, and all the pieces are somewhat different from each other, often built to the specifications of those who commissioned them."

Stone came over. "Barton, can we talk?"

Barton showed Stone and Holly to a little sitting area at one end of the shop, and they all took seats.

"Barton," Stone said, "I want to ask you about a couple of people you were in the army with. Will you tell me what you can about them?"

"If my memory is working properly," Barton said.

"The first is a Charles Crow."

Barton looked thoughtful.

"You remember Bob Cantor?"

"Oh, yes. My best squad lead, later my best platoon leader. I got him a field commission."

"Crow was a member of Cantor's original squad."

"Oh, yes. I remember him," Barton said, looking enlightened. "A real hustler; he was always buying or selling something, for less than it was worth when buying and considerably more when selling."

"Sort of like an antiques dealer," Holly interjected.

Barton laughed, showing a lot of teeth.

It was the first time Stone had seen him even smile, and he wondered if the joke would have gotten as big a laugh if it had come from him instead of Holly. "Did you ever see Crow after your outfit was back in the States?"

"I threw a party during our last week together, as people were beginning to be discharged or transferred."

"Was Crow discharged or transferred?"

"Why do I think you already know the answer to that question?" Barton asked.

"Sorry, Barton; I have to check your memory from time to time to see how it's working."

"Of course. Crow didn't re-up, as I recall. Neither did Cantor, though I thought he would have had a future if he'd stayed in the Corps."

"Do you have any idea what became of Crow after his discharge?"

"I remember that he was a New Yorker. I think he might have returned there, but I've no idea what he did after that."

"Another name: Abner Kramer."

"Ah, Ab," Barton said, smiling again. "A great success story. He was a big cheese at Goldman Sachs, then started his own investment bank, and he has a colonial estate up here. He's up practically every weekend."

"Tomorrow's Saturday," Stone said. "Do you think you might introduce me to him?"

"I could give him a call, I suppose. Why do you want to see him?"

"I'll be frank with you, Barton," Stone said. "I know about the, ah, transaction that took place among you, Cantor, Crow, Kramer and one or two others in Cantor's old squad."

Barton's eyebrows went up. "Do you, now? How much do you know?"

"Just the broad outlines," Stone said. "Will you fill in the gaps for me, tell me the whole story?"

"I think the whole business is better forgotten," Barton said.

"You understand, don't you, that you have no legal worries about that now. After all, it was back in the seventies, so the statute of limitations has expired, the government of South Vietnam no longer exists, and I very much doubt if the present government of Vietnam knows about the incident or has any interest in it."

"You doubt that, do you?"

"Do you have any reason to believe that they could be involved in what happened to you recently?"

Barton sighed. "All right, Stone; I'll tell you the story—under the protection of attorney-client privilege. And you, Holly, since you work for Lance, are unlikely to reveal this to anyone."

They both nodded.

"When you've heard it, you can tell me who you think might be involved." Barton settled into his seat, rearranged his features into a reminiscent mien and began to speak.

15

Barton settled himself and began. "We were pulling back from positions north of Saigon," he said. "We knew it was almost over, and we were just trying to do it in an orderly fashion. Some of the South Vietnamese commanders were in much more of a hurry.

"There was a ragged column of their forces pulling out of our joint fire base very early one morning, and I saw a South Vietnamese unit in several vehicles pulling out, one of them a truck with a fairly large object in the back, covered with a tarp and tied down. Later in the morning, when we finally began moving our equipment down the road to Saigon, our last two trucks caught up with Bob Cantor, riding point in a Jeep, and he took me forward a few yards on foot and showed me something through the reeds.

"The truck carrying the object was mired to its rear axle, along a riverbank, and they had the blanket off and were cutting the ropes tying it down. It was a large safe, quite an old one, from the look of it. The truck was listing toward the river at an alarming angle, and it looked as if it might tip over any moment.

"As we watched, the commanding colonel ordered a dozen of his men to get hold of the safe and tip it into the river. It made a big splash and disappeared into the muddy water. They abandoned the truck and got into another one and headed south.

"We were in less of a hurry than they, so several of us went into the water, got some cable around the safe and, using a winch mounted on our truck's front bumper, dragged it out of the river. We also had a wrecker with a crane, so we got it aboard a truck, covered it and began driving toward Saigon. We came under mortar fire twice and lost one man, but we finally made it to the city.

"I had rented a house there, with an attached garage, and Cantor and I, along with three enlisted men, got the safe in there and washed the mud off. Then we had to get the thing open, which turned out to be easier than I had imagined. It took Cantor about forty minutes to crack the safe. Who knew he had these skills?"

"Bob has many skills," Stone said. He knew because he had employed many of them.

"What was in the safe?" Holly asked.

"A lot of papers, mostly in Vietnamese, and six large leather sacks, containing hundreds of gold Chinese coins. They had been crudely struck, probably during or shortly after World War Two, and they weighed about an ounce apiece. I locked them in the garage, and we agreed to meet the next evening for dinner to talk about what to do with them. Two of my men got the safe onto the wrecker, drove it down to the river and made it go away."

"I don't get it," Stone said. "If the safe had gold in it, why didn't the Vietnamese officer open it and take the gold with him?"

"I can only guess," Barton said, "but I think he didn't have the combination. It was probably his commanding general's safe, and only he knew how to open it. I also think the Vietnamese colonel planned to go back for the safe when things cooled down. Fortunately for us, they never cooled down.

"Anyway, the city was pretty chaotic at the time, and when I happened to stop in at the headquarters of South Vietnamese intelligence to talk to an officer I knew there, I found them emptying their file cabinets and burning all the papers in their courtyard. The file cabinets were heavy and had combination locks. My officer friend was cleaning out his desk, and I asked him if I could have some of the filing cabinets. He was happy to give me six, along with the combinations, and I got a truck in there and took them back to the house.

"We put a sack of coins in each of the cabinets, then Cantor and I went to headquarters that night and typed up all the necessary shipping documents, put seals on the file drawers, secured them further with steel banding, labeled them as top secret and addressed them to me at my unit's headquarters at Fort Ord, California. Empty, except for the coins, they weighed about what they might have if they had been filled with documents.

"We met the others for dinner, told them about the plan and agreed that we would meet in San Francisco after returning home and decide how to deal with our newfound wealth. The next morning I got the file cabinets aboard a C-130 that was flying a lot of similar stuff home, and off it went.

"Ten days later, our unit arrived at Fort Ord in Monterey, and there were the cabinets, in a storeroom, waiting for us. Then it got a little tricky. We couldn't just walk into a coin dealer's and dispose of a huge quantity of very odd coins, so I went to a man I had known who was in the antique business in San Francisco. He was also an engraver, as were three earlier generations of the men in his family. One of them had been the first engraver at the San Francisco Mint, when it opened to deal with the proceeds of the 1849 Gold Rush.

"He had the equipment to melt down the coins and turn them into ingots weighing a kilogram each, and by spreading them around we were able to dispose of them over a period of a month, without attracting too much attention. As a result we accumulated a large amount of cash, and I threw a party for the men and distributed the proceeds. Each man got about three quarters of a million dollars."

"And you got considerably more," Stone said. "Half of everything, wasn't it?"

"That's correct, but apart from pulling the original safe out of the water, I had done all the work, with Cantor's help. He got a million dollars."

"And there was an argument among the men about this?"

"I heard later that one of them had objected to the arrangement."

"And what happened to him?"

"I don't know, exactly, but I have my suspicions. I was told about it, in veiled terms, as I was about to get onto an airplane for Washington."

"And that was it? Everybody was happy?"

"As far as I knew. There was one other facet to all this, though, and I've never told anyone about it."

Both Stone and Holly sat silently and waited.

"I'm afraid this is going to require a history lesson," Barton said finally.

16

Barton got up, went to his safe, opened it, opened a drawer inside and took out a small, suede pouch, closed with a drawstring. He came back and sat down, resting the pouch on his knee.

"After Franklin Roosevelt took office, in 1933, he took the country off the gold standard, in order to end the run on the banks and settle down the economy. All the gold coins were recalled and exchanged for paper money, and it became illegal to own gold coins, unless they were clearly rare and worthy of collecting. The last double eagles minted were the design by Augustus Saint-Gaudens; there were four hundred forty-five thousand five hundred minted, and they were dated 1933.

"Since gold coins were no longer circulated, all the Saint-Gaudens double eagles were melted down and converted to bullion. Two specimens were given to the Smithsonian. But somehow, examples of these double eagles began turning up here and there. It's believed that a high-ranking employee of the mint kept twenty or more and replaced them with other double eagles, so that the accounts balanced, but nobody knows exactly how many were thus liberated.

"My engraver friend in San Francisco, whose name was Isaac

Finkel, possessed a 1933 Saint-Gaudens double eagle. He wouldn't say how he got it, but I think that probably a relative of his worked at the mint and managed to retain one before they were melted down. Isaac wanted me to sell it for him, and I agreed to do so, on one condition: Using his Saint-Gaudens as a model, he would cut a new die for the coin, strike two for me, and I would pay him one million dollars for it.

"Isaac did as I asked, and the resulting two coins struck were absolutely undistinguishable from his original coin. I sold one of the two coins, representing it as original, to a Japanese businessman who had something of a reputation for collecting the uncollectible, for three million dollars, and gave a million to Isaac.

"There were other examples about. A Philadelphia jeweler came into possession of nineteen of the Saint-Gaudens double eagles. He sold at least nine of them to collectors, and the government confiscated eight of those. The ninth apparently passed into the possession of King Farouk of Egypt, and when he was deposed it came onto the market. But when the U.S. Government made extensive efforts to recover it, it disappeared, and what with the Feds' interest in the coins, dealers became reluctant to market them. In 2004, the Philadelphia jeweler's daughter found her father's other ten Saint-Gaudens among his possessions after his death, and she foolishly sent them to the U.S. Mint for authentication. I believe she may still be trying to get them back.

"But the most interesting story came when a British coin dealer turned up with the King Farouk Saint-Gaudens during the nineties in New York, where he tried to sell it to someone who turned out to be a Treasury agent.

"The government confiscated the coin, and the dealer promptly sued to get it back. During the lawsuit, which lasted for some years, the double eagle was deposited in the Treasury vaults at the World Trade Center. A couple of months before the 9/11 attacks the dealer and the U.S. Mint settled, agreeing to sell it at auction and divide the proceeds. The coin was removed from the vaults, monetized by the Treasury and sold at auction. It brought, including the buyer's premium, seven million five hundred and ninety thousand dollars."

"Holy shit," Holly said.

"What happened to your two coins, Barton?"

"I kept them for many years, then sold one to a collector, for... well, shall we say, for something less than seven million dollars. I used the money—some of it, anyway—to buy the Goddard-Townsend mahogany secretary that Holly so admires." He opened the suede pouch and emptied it into his hand. "This," he said, holding a gold coin up between thumb and forefinger, "is the original Saint-Gaudens from Isaac Finkel." He took Holly's hand and placed the coin in it.

Holly weighed it in her hand, then gave it to Stone.

"So this is what seven million dollars looks like," he said.

"Yes," Barton replied, "give or take."

"Barton," Holly said, "how much did you pay for the secretary?"

"That shall remain my secret," Barton replied, "but my investment in the piece is considerably more than the purchase price. You see, Isaac Finkel, by duplicating the Saint-Gaudens, had given me an idea. I had for years, with the help of two very fine cabinetmakers, been reproducing eighteenth-century pieces, small ones from old mahogany I had collected. You see it in the racks over there." He pointed.

"And you made the other secretary from that wood?" she asked.

"I believe I told Stone that, but it is not so."

"Then where did you get the mahogany?"

"Therein lies another tale," Barton said. Having begun to tell the truth, he was obviously relishing his own stories. "I traveled to Central America in search of exactly the right mahogany. After moving about for several weeks and asking a lot of questions, I heard a story about an early-nineteenth-century shipwreck in a river not far from where I stood. The ship had been carrying a cargo of mahogany logs timbered upriver, and the logs went down with the vessel.

"I bought scuba equipment, hired a boat and began searching for the wreck. It took me nearly two weeks, but I found it. I managed to raise a magnificent log and transport it to a sawmill, where I had it ripped into lumber. I then went on a search for the biggest piece of furniture I could find. I found a huge sofa, and I built a crate for it from the mahogany lumber."

"Why?" Holly asked.

"Because it was illegal to export old mahogany, since it was considered a national treasure. I shipped the sofa back to the United States in the mahogany crate. Some weeks later, I got a call from the shipping company saying that my shipment had arrived and that it would be delivered the following day.

"When the truck arrived here, I went out to greet it in a state of great excitement, and there, on the back of a flatbed truck, was the sofa. No crate."

"What did you do?" Holly asked, transfixed.

"I went, to put it politely, apeshit," Barton replied. "I got the head of the shipping company on the phone. 'Good Lord,' he said, 'that crate weighed so much that it would have cost another couple of thousand dollars to ship it to you, so we uncrated your sofa.'

" 'And where is my crate?' I asked.

" 'Oh, some of my employees liked the wood and took it home.'

"I explained to the gentleman that, if he did not recover my mahogany at once, I would find him and do very bad things to him, and by God he did. It was delivered a few days later, and over the next year, we built our replica of the Goddard-Townsend secretary from that single, very old mahogany log."

"What a story!" Holly said.

"Yes," Barton agreed. "It's a pity I can never publish it."

"Barton," Stone said, "you forgot an important detail in your story about the Saint-Gaudens double eagle."

"Oh?" Barton asked innocently.

"What happened to the die that Finkel made for you? The one that the two replica double eagles were struck from?"

"Oh, that," Barton said. "It was in a drawer of the secretary that was stolen."

"I see," Stone said. "And I think I'm beginning to get the full picture. And which of the secretaries was stolen? The original or the replica?"

Barton shrugged. "It hardly matters, does it?"

17

That evening Barton took Stone and Holly to dinner in Litchfield, ten miles away.

"I think you'll like this place," Barton said as Stone parked the car on the pretty street. "It's called the West Street Grill."

He led them inside, where they were greeted by and introduced to the owners, James and Charles, and given a booth in the center of the restaurant. They ordered drinks, and menus were brought. They had just ordered dinner when a couple stopped at their table.

"Good evening, Colonel," the man said. He was tall and slim, with iron-gray hair. Stone thought he had seen him before. The woman was very beautiful, with shoulder-length chestnut-colored hair and a lithe and curvaceous body.

"Good evening, Ab," Barton replied. "Charlotte, how are you?"

"Very well, Barton; we had a wonderful dinner."

"May I introduce my friends Stone Barrington and Holly Barker? This is Abner Kramer and his wife, Charlotte."

Hands were shaken all around.

Barton moved over a bit in the large booth and signaled Stone to do so as well. "Please sit and have a drink with us."

The couple sat down, and brandy was brought for them.

"How have you been, Bart?" Kramer asked.

"Oh, I was under the weather for a few days, but I'm fine, now."

"Are you ready to sell me that Goddard-Townsend secretary?"

"Oh, I'm not sure I'll ever part with that, Ab. If you're very nice to me, maybe I'll bequeath it to you in my will."

Kramer laughed. "I'm not sure I could wait another fifty years for it."

"Well, maybe I can find you something to substitute until I kick off."

"You'll outlive me, Bart."

"I promise not to do that, Ab. I've been telling Stone and Holly about your place up here, and they've expressed an interest in seeing it. Would it be convenient if I brought them by for a while tomorrow some time?"

"I'm afraid not, Bart; we've got the painters in as part of an extensive project, and the place is a mess. We only came up here for the night just to have a word with the painting contractor; we'll go back tomorrow morning. It's difficult to sleep with the smell of paint in the house, and the stuff has been custom-mixed to match the original eighteenth-century formula and takes forever to dry. Perhaps another time."

"Soon, I hope," Stone said.

"I'm afraid it may be a while before the house will be viewable."

"I have a place in Washington, and I'm up here from time to time. I hope I'll have another opportunity."

"We'll see that you do," Kramer replied. "I know your name, I believe."

"I've had the place here for a while, now."

"No. I mean from New York. Are you an attorney?"

"I am."

"Something about your involvement with the death of that Mafia guy... What was his name?"

"Carmine Dattila?"

"That's the one. Dattila the Hun they called him."

"I wasn't involved with his death; I just represented the man who was accused of shooting him."

"But he was never tried, was he? Was he innocent?"

"Innocent is too strong a word," Stone replied. "Let's just say that the D.A. decided that they didn't have sufficient evidence—or perhaps the inclination—to bring him to trial."

"That's an interesting locution," Kramer said. "Perhaps at our next meeting you would be kind enough to tell me the details."

"I'd be happy to," Stone said. "At least those details that don't violate the confidence of my client."

"The Colonel and I are both very interested in situations where a crime has been committed but gone unpunished," Kramer said. "Now, if you'll excuse us, we'll get home and try to sleep for a while in our paint-scented atmosphere."

Stone shook both their hands. "It was good to meet you. I look forward to seeing your house when it's back together."

"And we look forward to showing it to you," Kramer said. They shook the hands of Holly and Barton, then left.

"I wonder what he meant by that?" Holly asked.

"By what?" Barton asked, innocently.

"That business about both you and he being interested in unpunished crimes."

"Oh, that was just a little joke," Barton said. "He often talks that way when we're together."

"Barton," Stone said, "is Ab Kramer the only one of your former men that you see in the ordinary course of things?"

"Yes, he is, I suppose, and I ran into him only because he bought a place here and asked me to advise him on some of the pieces he was collecting. He has a fine collection of American furniture, perhaps one of the dozen best in a private home."

"A home he doesn't want Holly and me to see," Stone said.

"I wonder why," Holly said.

"Maybe he has a new piece of furniture in his collection, one that he doesn't want us to see," Stone replied.

"So," Barton said, "you think Ab Kramer might be behind the theft of the secretary?"

"It's cheaper than buying it at auction, isn't it?"

"Ab is a very wealthy man; I'm sure he could write a check for the piece if it came on the market."

"Yes, if it came on the market. On the other hand, if he thought that you were never going to sell it... Well, it's one of only two in private hands, isn't it? And the other is on the West Coast?"

"You have a point," Barton said. "Certainly, Ab is accustomed to getting what he wants, one way or another."

"Are you aware of any circumstances in which he acquired some possession by means other than strictly legal?" Stone asked.

"Well, not for the last twenty-odd years," Barton replied, "but, of course, I haven't seen all that much of him since Vietnam."

"Exactly how much have you seen him?"

"I was invited to dinner once, along with a large table full of people. I went to the house on another occasion to see a piece he'd bought; I think he wanted to know if he'd paid too much for it. He had. That's about the extent of our recent acquaintance."

"How did he know you had the secretary?"

Barton looked a little sheepish. "I think I may have mentioned it when I bought it. I was very excited about it, and it was difficult to keep it to myself."

"Who else did you tell, Barton?"

"No one. No one at all."

"That's very interesting," Stone said. "I wonder how we could get a look inside that house."

18

Saturday morning dawned bright and beautiful, with the nip of autumn in the air, and Stone and Holly slept in each other's arms.

Holly stirred. "Why don't you stay for the weekend?" she asked. "There's nothing for you to do in the city, is there?"

"Except find Barton's secretary," Stone muttered.

"You might be more likely to find it here," she said.

Stone opened an eye. "Are you suggesting what I think you're suggesting?"

"Well, one of the things about attending classes at the Farm is that they turn you into a pretty good cat burglar." The Farm was the CIA's training facility.

"Yeah, but they yanked you out after only a few weeks and put you to work."

"That's true, but I've been going back a couple of days a week to complete my training. Lance says it will look better on my record when promotion time comes."

"So what have they taught you at the Farm?"

"Oh, lock picking, safecracking, the foiling of alarm systems, silent killing—all sorts of good stuff. Oh, and I can kill you with my thumb."

"Please don't. Have you killed anybody?"

"Not yet, but you don't want to cross me."

Stone kissed her. "What can I do to keep you sweet?"

"You know what," she breathed in his ear.

He knew, and he did it.

After a long lunch at the Mayflower Inn, they called Barton and went back to his house. He took them into the study.

"We want to get into Abner Kramer's house," Holly said.

"Correction," Stone said. "*She* wants to get into Kramer's house."

"I think that's a terrible idea," Barton said.

"How else are we going to know if he has your secretary?" Holly asked.

"I don't think Ab has it," Barton replied.

"Have you got a better candidate?" Stone asked. "You've said he's the only person you told about it. You've also said that, when he wants something, he gets it, and the implication was that he doesn't care how."

"He wouldn't steal from *me*," Barton said. "After all, I gave him the basis of the fortune he's made."

"And you cut him and the others out of the deal on the Saint-Gaudens double eagle," Stone pointed out. "Ab could be nursing a grudge, and how better to get back at you than to take your most prized possession?"

"We just want to look around," Holly said.

Stone pointed at Holly. "*She* just wants to look around."

"Oh, yeah?" Holly said. "What do you want to do, hold my coat?"

"I'd be happy to hold your coat," Stone said.

"Holly," Barton said in a fatherly tone, "why do you think you can even get inside the place? Ab, no doubt, has state-of-the-art security in place."

"I've been trained by the best to breach state-of-the-art security," Holly said. "All I need is a few tools that I can buy at the local hardware store."

"Come on, Barton," Stone said, "let her at least case the joint."

"Is there some vantage point from which we could take a look at the estate from a distance?" Holly asked.

"As a matter of fact, there is," Barton replied.

They followed Barton's directions, turning off the highway and onto a dirt track that wound for miles through the woods. Twice they had to get out of the car and move fallen tree limbs aside in order to pass. Finally they got out of the car, and Barton, carrying a binocular case, led them a few yards into the trees.

The hillside fell away, and they found themselves looking across a small lake at the back of a large house, perhaps half a mile away. A barn and some outbuildings stood to one side, enclosed by a stone wall.

Barton took his binoculars from the case and handed them to Holly. "Here you go. They're fifteen power at full zoom, so you'll need to brace against a tree to hold them steady."

Holly braced herself and synchronized the two eyepieces. "Wow," she said softly. "These things are great."

"Let me take a look," Stone said. He received the binoculars and braced against a tree. " 'Wow' is right," he said. "I can see a picture on a wall, right through a window."

"Do you see a large mahogany secretary?" Barton asked.

"Sorry, no."

Holly tugged at his sleeve and demanded the binoculars back. "He wasn't lying about the painters," she said. "I can see a corner of a van behind the stone wall, and a man in white coveralls just came and took a bucket out of it and went back into the house."

"There's got to be a caretaker," Stone said.

"There is," Barton replied. "I know the fellow. He would probably live in the little house you can see a part of behind the barn."

"So when the painters leave, there'll still be somebody there."

"Of course. You don't just drive away and leave a house like this, containing an important collection, all by itself."

"What kind of security is there likely to be, Holly?" Stone asked.

"Oh, every door and window in the house will be wired, and there'll be motion detectors galore, sensors under the rugs. Like that."

"Will there be battery backup?"

"Of course, and maybe a generator, too."

"So, if we could cut the power, the generator would come on automatically?"

"Yes."

"So we could fix the generator so it wouldn't come on, then cut the power?"

"But there'd be a battery backup. It would be crazy not to have that."

"Where would the batteries likely be?"

"Inside the house, probably. But the generator would be outside, since it's noisy when it comes on."

"How noisy?"

"Probably like a big truck idling. They'd have a big one for a place like this, at least twenty kilowatts, I'd imagine."

"Right," Stone said. "When you've got that much money, you don't tolerate the slightest inconvenience. The power goes off in the middle of your favorite TV program, you want it back on instantly."

Holly panned the scene with the binoculars. "I see a power transformer on a pole about a hundred yards from the house," she said. "We'd have to knock that out in such a way that it would appear to be a normal failure. Short it out. Could take them a while to reset it."

"Then what?" Barton asked.

"I want to watch the painters leave for the day," she said, "and then I want to go to the hardware store before it closes."

"Impossible to do both," Stone said. "Give me a list, and I'll go now. I can be back in an hour."

Holly took a notebook from her pocket and began scribbling. She handed it to Stone. "No shortcuts, no substitutions."

"Right."

"Stone," Barton said, "there's a gate where you can drop us along the way. It's closer to the house."

"All right."

Stone dropped them a mile back down the dirt road.

"We'll leave the gate open," Barton said. "You can drive closer to the house with your lights off, but don't slam any car doors."

"I'll be back shortly," Stone said. He drove away reminding himself that he was not—*not*—going to enter that house.

19

Stone drove into town to the Washington Supply and walked around, filling Holly's order. He picked up a small screwdriver set, needle-nose pliers, wire cutters, electrical tape, a small roll of wire, an electrical meter, some alligator clips, two tiny flashlights and lithium batteries and, of course, a roll of duct tape. He also bought her a nylon tool belt with a pouch, and three pairs of paper socks that workmen wore over their boots to keep from tracking up nice houses. As an afterthought, he grabbed a box of latex gloves, then he went to the cashier's counter.

"Stocking up, huh, Mr. Barrington?" the man at the counter asked.

"Yeah, just a few things for around the house, do a few repairs." He charged the goods to his account and left. Half an hour later, he turned off the dirt road and through the opened gate onto an almost grown-over lane. It was getting dark, and he switched off his lights to avoid being seen from the house. The lane ended in a little clearing, perhaps a hundred yards from the house. He stuffed all his purchases into the tool belt and its pouch, then, carrying the socks and the latex gloves, he followed Holly's and Barton's tracks through some fairly tall grass until he found them behind the barn.

"Hey," Holly whispered. "Did you get absolutely *everything*?"

"Of course. That and a bit more." He handed her the tool belt and issued everybody latex gloves and paper socks. "Wait until we're inside the house before you put on the socks over your shoes," he reminded them.

A vehicle door slammed, and they peeked around a corner of the barn.

"The painters are packing up," Holly said.

"Hey, Randy!" somebody yelled.

A door opened at the caretaker's house, and a man stepped out. "Yeah?"

"We're done for the day; you can lock up and do the security thing."

"Okay, as soon as I finish dinner. See you guys on Monday." He went back inside and closed the door. The van drove away.

"Holy shit," Holly said. "The house is wide open, and the alarm hasn't been set. Let's go!"

"I'll wait here," Stone said.

"Oh, come on. I don't even have to do the burglary thing."

"Oh, all right." He followed along behind Holly and Barton, keeping low behind the stone wall. All the lights in the caretaker's house seemed to be on, and there were one or two, probably night-lights, on in the big house. Holly led them straight to the back door, and they simply opened it and walked inside. They were in a mudroom, and half a dozen pairs of gumboots were lined up against the wall under a row of pegs holding various outerwear.

"Okay, socks and gloves on," Holly said, and they all slipped the paper things over their shoes and pulled on the latex gloves. "There's the security box," Holly said, pointing, "and I'll bet the backup batteries are in that cabinet below. You lead the way, Barton; you've been here before."

Barton led them through the mudroom into the butler's pantry, then through the kitchen and into the dining room.

"Hey, some table," Stone said, as they walked through.

"Sheraton. It seats sixteen," Barton said. "I authenticated the chairs for him."

They continued into the living room. Practically everything was covered in painters' drop cloths. The pictures had been removed from the walls, stacked along one side of the room and covered. Barton was looking under drop cloths, identifying furniture.

"There's nothing big enough in here to be the secretary," Stone said, looking around.

"It's in two pieces," Barton said, "desk and bookcase, which rests on top of the desk. It will look smaller under a cloth."

The three of them spread out in the very large living room and began looking under drop cloths.

"Not here," Barton said finally. "Let's try the study." He led the way into the next room. It was completely dark outside now, but a rising moon offered some light. Holly gave him one of the little flashlights.

They repeated the process from the previous room. "Not here," Barton said.

"But look at that," Stone said, pointing.

"What?" Holly said. "I don't see anything."

"Exactly. It's an empty space in a room otherwise stuffed with furniture. What goes there?"

"The secretary," Holly said.

"It's the right size and the right place in the room for it," Barton said. "It's where I'd put it."

Then, from the back of the house, they heard a noise.

"Back door," Holly said.

They froze in their tracks, then a few seconds later tiny lights began to flash around the corners of the ceiling, and a steady beeping, every second, started. They heard the back door slam.

"The security system is booting up," Holly said. "We've got maybe thirty seconds to get out of the house. Let's go!!"

She ran out of the study, through the living room and into the dining room. More tiny lights were flashing. "Cameras and motion detectors," she said. "Hurry!"

They made it to the mudroom and Holly tried the back door. Locked. She reached into her tool kit and began fiddling with the door.

"The thirty seconds has to be up," Stone said.

"If we're lucky, it's set for sixty instead," Holly replied.

The door came open, they all stepped outside and Holly closed the door behind them. "Run!" she said.

The three of them sprinted back along the path they had come, and as they ducked behind the stone wall, spotlights came on around the eaves of the house, and there were three short sharp blasts from a loud horn.

They huddled behind the wall, panting.

"That noise means the system is now fully armed," Holly said. "Another second and the exterior motion detectors would have caught us."

"Why didn't you disarm the system as soon as we were inside?" Stone asked, panting.

"How could I know the caretaker is a fast eater?" she replied. "Anyway, it's lucky I didn't, or he would have found the system inop and called the cops."

"Well," Barton said, "that's the most fun I've had in a long time."

"Stone, lead the way to the car," Holly said, handing him a flashlight. "And don't use that any more than you have to."

Half an hour later they were back on the main highway, headed for Barton's house.

"He doesn't have the secretary," Barton said. "It's not in the house."

"Maybe it's upstairs in a bedroom," Stone said.

"No, he'd never put it there; he'd want it on display, for all to see."

"Well," Holly said, "he's made a space for it. My guess is it'll be here as soon as the painting's done."

"It could still be in New York," Stone said.

"Probably is," Barton agreed. "There's nowhere around here he could store it without causing comment."

"Barton," Stone said, "we could just wait for his paint to dry, wait for him to move it up here, then report it stolen, get a search warrant and go get the thing."

"No," Barton said. "If the police get into this and it makes the press—and it will—then everything will be ruined."

Stone wondered what he meant by *everything.*

20

Stone and Holly went to the Mayflower Inn the following morning for Sunday brunch and lingered over their food.

"Stone, where would Abner Kramer hide the secretary in New York?"

"Kramer strikes me as the type who would be very well prepared," Stone replied. "He may have rented storage space for it."

"Or it could be in his house or apartment."

"That's a possibility, too."

"So, let's go to New York and break into his place."

"Well," Stone said, "I now have a fairly complete set of burglar tools. It would be a shame not to put them to use."

"Good."

"I'm kidding. I've had enough of housebreaking; I don't have the innate sneakiness required for the work."

"Are you saying I'm sneaky?"

"Let me be clear: You are sneaky. Isn't that one of the prime requisites for working at the CIA? I'll bet you aced the Sneaky 101 final at the Farm."

Holly giggled. "You know me too well."

"Are you going to stick around here for a few more days?"

"Well, it's a paid vacation, isn't it? And I've got a free house. I miss Daisy, but she's staying with my housemate."

"You have a housemate? I'm jealous."

"It's a female-type person. The place had a spare bedroom, so I cut my rent in half."

"Sounds sensible." Stone waved for a check. "I'm going to have to go back to the city."

"Why don't you just hang out here with me?" Holly asked.

"Well, I do have a law practice that requires my attention from time to time if I want to earn a living, and I have to look into the other guy from Barton's Marine outfit.... What's his name?"

"Charles Crow."

"Right. From the Bronx."

"That's the one."

"Watch your ass, Stone."

"You mean more than usual?"

"Remember, Crow is the operator, according to Barton. Sounds like a guy with few, if any, scruples."

"Okay. I'll watch my ass."

Stone got back to the city late in the afternoon, went through his mail and checked his phone messages. Alarmingly little business activity, he thought. He was going to have to make some money pretty soon.

Dino was already at Elaine's when Stone got there.

"How was the country?" Dino asked.

"Gorgeous. The leaves have started to turn."

"Not here, yet."

"Soon. Trust me."

"What did you find out up there?"

Stone gave him a rundown of his activities in Connecticut, including their housebreaking adventure.

"You're not sneaky enough to be a burglar, Stone."

"Exactly what I told Holly."

"If you don't watch it, I'm going to be bailing you out of some country jail."

"I hope not. Have you spread the word about the secretary among your colleagues in blue?"

"I have, discreetly."

"And a photo?"

"Yes. Otherwise they wouldn't know what the fuck I was talking about. They're cops, not readers of antiques magazines."

"Granted. I've got to look into the other member of Barton's outfit who seems a candidate for all this. Can you do a search on arrests and convictions for a Charles Crow?"

"The real estate guy?"

"There's a real estate guy named Charles Crow?"

"You don't ever read the papers, do you?"

"Every day."

"Not the *Times*, the *Daily News* and the *Post*."

"Dino, I know you consider those rags newspapers, but there's nothing in them that I need to know."

"If you read them, you'd know about Charlie Crow."

"What would I know?"

"Crow is this hotshot real estate... speculator, I guess you'd say. Made a bunch of money, got himself a trophy third wife and a publicist to get him on Page Six. You know what Page Six is?"

"Of course, Dino." Page Six was the *Post*'s gossip page.

"Well, Mr. and Mrs. Crow make an appearance there at least once a week, every day during the trial."

"Trial?"

"Yeah, he got caught in some sort of property swindle, but he got off. Cost him a couple of million in legal fees, though."

"That could put a dent in a fellow's wallet, couldn't it? Especially if he has a trophy wife and a publicist to support."

"I guess so. Charlie Crow was in Barton's outfit?"

"Yeah, and Barton says he was a wheeler-dealer even then."

"Are you sure it's the same Charlie Crow?"

"No, I'm not," Stone said. "That was your contention. Is he from the Bronx?"

"Yeah, and you can take the boy out of the Bronx, but..."

"I get the picture," Stone said. "Charlie is still a little rough around the edges, then?"

"Correct picture."

"I'd like to know if he has a sheet for anything besides his real estate scam."

Dino unsheathed his cell phone and made the call. "They'll get back to me," he said, putting the phone away.

"Who's Charlie's publicist?" Stone asked.

"Ask the guy behind you."

Stone turned and found Bobby Zarem, ace publicist, at the next table. "Hey, Bobby," he said.

"Hey, Stone."

"You ever heard of a guy named Charlie Crow?"

"Hasn't everybody?"

"You don't, by any chance, represent him, do you?"

"Too sleazy for my taste," Zarem said. "He's one of Irv Kaplan's clients. They're well suited to each other."

"Thanks, Bobby." Stone turned back to Dino. "You hear that?"

Dino held up a hand while he opened his cell phone. "Bacchetti. Yeah? Yeah. Read it to me. Thanks." Dino hung up. "Charlie had a juvey record, small time stuff: joyriding in other people's cars, petty theft. Nothing after that. Maybe the Marines straightened him out."

"From what Barton says, they just made him a better criminal."

"Barton should talk."

"Oh, I forgot to tell you about the gold double eagle." Stone told him the story.

"So, when Barton gets a little short, he can always stamp out another twenty-dollar gold piece and sell it for a few million?"

"He's admitted to doing that twice but not recently."

"Our Barton is quite the card, isn't he?"

"He certainly is," Stone agreed. "Did I mention that the die for the gold coin was in a drawer of the secretary when it was stolen?"

"You did not mention that, but I guess it makes Barton more anxious than ever to get the furniture back."

"Yes, it certainly must," Stone said.

"Well, let's hope whoever has the thing doesn't go through the drawers; he might recognize it. What does a die look like, anyway?"

"I'm not sure, but I once had a tour through a factory that makes class rings, and they had this good-sized machine that stamped them out. They'd put a blank piece of gold, already cut to shape, into the thing, and bang, the thing stamped the design onto it. The die part was pretty small, though, not a lot bigger than the ring it stamped out."

"So you could put the die in your pocket?"

"Or in a small drawer in a large piece of furniture."

"Having the die would be like having a license to print money, wouldn't it?"

"It would be like not having a license to print money, just a printing press."

"That would do me," Dino said.

21

Stone was at his desk at the crack of ten. Joan had left a list of the bills needing to be paid, and it turned out to be a rather depressing list, since there was not enough cash in his bank account to meet them.

Joan came to his office door. "Good afternoon," she said archly.

"Don't start, Joan."

"You saw what we owe?"

"Yes."

"And what we have in the bank?"

"Yes. Use your own judgment as to which and how many to pay."

"Is there any oil in the pipeline?" she asked.

"There is oil in the ground, and as soon as I locate it, there will be an abundance in the pipeline."

"So much for geology," she said, then returned to her office.

Stone called Bob Cantor.

"Good morning," he said.

"Bob, you sound a little down."

"I guess you could say that."

"What's the problem?"

"I can't go into it."

"Let me ask you a question: Was the guy you saw at Clarke's Charlie Crow?"

There was a dead silence.

"Bob?"

"How did you know that?"

"The information came my way in connection with some work I'm doing for a client."

"I don't believe you."

"Bob, how else would I be able to guess that? And it was a guess."

"I only saw him for a minute."

"And he saw you."

"Well, yeah."

"Why didn't he speak to you?"

"Look, we made a pact a long time ago not to contact each other."

"Do you think his presence at Clarke's was just a coincidence?"

"It's a popular place; a lot of people drink there."

"Do you think it was a coincidence?"

Cantor sighed. "I don't know," he said. "I just didn't expect him to pop up on my radar."

"Another of your former Marine buddies has popped up, this time on my radar."

"Huh?"

"Ab Kramer."

"Holy shit. How'd you run into *him*?"

"I was having dinner at a restaurant in Litchfield, Connecticut, with Barton Cabot, and he stopped by our table to say hello, then stayed for a drink."

"Why were you having dinner with the Colonel?"

"At his invitation. I'm trying to help him recover the property he lost when he was, well, mugged, shall we say?"

"How is he?"

"He seems to have recovered himself, except that he can't remember anything about being beaten up."

"Do you believe that?"

"I don't think he would conceal anything from me that would help find his property."

"The Colonel is a complicated man," Cantor said.

"You mean he lies a lot?"

"I wouldn't put it quite that way. Let's just say that he plays his cards very close to his vest. Always."

"You know that Kramer has done well on Wall Street?"

"I read the business pages."

"What do you know about Charlie Crow's business life?"

"I read Page Six in the *Post,* too."

"So you know that Charlie seems to have an unscrupulous side to his nature?"

"Charlie Crow was *born* with an unscrupulous side to his nature. When we were in 'Nam, if there were two ways to get something done, he would always choose the crooked way, and he'd always make a profit doing it."

"Would you say that Charlie has a tendency to hold a grudge?"

"Forever," Cantor replied.

"So, you think he might still be just a tiny bit peeved about the split in your caper with the gold coins?"

"How'd you know about the gold coins?"

"The Colonel told me."

"Oh. One of the many reasons I was glad to agree never to contact any of the others again was that I would never again have to listen to Charlie Crow bitch about his cut. If he walked in here right now, the first thing he'd say to me would be 'Y'know, I got screwed on that deal with the Colonel.' "

"Did Charlie have violent tendencies?"

"Shit, we were in a jungle war; we *all* had violent tendencies. That's why we're still alive."

"Would Charlie have trouble letting go of that after reentering civilian life?"

"I wouldn't be surprised. If an argument got heated, Charlie always threw the first punch. Or, more likely, the first kick in the balls."

"A street fighter, then?"

"He wouldn't need a street; he was ready to go anytime, anywhere."

"What about Ab Kramer?"

"Ab was smarter than Charlie and cooler, too. He'd pick his moment to take a swing at somebody, but he'd get around to it, if he was mad enough. He knew how to stay mad but not show it."

"Did either of them ever kill anybody who wasn't wearing black pajamas and carrying a Kalashnikov?"

"Let's not get into that."

"Let me put it another way: Would Charlie hesitate to kill somebody who made him mad enough?"

"He might; maybe he grew up some over the years."

"Would Ab?"

"Ab was too smart for that. If he wanted to do more than just throw a punch, he'd find a way to do it so that the other guy never forgot it. I saw him maneuver a guy right into the stockade once. The guy did a year, and when he got out, Ab walked up to him in a bar in Saigon and asked him how he enjoyed his stay. Ab was fearless."

"Which one of them would be more likely to have stolen the Colonel's piece of antique furniture?"

"Stone, Charlie Crow might take a broken bottle to somebody who'd crossed him, but he wouldn't know his ass from antique furniture."

"Thanks, Bob. I think I get the picture."

Joan buzzed Stone. "Bill Eggers is on line one, and he's whispering."

"Why is he whispering?"

"You'll have to ask him."

Stone picked up the phone. "Bill?"

"Stone," Eggers said in a raspy whisper, "get over here."

"What?"

"Right now." Eggers hung up.

Stone slipped into his coat and stopped at Joan's desk. "Bill wants me to come over there in a hurry."

"Why was he whispering?"

"I forgot to ask. See you later."

Five minutes later, Stone got out of a cab at the Seagram Building on Park Avenue at Fifty-second Street, where the law firm of Woodman & Weld occupied four high floors.

Woodman & Weld was often referred to as the gold standard of New York law firms, with a reputation for high-quality legal services, solid integrity and complete discretion. Every law firm, however, has clients and cases with whom it would prefer not to be publicly associated, and for that reason W&W employed Stone. He and Bill Eggers had been classmates at NYU Law School, and when Stone had been invalided out of the NYPD, Eggers had brought him aboard.

Stone got off the elevator, and the receptionist didn't even speak, just waved him in the direction of the corner office of the managing partner.

Stone rapped lightly on the door, opened it and stuck his head in. "Good morning?"

"Stone!" Eggers said, rising from his chair. His companion did not rise. "Come in, come in! I want you to meet someone."

At this, the other man rose. He was of medium height and build, wearing a very good suit but somehow unprepossessing. He was bald, with a fringe of blond hair, and wore rimless spectacles. Stone knew who he was immediately.

"Stone, this is Harlan Deal. Harlan, this is my colleague, Stone Barrington."

Stone shook Deal's hand. His grip was firm and cool, but his demeanor was dour. He looked as though he had not slept well for some time. "How do you do, Mr. Deal," Stone said.

"Hello," Deal replied. "Please call me Harlan; everybody does."

What most people called him, Stone reflected, was The Deal. Harlan Deal had inherited a portfolio of grimy real estate in the nether regions of the Bronx and Queens and had turned it into a giant holding company, called Real Deal, with a worldwide reach. It was a great American success story, but Deal, personally, remained low-powered socially. He contributed to good causes, even had his own foundation for that purpose, but he was not high on the dinner-party list of anyone who did not wish to borrow money from him. There were stories of dinner partners who had not heard him speak during a five-course meal.

"Sit down, Stone," Eggers said. "Harlan has a little problem that I think you might be able to help him with."

"Well, I'll certainly try," Stone replied.

"Heh, heh," Eggers chortled. "I think you'll find, Harlan, that Stone's efforts are of a very high order."

Stone stared at Eggers. What was he promising this guy? Stone had no clue as to why he was there. "Well, Bill," he said, "let's hear about the problem before we start making promises. Perhaps Mr. Deal will tell me about it."

"Harlan," Deal replied.

"Of course, Harlan, and please call me Stone."

"What sort of work do you do, Mr. Barrington?"

"I'm an attorney, of counsel to Woodman and Weld."

"Of counsel? What does that mean, exactly?"

"I think Bill could explain that better than I."

Eggers had not been ready for this, but he caught the ball. "Stone is a generalist, where most of our people specialize. That sometimes gives him a better view of the big picture. He is a very, very capable attorney, I assure you."

"I see," Deal said, obviously not seeing at all. "And how are you going to help me, Mr. Barrington?"

Stone fixed a benevolent smile on his face. "I'm afraid I won't be able to help you at all, until you tell me your problem, Mr. Deal."

"It's Harlan, please."

"And please call me Stone."

"I assure you, Harlan," Eggers said, "all this will be kept in the closest confidence, under the full force of the attorney-client relationship."

"I should certainly hope so," Deal said, but he still made no move to explain his problem. He sighed deeply and finally said, "It's my wife."

Stone and Eggers sat silently, hanging on his every word.

"Oh, sorry," Deal said. "I mean my fiancée. Soon to be my wife."

"Yes, go on," Stone said.

"There's not much to tell," Deal said.

Stone had that impression. "Perhaps you could tell me the nature of the problem with your fiancée."

"I hope you understand that this is deeply embarrassing for me," Deal said.

"Harlan," Eggers said. "You're among friends. Please feel free to speak candidly."

"All right," Deal said, but then he became silent again, staring out the window of Eggers's office toward the East River.

Stone and Eggers waited patiently. Stone fought the urge to doze off. He was beginning to understand the reluctance of people who gave dinner parties to invite Harlan Deal.

"Harlan?" Eggers asked, expectantly.

"Yes, Bill?"

"You were about to tell us about the problem with your fiancée."

"Oh, yes." But still Deal said nothing.

"Tell me, Harlan," Stone said, "if I may call you that."

"Of course. Please call me Harlan, Mr. Barrington."

"And call me Stone."

"Of course."

"Tell me, do you think that your problem with your fiancée might require a legal solution?"

"Well, certainly," Deal replied. "Why else would I come to my law firm?"

"Of course," Stone said. "Could you give me some idea of what might be the legal action you consider necessary?"

"Well, I don't want to sue," Deal replied. "That would just be all over the papers."

"*Discretion* is the byword in these cases," Stone said, although he had no idea what cases he was talking about.

"Well," Harlan said, rising to his feet. "I'm glad you understand, Mr. Barrington." He offered his hand. "May I say that it has been a real pleasure meeting you." He shook Stone's hand warmly, then Eggers's, then walked out.

Stone turned to Eggers. "Bill, what the fuck was that all about?"

"I apologize for Harlan," Eggers said. "He has difficulty articulating problems that are not related to his business."

"You seem to be having difficulty articulating, too, Bill. *What is the problem?*"

"The young lady won't sign the prenup," Eggers said.

23

Stone sank into a chair. "Bill, how the hell am I supposed to get a woman to sign a prenup she has already declined to sign?"

Eggers leaned across his desk and handed Stone a two-page document. "Read it. I wrote it myself."

Stone scanned the agreement. "She gets an allowance of half a million dollars a year, adjusted annually for inflation, and if she leaves him, she gets a million dollars for every year they've been married, calculated to the nearest month?"

"Not bad, huh?"

"Not bad, if she's considering it as employment. Not good, if we're talking about Harlan Deal's very large fortune."

"Stone," Eggers said, "a good prenup should accomplish two things: one, insure the financial welfare of the wife in the event that the husband changes his mind about how beautiful and sexy she is, and two, prevent an avaricious woman from looting the husband's fortune when she decides she can be just as rich divorced as married. I think this document satisfies both those requirements."

"Well, this certainly accomplishes the second, but there's nothing in here about housing after a divorce. She's not going to be able to buy a nice apartment in New York—I'm assuming we're talking New York—on a stipend of a million a year."

"Good point. I think I can get Harlan to kick in, say, two million for an apartment."

"Make it three million; you can't get much for two these days."

"All right."

"Does the lady have any children?"

"Not that I'm aware of."

"Is she young enough to get pregnant, assuming Harlan is fertile enough to get her that way? If we don't make provision for possible children, and she has some, it will never stand up in court."

Eggers stared at him, annoyed. "Okay, what do you suggest?"

"If she has his kids, five million for an apartment, half a million a year per kid in child support, a twenty-million-dollar trust fund per kid and the same as a bequest in an irrevocable codicil to his will."

"That's upping the ante quite a lot," Eggers said, frowning.

"It's a small fraction of what he'd pay without the prenup. Anyway, he can always get a vasectomy and cut his costs."

"You're sounding a lot like the lady's lawyer."

"Believe me, she's going to get one before she signs this thing, so we'd better anticipate."

"All right, I'll talk to Harlan. Anything else, before I call him?"

"She's almost certain to want other things; we have to consider them, if he wants to marry the lady."

Eggers looked at his watch and picked up the phone.

"Has he had time to get back to his office?" Stone asked.

"His office is two floors up," Eggers replied, dialing a number. "Harlan? Bill Eggers. Stone and I have talked this over, and he has made some very important suggestions to be included in the prenup, ones that might make her more amenable and, at the same time, make you look more generous." Eggers went through the list, then listened. "Harlan, a twenty-million dollar bequest to each kid isn't all that much, and since you'll be dead, you won't miss it. And you can always get a vasectomy." Eggers listened some more. "All right, but remember, she's bound to talk to her own attorney about this; in fact, we want her to do that, because we may have to make this agreement stand up in court. There may be other things she wants, so let's make our objective to just keep her reasonable and, of course, happy. After all, you'll have to live with the lady."

Stone spoke up. "Tell him, if she signs it, to send her two dozen roses and a bigger ring."

Eggers ignored him. "We'll get back to you, Harlan. Give us a few days." Eggers hung up. "I'll tell him that later. Now you'd better get going."

"Do I get to know who the lady is?" Stone asked.

"Oh, yeah. Her name is Carla."

"Come on, Bill, what's her last name?"

"She doesn't use one, and Harlan doesn't know it."

"Wait a minute, there's a woman who plays piano and sings at Bemelmens Bar in the Carlyle Hotel."

"That's the one. She lives in a suite in the hotel."

"I've heard her a couple of times; she's very good."

"Well, it's nice that you're a fan; it will give you two something to talk about."

"All right," Stone said, getting to his feet, "I'll give it a shot."

Eggers rose with him and walked him to the door. "You'd damn well better give this a lot more than a shot, Stone. Harlan Deal spends one hell of a lot of money with this firm, and losing him would impact us in all sorts of ways, including having to trim our expenses, like what we spend on of-counsel attorneys."

"I get the picture, Bill. No threats, please."

"Oh, that wasn't a threat, Stone; that was just a clear picture of what the landscape around here would look like if we should lose Harlan Deal's account. These offices would look like a nuclear test site."

"I get it, I get it," Stone said. He didn't let the doorknob hit him in the ass on the way out.

24

Stone went back to his office, ordered in a sandwich and had lunch at his desk. He had nearly dozed off on his sofa when Joan buzzed him. "Bob Cantor on line one."

Stone staggered back to his desk, slapped himself a couple of times to wake up and picked up the phone. "Hi, Bob."

"Hi, yourself. I thought you might like to know that I had an unexpected call from Charlie Crow."

"That's very interesting. What was it about?"

"He wants to have lunch."

"I thought you had all agreed not ever to contact each other."

"We did, and I've stuck to that. I don't know about the others."

"How do you feel about having lunch with Crow, Bob?"

"Nervous."

"What exactly did he say when he called?"

"He said he thought that enough time had passed that it wouldn't matter, that he'd always liked me and that he'd like to renew our friendship."

"Was he lying about liking you?"

"We got along in 'Nam, but that's about all. Renewing our 'friendship,' as he put it, is not all that appealing."

"Was there anything sinister in his tone?"

"No, he was affable, I guess you'd say. Charlie could always be affable if he felt like it. Some thought he had a lot of charm. It was pretty much lost on me, though."

"Are you going to see him?"

"I faked another call coming in and said I'd get back to him."

"I think it might be a good idea to see him, Bob."

"Why?"

"It might help us help the Colonel."

"Yeah, I guess it might."

"You've got to play dumb, though. You can't give him the slightest idea that you know about the Colonel's problem. Remember, it wasn't in the papers, so you can't possibly know about it. If he brings up the Colonel, and I suspect he will, then you can talk about him."

"All right. I'll call Charlie back."

"Bob, before we had lunch and had our first conversation about Colonel Cabot, did you know anything about his life after Vietnam up to now?"

"I never heard a word about the guy. I guess we travel in different circles."

"Another thing: You have an unlisted number, don't you?"

"Yeah."

"Then how did Crow get hold of it?"

"It's not all that hard to get an unlisted number; I've done it for you from time to time, remember?"

"I remember. Okay, call Crow back and make the date. And I think having a recording of the conversation would be nice. Can you wire yourself in a way he can't detect?"

"Yeah, I can wear a transmitter that looks like a pen and a tiny mike."

"Where would it transmit to?"

"It has a range of about a mile. I can put the recorder in my van and park near the restaurant. Otherwise, I'd have to wear a recorder, and that would be easy to find in a pat-down."

"Is he likely to pat you down?"

"How the hell should I know? Depends on how paranoid he is, I guess."

"Better pick a quiet restaurant; don't do it at P. J. Clarke's."

"A good point."

"Don't tell him anything about your expertise with electronics. There's no reason why he would know about that, is there?"

"None. I didn't get my first computer until '79."

"I'd love to know if he'll admit having had any contact with Abner Kramer."

"I guess I can ask him if he's seen any of the other guys, give him an opportunity to say so. I'll call you after."

"Thanks, Bob." Stone hung up. This, he thought, was a move in the right direction, especially since he had little or nothing to go on. He needed a break badly.

Stone met Dino for dinner at Elaine's. "Anything to report?" he asked.

Dino gave him a smart salute. "Nothing to report, sir!"

"I'd hoped one of your people could give us something to go on."

"What, you think somebody is just going to stumble across this piece of furniture?"

"I'd like that," Stone said, "as unlikely as it is. Maybe there's something else your guys can do."

"I can't wait to hear this," Dino said.

"I need to know a lot more about Charlie Crow, not your Google sort of stuff—I need to know where he goes, who he hangs out with. Especially who he hangs out with."

"You're actually asking me to put New York City police officers on a tail unconnected to any crime?"

"It is connected to a crime: the beating of a man and the theft of an extremely valuable object."

"It's not like I can open a file on it, Stone. I mean, there was a time I could have opened a file, then shredded it when it was over, but these days, once you put something in a computer it's there forever."

"Well, for God's sake, don't put anything in a computer. Just put a couple of guys on tailing Mr. Crow for a few days. I especially want to know if he's in touch with Abner Kramer."

"Maybe I can do that. Why don't you put Bob Cantor on this? Get him to tap Crow's phones."

"Fortunately, Crow called him and invited him to lunch, and he's going to wear a wire."

"That might produce something."

"I'm counting on it, since I have nothing else."

"How was your time with Holly?"

"It was very good, thanks. I'm sure she's already reported back to Lance."

"Well, she does work for him, after all. Is she enjoying being a spook?"

"Seems to be. I think she likes it better than being a small-town police chief. She doesn't have to do traffic tickets and penny-ante drug busts. Also, working for Lance, she must be privy to a lot of very interesting information."

"You think Lance's job is all that interesting?"

"Jesus, Dino, he's the fucking head of CIA operations."

"Then he must know everything in the world."

"I would think so."

"Then how did he lose track of his brother for thirty years?"

"That's an interesting question, and he hasn't answered it very satisfactorily. My guess is when somebody doesn't want to be found, he's hard to find."

"I don't buy that."

"Neither do I, entirely, but I don't see how it affects what I'm doing for Barton."

"Everything affects everything," Dino said.

25

Stone left Dino at Elaine's and took a cab to the Carlyle Hotel on Madison Avenue at Seventy-sixth Street. As he entered the Madison entrance, the Café Carlyle, former home of the late, great singer/pianist Bobby Short, was on his right, but he turned left, into the Bemelmens Bar.

The place was, maybe, three-quarters full, and the grand piano, in the middle of the room, was unoccupied. A maître d' appeared. "I'd like that table there," he said to the man, pointing at a tiny table with an unobstructed view no more than eight feet from the piano.

"You're alone, sir?" the man asked, as if he were asking for a king-size bed.

Stone passed him a twenty and was seated immediately. He ordered a cognac and a small bottle of San Pellegrino and waited for Carla to finish her break.

Five minutes later, she arrived, along with her bass player, who picked up his instrument and did a little tuning. Carla was a tall, Scandinavian-type blonde, clad in a long, slinky black dress set off by a diamond necklace that was either a fake or supplied by Harlan Deal, because she could never have afforded it on a singer/pianist's income. She played a few chords, then swung into a medium-tempo version of "Day In, Day Out," then followed that with songs by Rodgers and Hart, Cole Porter and Jerome Kern.

The music suited Stone to his core; it was what his parents had listened to, and he had grown up dancing to it in their home and at school dances. Then Carla did something that riveted him to his seat. She sang a Gershwin tune called "Do It Again" slow and sexy, and she sang it directly to him. Suddenly, beads of perspiration popped out on his forehead.

When she finished he smiled and applauded enthusiastically. She ignored him for the next three songs, then announced a break and stood up.

Stone stood, too, and she seemed to see him again. He walked the few steps between them and said, "My name is Stone Barrington. Would you join me for a few minutes?"

She said nothing but walked to his table and sat in the chair he held for her.

"Would you like something to drink?"

"This will do," she said, taking his glass of Pellegrino.

"That was a wonderful set," he said. "Especially the Gershwin tune."

She leveled her gaze at him. "I don't sing it often."

"Then I'm all the more grateful for hearing it."

"Who are you, Mr. Barrington?"

"I'm an attorney, and I'm here on business as well as pleasure."

"Oh?" she said. "Are you suing me?"

"Far from it," he said. "I'm here to see that you never have to work another day in your life, unless you want to."

"Fortunately, I enjoy my work," she said.

"That's apparent from the way you do it."

"Does this have something to do with Harlan Deal?"

"It does, and I'll be brief, so that we can talk like two human beings again." He took an envelope containing two copies of the prenuptial agreement and put it on the table. "I had a meeting with Mr. Deal this morning, and with his approval, I've made some substantial changes to this document. My advice to you, which is confidential, since it represents a conflict of interest, is to read it, consult a good attorney, then make a few more demands. He handed her his card. Have your attorney call me directly, and I'll see if I can help with Mr. Deal."

She tossed her head in a way that flipped her long, nearly white blonde hair over her shoulder. "Well, Mr. Barrington, you're taking a risk; I could get you disbarred for that advice."

"Not unless you're wearing a recording device," he said, looking her up and down, "and frankly, I don't know how you could conceal one in that dress."

She gave him a small smile, then picked up the envelope, opened it and carefully read the prenup. "Do you have a pen?" she said.

Stone held up his pen. "I do, but, again, I think you should consult an attorney."

"I believe I just have," she said, then took the pen from his hand and signed both copies of the agreement. "I think it's generous as it is."

"We'll need a witness," Stone said.

She beckoned her bass player, a very large and handsome African-American man who was sitting nearby. He came over, witnessed the documents and returned to his seat.

She handed Stone a copy, then folded the other and tucked it into her tiny purse. "Now, perhaps we can talk, as you said, like human beings."

"By all means. Tell me, what is your surname?"

"I don't have one," she said. "I never liked my name much, so I stopped using it when I got out of college, which was fifteen years ago, and I had it legally changed ten years ago. Since then, I've managed to forget it."

"I see," Stone said. "Of what national extraction are you, or have you forgotten that, too?"

"My father was Italian; my mother, Swedish."

"You seem to have taken on more Swedish characteristics than Italian ones," he said.

"Don't count on it," she replied. "I still know how to use a stiletto on a dark night. Figuratively speaking."

"I don't doubt it for a moment."

"I have one more set to do," she said. "I live in the hotel; perhaps when I'm finished, you'll come up for a drink."

She had managed to say that without sounding in the least like Mae West, but Stone still gulped. This was *really* a conflict of interest. "I'd like that," he said, tucking away his legal ethics.

She played and sang another dozen songs, then thanked her audience, got up and walked past Stone's table. She shook his hand, and her palm contained a card. "Give me ten minutes to freshen up," she said.

Stone finished his drink, paid his check and stopped by the men's room for a little freshening of his own, then he walked out onto Madison Avenue and hailed a cab. "Drive over to Park, then turn right on Seventy-sixth and let me out at the hotel entrance there."

"Big spender," the driver said.

"I'll make it worth your while." Stone didn't know if anyone was watching Carla or him, but he wouldn't put it past Harlan Deal, not to mention Bill Eggers. He got out at the Seventy-sixth Street entrance, checked Carla's card for the room number and took the elevator to a high floor.

The door was cracked, held just open by the plastic DO NOT DISTURB sign hanging on the doorknob. He pushed it open and entered, finding himself in a nicely furnished living room with a spectacular southern view of the city. "Hello?" he called.

"I'll be with you in just a minute," she called back. "Fix us both a cognac."

Stone went to the wet bar/kitchenette and found glasses and a bottle of Rémy Martin, then went back into the living room and set them on the coffee table. She came out of the bedroom wearing a flowing silk dressing gown that looked like something out of a 1950s movie, costumes by Edith Head. He had little doubt that she had nothing on under it.

She took the brandy, then stood on tiptoe and kissed him full on the lips. "I wanted to do that all evening," she said.

"So did I," Stone said. Sadly, he remembered the conflict of interest present here. "But I am prevented from doing what I really want to do."

"I'm glad to know you have at least *some* ethics, Mr. Barrington, but I believe I can relieve your conscience."

"How would you do that?" he asked.

"It's quite simple," she replied. "I have no intention whatever of marrying Harlan Deal."

"In that case," Stone said, taking her in his arms, "I am entirely unconflicted."

A moment later, he found he had been right about what she was not wearing under the dressing gown.

26

Stone woke up early, a little after six. Carla was inert beside him, the sheet failing to cover one breast. He slipped out of bed, went into the bathroom, showered, then dressed. He debated whether to wake her, then decided not to; he would phone her later.

The morning was crisp, and he walked downtown to his house and let himself in by the office door. He left the signed prenup on Joan's desk with a note telling her to messenger it to Eggers ASAP, then went into the kitchen, where Helene was bustling about.

"You are up very early," she said in her Greek-accented English, "and you are dressed, which means you slept somewhere else."

"Stop being a detective and scramble me some eggs, please, Helene." The *Times* was on the kitchen counter, and he read it while Helene cooked. The headline story on the first business page was of an acquisition by Harlan Deal of an aircraft-leasing company. He wished he'd known the day before; he wasn't above a little insider trading. Too late, now.

The acquisition and the prenup were Deal's good news for the day, he thought. The bad would follow when Carla broke her news.

He was at his desk when Joan arrived.

"Slept somewhere else, huh?"

"Joan..."

"You're wearing yesterday's suit."

"I like the suit; why can't I wear it two days in a row?"

"Okay, stick with that story."

"There's something on your desk for immediate action."

Joan left, and he heard her calling the messenger service.

Stone finished reading the *Times* and had started the crossword when Joan buzzed.

"Bill Eggers on line one."

Stone picked up the phone. "Good morning, Bill."

"How the hell did you do it?" Eggers asked. "How did you get her to sign?"

"I simply asked her nicely," Stone replied. "Apparently, no one had bothered to do that."

"I've already talked to Harlan, and he's thrilled. He announced a new acquisition this morning, too."

"I saw it in the *Times*. I guess you knew about this yesterday, Bill."

"Sure. We did the legal work."

"You might have dropped a hint."

"Yeah, sure, and have the SEC all over us both like a case of the flu. Don't worry; Harlan is sending you a check. I told him to pay you directly."

"And I get to keep it all? Gee, whiz!"

"Don't worry, the aircraft-leasing deal left us flush."

"I never worry about you, Bill. Thanks." He hung up, and Joan buzzed again.

"Yes?"

"A messenger just delivered a check from Harlan Deal for twenty-five thousand dollars! What the hell did you do for Harlan Deal? I didn't even know you knew him!"

"Met him yesterday, did some work for him last evening."

"Now I can pay the rest of the bills!"

"See how good I am to you?"

Bob Cantor met his old service buddy at "21." He hadn't been there in years, but Crow had, judging from the way they were greeted and seated. They were at a corner table on the ground floor, away from the hubbub of the horseshoe-shaped seating areas.

"So, Bob," Crow said, "how you been?" Charlie was dressed in a five-thousand-dollar suit, a five-hundred-dollar shirt and a two-hundred-dollar necktie with a matching one-hundred-dollar pocket square. He still managed to look like a real estate tycoon who sold used cars on the side.

"I been good, Charlie, and from what I read about you in the papers, so have you."

"Oh yeah. Boy, it's been sweet." He ordered martinis for both of them.

Cantor took a small sip of his drink. "I was kind of surprised to hear from you, Charlie, after that blood oath we all took."

"Come on, Bob, it's been thirty years; we can talk now without any problems."

"Yeah, I guess so."

"How have you spent the last thirty?"

"Well, I joined the NYPD when I got back from 'Nam and did twenty-five years there, fifteen of them as a detective, then I retired."

"How do you spend your time now?"

"Oh, I dabble in photography," Cantor said, not mentioning that he sometimes kicked in a bedroom door before dabbling. "And you're in the real estate game?"

"I am."

"Married?"

"Third time lucky, I hope. How about you?"

"Nah, I stayed a bachelor. I got a couple girls I see from time to time."

They ordered lunch and chatted amiably, as if they were dear old friends. Cantor finally popped the question. "Seen any of the other guys?"

"You know," Crow replied, "I was thinking we should have a reunion of the old band of thieves."

"You in touch with them?"

"I could probably track them down," Crow said.

"Any idea what they're doing?"

"Well, Ab Kramer is a big deal in the stock market, filthy rich, too. He's in *The Wall Street Journal* pretty often, does the odd appearance on CNBC, too. I've heard a rumor he might be the next secretary of the Treasury, if the Democrats hang on to the White House."

"Yeah, I've seen the business news stuff about him; I didn't know he had political connections, though."

"Big fund-raiser for the Democrats, the bastard," Crow said.

"I take it you're a Republican, Charlie."

"You bet your sweet ass; that's where the money is, boy. You give, you get; that's my policy."

"What about Harry Collins, you seen him?"

"Funny, I saw him at the track not long ago, and at the hundred-dollar window, too."

"Did you speak to him?"

"Nah."

"Just like you didn't speak to me at P. J. Clarke's the other day."

"Well, I just happened to be there for a drink; given our previous arrangement, I didn't know if you'd want to talk."

"Well, like you say, it's been a long time. You ever see Ab?"

"Funny you should mention that; he kibitzed on a deal another guy at his firm did for us. He's an investment banker, you know."

"How about the Colonel, you ever hear anything about him?"

"Ab says he's in the antiques business up in Connecticut. Ab has a place up there and said he ran into him."

"Antiques? The Colonel? That doesn't sound like him."

"Well, you and him did okay in the gold coin business, remember? That's antiques, sort of."

"You still pissed off about not being in on that, Charlie?"

"Of course not," Crow said, clapping Cantor on the forearm. "I've done real good; why should I care? Say, how did you spend your cut?"

"I bought a car and some clothes, bought a little apartment and put the rest in the stock market and left it there."

"Good for you, Bobby! I guess you're a rich man now, huh?"

"I've done okay. At least I don't have to live on my pension."

They had coffee, and the waiter brought the check. Crow paid it with a black American Express card.

"Well, Bob," Crow said, "do I have your permission to arrange a class reunion?"

"What'd you have in mind?"

"I don't know, maybe some good steaks and a few bottles of fine wine. You up for that?"

"Sure. I guess so."

"They've got some private rooms here; maybe we'll do that."

"Fine by me."

They got up and walked to the front door; there was a silver Rolls-Royce, the new one built by BMW, waiting at the curb, a uniformed chauffeur braced with the door open.

"Drop you someplace, Bob?"

"Nah, it's a nice day; I think I'll walk for a while."

"I'll be in touch," Crow said, shaking his hand.

"Might be nice to see the old crowd at that," Cantor said, waving good-bye and turning up Fifty-second Street, toward Fifth Avenue, while Crow's Rolls glided toward Sixth.

Cantor had no doubt that Charlie wasn't going to arrange a class reunion. "I wonder what that guy is up to," he said aloud to himself. He looked back toward Sixth Avenue and saw the Rolls turn the corner, so he crossed the street and went into a parking garage. He checked the recorder in his van and found that it had worked perfectly.

27

Stone waited until after lunch to call Carla.

"Hello?" She didn't sound sleepy.

"I hope I didn't wake you."

"Are you kidding? I've been awake for all of ten minutes."

"Well, you worked late."

"So I did. Why did you sneak out without waking me?"

"Because you worked late. Anyway, I kissed you before I left, but you didn't notice."

"Liar. I would have noticed."

"Before we go on with this, when are you going to break your news to Harlan?"

"I'm having a drink with him early this evening, before I go on. Don't worry, he'll take it like a man."

"What does that mean?"

"He'll look shocked and hurt, then he'll go out and get laid."

"Oh. In that case, do you ever get an evening off from your gig?"

"Three of them. I only work four days a week."

"Want to drive up to Connecticut on Sunday and stay for a night or two?"

"As long as we don't leave before three o'clock."

"Three it is. I'll call you when I'm five minutes from the hotel. I'll be in an evil-looking black Mercedes, at the Seventy-sixth Street entrance."

"What clothes shall I bring?"

"Tweeds."

"Oh, come on."

"Country clothes, then."

"If you say so."

"You were a wonderful surprise last night," he said.

"So were you."

"Are you taking me to Connecticut so Harlan won't find out?"

"I think it might be politic to avoid being seen together in the city for a little while, don't you?"

"I guess it couldn't hurt," she admitted.

"I wouldn't want him to get mad and take it out on the law firm; he's an important client. Let him down easy, will you? Let your Swedish side handle it, not your Italian side. The stiletto wouldn't look nice, protruding from between his shoulder blades. Figuratively speaking."

"You're a card."

"It was your line."

"See you Sunday at three." She hung up.

Joan buzzed him.

"Yes?"

"Lance Cabot on line two."

Stone picked up the phone. "Hello, Lance."

"It's Holly," she said. "Hang on, I'll get him for you."

"Did you enjoy your stay in Connecticut?"

"Not so much, after you left."

"A man's gotta work."

"A woman, too. Hang on for Lance." She put him on hold.

He was on hold for an annoyingly long time before Lance spoke. "Stone?"

"Yes, Lance."

"Sorry to keep you waiting. I plead national security."

"You must be a Republican."

"I don't do politics; it's bad policy in my line of work."

"I agree."

"I want to thank you for looking in on Barton. I'm much relieved to know that he's doing better."

"Better, except he still can't remember the assault."

"That's understandable. I once took a cricket bat to the head and didn't remember twelve hours. Still don't."

"I didn't know cricket was a contact sport."

"The incident did not take place on a cricket pitch," Lance said, "and the batter was a woman."

Stone chuckled in spite of himself. Lance didn't have much of a sense of humor, usually. "Lance, what do you know about Abner Kramer?"

"Financial bigwig, Democratic Party contributor; rumors about a cabinet post, if Will Lee gets reelected."

"I can read that in the *Times*. I'd expect more from a highly placed member of the intelligence community."

"It's all I need to know about him."

"You might need to know more."

"Why?"

"He and Barton had a brief exchange about the mahogany secretary when we saw him in a restaurant in Connecticut."

"Oh yes, I hear you were breaking and entering up there."

"Kramer wants to buy the secretary from Barton. Did Holly tell you about the empty space in his study? Just the right size for the secretary."

"But it was an empty space, not a piece of furniture."

"It crossed my mind that, if Barton wouldn't sell it, Kramer might want it anyway. You know that he and Barton did some business when they were in the Marines."

"I heard. I'll put out a couple of feelers on Kramer."

"I'd especially like to know if he's had any shady dealings the past few years."

"I expect the president might like to know that, too."

"That's up to you."

"Anything else you need?"

"Well, there's a character named Charlie Crow, who was part of the Marine unit, too, and another named Harry Collins; everybody else is dead."

"You left out your friend, Cantor."

"I know enough about him."

"Okay, I'll put Holly on it."

"Thanks. I think that could be helpful. Barton liked Holly a lot."

"My brother was always fond of the ladies, and Holly corresponds to a type I used to see him with."

"Did that cross your mind when you sent her to Connecticut?"

"I don't remember."

"You're getting as bad as Barton. I hope his memory isn't as selective."

"You think he's holding out on us, Stone?"

"I think he's a craftier man than he lets on."

"He is that."

"Lance, how hard did you try to find him during your years apart?"

"Hard at first; after I was transferred to London, less hard. I didn't use agency resources, if that's what you mean."

"Why would he want to stay out of touch with his younger brother?"

"I haven't asked him that."

Maybe you wouldn't like the answer, Stone thought. He said good-bye and hung up.

28

Stone and Dino were still on their first drink when Bob Cantor walked into Elaine's.

"Hey, Bob," Dino said. "It's after dark, and you're out of your coffin!"

"Very funny. I usually work at night, you know."

"My very point," Dino said.

"It is unusual to see you in here," Stone pointed out.

"I live downtown, okay? I hate the subway, cabs are expensive and there's never any parking around here, except at twenty bucks an hour."

"All good reasons," Stone said.

Cantor took out a small tape player and handed Stone an earpiece. "I wanted you to hear this," he said.

Stone listened to the lunchtime conversation, then handed the earpiece back to Cantor.

"Don't I get to hear?" Dino asked. "I'm on the team, too, you know."

"He is?" Cantor asked.

"He is," Stone replied. "Why does Charlie want to have a reunion?"

"Dunno," Cantor said. "Maybe he's getting all sentimental in his old age, but I doubt it."

"But what would he have to gain by getting you, Ab Kramer and Harry Collins together all in one place?"

"You're forgetting the Colonel."

"Him, too."

"I can't think of any reason, and I doubt Charlie plans to do it. It would be like him to suggest the opposite of what he intends to do."

"Okay," Stone said. "Suppose he beat up the Colonel and took his mahogany secretary. He's already got it, so what does he want to do, gloat?"

"Ransom it," Dino said. "He'll say he knows somebody who can get it back for half what it's worth. That way, he makes a quick twelve million, and the Colonel sells it and gets the rest."

"That sounds like Charlie," Cantor said. "It's what he would do."

"On the tape," Stone said, "he says he bears no hard feelings about the gold coin thing that you and the Colonel profited from. Does that sound like him?"

"No, it doesn't; Charlie would hold a grudge forever."

"Wait a minute," Dino said, "what's this about a gold coin?"

Stone gave him a quick version of the story.

"Ah," Dino said, "if he's got the secretary, and he found the die in the drawer, then he can afford to be magnanimous about the coin deal, since he's in a position to make his own coin and repeat the deal."

"That makes a lot of sense," Stone said.

Cantor shook his head. "Just because Charlie had the die wouldn't make him magnanimous; he would want to gloat. No, all this seems logical, but it's not right. It's not Charlie. He doesn't want the reunion; he wants something else."

"Wants what?" Stone asked.

"Who knows? It could be something completely off the wall."

"Maybe he wants to impress the Colonel with how well he's done over the years," Stone said.

Cantor nodded. "Now *that* makes sense, showing off for the Colonel. Funny, though, he didn't mention the Colonel. I brought up his name."

"Did you agree to the reunion?" Dino asked.

"Yeah, I said okay," Cantor replied.

"Dino," Stone said, "have your people tailed Charlie Crow yet?"

"Yep," Dino said. "In fact, they planted a very nice little GPS device on the Rolls. I can follow it on any laptop."

"Dino, you said you weren't going to put anything on a computer."

"Nah, this device is off the books, and so is the website that tracks it."

"So, where'd he go?"

"His lawyer's office, for a little over three hours, then his own office, then home. He and his wife ordered in Chinese."

"Pretty dull life," Cantor said.

"Yeah," Stone agreed, "but I wonder about the trip to his lawyer's office. Two hours is a long time for a client to sit with his lawyer. Three is forever."

"Maybe he's got a deal cooking," Dino offered.

"Still, three hours is a long time. I can't ever remember meeting with a client for three hours."

"Yeah," Dino said, "but it's hard to spend three hours talking about a DUI or a divorce. Crow has a *business,* remember?"

"My clients have businesses, too," Stone said defensively. "I met with Harlan Deal yesterday, and it didn't take three hours."

"Harlan Deal is *your* client?" Dino asked.

"He is." Long pause. "Well, I consulted on a matter."

"For how long?"

"Well, the meeting lasted only a few minutes, but I had to spend several hours sewing up everything."

"Sewing up what?" Dino asked.

"That's privileged," Stone replied. "Let's just say that I completed a negotiation that Harlan couldn't, and in the process, I saved him a substantial chunk of his fortune."

"That sounds like a paternity suit," Dino said.

"It was a good deal more important than that," Stone replied, "and I think I can safely say that the outcome was favorable for all concerned, including me."

"How was it favorable for you?" Dino asked.

"Harlan sent me a check for twenty-five grand this morning by messenger."

"Now I'm impressed," Dino said.

"Me, too," echoed Cantor.

"And well you should be," Stone said, drawing himself up to his full height. "Harlan certainly was."

"Is that what you call him? Harlan? Not Mr. Deal?"

"Yeah, sure."

"And what does he call you?"

"He calls me Mr. Barrington."

"Sounds a little standoffish," Cantor said.

"Our relationship is perfectly cordial," Stone replied.

"I thought maybe this had something to do with that story in the *Times* business section this morning," Dino said.

"His acquisition of the aircraft-leasing company? That was the icing on the cake. Harlan had a good day."

Cantor, who was sitting facing the door, suddenly sat up.

Stone and Dino followed his gaze to the bar. A heavyset, florid-faced man was taking a stool.

"What?" Stone asked.

"I'd swear to God that's Harry Collins," Cantor said.

"Who?" Dino asked.

"The other guy from the Colonel's old outfit. Charlie mentioned seeing him at the track. I mean, he's gained a lot of weight, but I think that's Harry."

"Now that's interesting," Stone said. "First Charlie Crow walks into P. J. Clarke's when you're there, and now Harry Collins walks into Elaine's when you're here. And you're hardly ever here."

"Well, I'm not speaking to him," Cantor said. "I'll leave that to Charlie." He picked up a menu and ordered dinner; they all did. By the time their first course arrived, Harry Collins had finished his drink and left.

29

Stone was throwing a few things in a bag on Sunday afternoon, getting ready to pick up Carla for their trip to Connecticut, when his phone rang.

"Hello?"

"It's Eggers." He sounded dour.

"Hi, Bill. What has you making phone calls on a Sunday?"

"I had lunch with Harlan Deal."

"That sounds like a reason for indigestion, not a Sunday phone call."

"His girlfriend dumped him," Eggers said.

"The one who signed the prenup?"

"The very one."

"Well, the poor guy."

"He blames you."

"Hey, wait a minute. I got her to agree to the prenup; I didn't sign on to see that they lived happily ever after."

"Harlan says he's heard about your reputation with women, and he thinks you stole her."

"What reputation with women? Usually, I get dumped!"

"What happened to that emergency room doctor you were going out with?"

"A perfect example," Stone said. "A couple of weeks ago, she called and said she had to talk to me right away."

"Sounds like she was pregnant."

"That crossed my mind, but it wasn't what was on hers. We met for lunch, and she broke the news to me that she'd been seeing a doctor at her hospital and that he had asked her to marry him."

"Sounds like the signal for you to jump in and see the doc's raise."

"Well, I wasn't quite up to seeing the doctor's raise, and, anyway, it wasn't a card game."

"Did you think she was bluffing?"

"That crossed my mind, too, but like I said, it wasn't a card game."

"So how did you handle the doc's raise?"

"Since it wasn't a card game, I wished the two of them every possible happiness."

"Now, *that* sounds like a bluff."

"Why are you poker-obsessed today?"

"I know a poker game when I see one. Did she call your bluff?"

"She pecked me on the cheek, said it had been fun and left the restaurant."

"So she called your bluff."

"In a manner of speaking."

"Did you run after her?"

"Not exactly."

"Why not?"

"I hadn't paid the check. And it took a few minutes to get it out of the waiter."

"Plenty of time for her to marry the doc."

"Figuratively speaking, I suppose so."

"Heard from her since?"

"No."

"Have you called her?"

"Ah, no."

"Game over."

"Not until she marries the doc."

"How do you know she hasn't?"

"Because Dino's girl, Genevieve, works with her at the hospital, and she would have told Dino, and since Dino loves to gloat, he would have told me."

"So you're sure she hasn't married the doc?"

"Not absolutely entirely."

"Why not?"

"Because Dino's girl isn't speaking to him right now."

"Why not?"

"He has no idea."

"She won't tell him?"

"No."

"I've played that game and lost," Eggers said. "What's he going to do about it?"

"He's afraid to do anything, and he won't take my advice."

"Which is?"

"Pretend nothing has happened, and call her and ask her to dinner."

"That's not bad," Eggers said, a touch of admiration in his voice.

"I thought it was pretty good."

"If it's such good advice, why don't you follow it yourself?"

"You mean call Dr. Eliza and just ask her to dinner, as if nothing has happened?"

"Exactly."

"I can't do that."

"Why not?"

"Because she's decided to marry another guy."

"No she hasn't."

"Haven't you listened to anything I've said to you?"

"Sure I have. She told you another guy has asked her to marry him; she didn't say she'd said yes, did she?"

"Well..."

"Well, what?"

"Shut up. I'm mentally reviewing the conversation."

Eggers was quiet for three seconds. "So?"

"Well, maybe she didn't say exactly that, but I think I'm entitled to draw that inference."

"This isn't a dispute over a contract, Stone."

"Well, in a way it is."

"You didn't have a contract with her, did you? Either written or implied?"

"Well, she must have thought so, because she felt it necessary to report this proposal of marriage to me."

"Listen," Eggers said, "I'm getting lost here. What was your original point?"

"I don't remember," Stone said. "What was the original question?"

"Uh...oh, the question was Harlan Deal's."

"I don't remember."

"I think it was more of a contention than a question. He thinks you stole his girl."

"I wasn't hired not to steal his girl, was I?"

"You mean you stole his girl?"

"Certainly not. In no way, shape or form."

"That doesn't sound like a complete denial to me."

"What kind of denial would you like?"

"Answer the question directly: Did you steal his girl?"

"No."

"You're sure."

"Bill, if the girl decided to dump Harlan, it wasn't because I got her to."

"What did you advise her to do?"

"My only advice to her was to read the prenup and consult a lawyer before signing."

"Did she consult a lawyer?"

"Well, she says she did."

"Where were you at the time?"

"At a table at Bemelmens Bar at the Carlyle."

"Was another lawyer sitting at the table?"

"No."

"So the lawyer she consulted was you?"

"That would be a conflict of interest, Bill."

"It certainly would, Stone. Did you advise her to dump Harlan?"

"Certainly not! Why would I do that? Marrying Harlan looked like a pretty good deal to me."

"Did you tell her that?"

"No."

"Maybe you should have."

"I couldn't give her advice, Bill; she wasn't my client."

"And what, exactly, is she to you?"

"Harlan Deal's ex-girlfriend, what else?"

"Which is a good enough reason for you to steal her from Harlan."

"If she had already dumped him, she couldn't be stolen, could she?"

"This conversation is exhausting me," Eggers said.

"Me, too."

"What do you want me to tell Harlan?"

"Tell him? I don't want you to tell him anything."

"All right, I'll tell him you didn't steal his girlfriend."

"That would be the accurate thing to tell him. Now I have to go, Bill; I have a date."

"I hope to God it isn't with Harlan's ex-girlfriend, because he'll find out."

"Good-bye, Bill!" Stone hung up, then he picked up the phone and called Harlan Deal's ex-girlfriend. "I'm on my way. I'll be there in ten minutes. Meet me in the garage, instead of on the street, okay?"

"Okay," she said.

30

Stone pulled into the Hotel Carlyle garage and looked around. No Carla.

The attendant approached. "Parking, sir?"

"Picking up," Stone replied.

The attendant looked around. "Anyone in particular?"

"A lady."

"There's no lady, sir."

"There will be shortly. I'm going to turn around." Stone did a quick three-pointer, putting the passenger door close to the garage's lobby door.

The attendant walked over. "I'm sorry, sir, you can't park there."

"I'm not parking, I'm waiting."

"For the lady."

"You've grasped it."

The attendant reached into a hip pocket and produced a stack of tickets. He was about to tear one off.

"I don't need a ticket," Stone said.

"But you're parked."

"I'm just waiting."

"Sir, after you've waited for a while, you're parked. We're busy here."

Stone looked around. "I don't see any other cars coming in or out."

"Sort of like ladies," the attendant said.

At that moment the lobby door opened, and Carla emerged carrying one of those plastic duffels with blobs all over it that cost a couple of thousand dollars. The attendant took the bag, and Stone popped the trunk for him, then he leaned over and opened the door for Carla. "Duck," he said, pulling her down until her head rested on his thigh.

"Can't you wait until we get to Connecticut?" she asked.

"Harlan may be having us followed."

"So you want his people to catch us like this?" She bit him on the thigh.

"Ouch!" He put the car in gear. "I just don't want anyone who's watching to see you in the car."

She bit him again, higher up. "Or doing this."

"Exactly," he said, "and that hurt."

"It was supposed to."

Stone got over to Fifth Avenue, then down to Sixty-sixth Street and turned into the park, checking his rearview mirror. "Just another minute, until I'm sure there's no one on our tail."

"Oh, take your time," she said, biting him again. "I'm enjoying this."

Stone reached the other side of the park and turned up Central Park West, then left on Seventy-second. "Okay, you can sit up now; I think we're tailless."

"Speak for yourself," she said, biting him again.

"Carla, I'm going to have teeth marks from my knee to my crotch."

"Closer to your crotch, but who's mapping?" She sat up. "What a beautiful Sunday afternoon! I hadn't seen it until now."

Stone turned onto the West Side Highway and accelerated past a dozen cars, then settled in the right lane and watched his mirrors.

"Why do you think Harlan is having us followed?" Carla asked.

"Because Bill Eggers called me half an hour ago and said Harlan thought I had stolen you from him."

"Who's Bill Eggers?"

"Harlan's lawyer."

"I thought you were Harlan's lawyer."

"I was, ah, sort of on special assignment."

"You didn't perform very well, did you?"

"What do you mean? I got the prenup signed, didn't I?"

"Among other things. But you did steal me from Harlan."

"You had already made the decision to leave him," Stone said.

"Well, that's what I told you. I had to take your ethical considerations into account, didn't I?"

Stone checked the mirror again and saw a black SUV barreling up the passing lane. "Duck," he said, pulling her down into his lap again. She promptly unzipped his zipper and began extracting him. The SUV abruptly pulled alongside and paced him. Stone looked left and saw two beefy men through the open window: one driving, the other eyeing him suspiciously. The Hudson River flashed on the other side of the pursuing car.

Carla had achieved her objective and was entertaining Stone.

Stone was able to make small noises but couldn't speak, because the thug in the car next to him would see his lips move and know he was talking to someone.

The black SUV suddenly accelerated and pulled ahead of him. "Now they're checking us out in their mirrors," he said, attempting ventriloquism.

She stopped for a moment. "Who cares?" she asked, then resumed.

Stone tried to focus on the rear of the SUV. It was a Porsche

Cayenne Turbo; no wonder it was so quick. Then, without much warning, he climaxed.

Carla kept going for a minute, then pulled back and dabbed at him with a tissue. "There, dear, is that better?"

"It is incomparably better," Stone said, panting, "but you still have to keep down."

Then the Cayenne accelerated as if shot from a cannon and flew off at the next exit.

"I think we're safe, now," Stone said. "You can come up for air."

Carla rezipped him, sat up and checked herself in the vanity mirror, dabbing at her lipstick. "You owe me one," she said.

Stone patted her on the knee. "And you shall be repaid in full, my dear."

"And in kind, I hope."

"Whatever your heart desires."

"We're not talking about my heart."

"Whatever the relevant part of you desires."

"That's more like it."

"You're lucky I didn't drive into the Hudson," Stone said. "In fact, I'm still a little woozy."

"Oh, I knew you'd maintain control of yourself."

"I don't think I would have described myself as in control."

"It's wonderful how men can do it anywhere, like dogs."

"You were doing the doing; I was just hanging on for dear life."

"I suppose you could look at it that way," she said. "How soon will you be able to do it again?"

"Not until I'm out of the car," Stone said, "and indoors."

"Don't you like sex outdoors?"

"I prefer beds or bearskin rugs before fires."

"Does your house have a bearskin rug before a fire?"

"It has a fireplace."

She sighed. "Well, I guess that will just have to do."

31

Stone kept checking his mirror, looking for the black Cayenne, and once, near Bedford, he turned off the Sawmill River Parkway and stopped for gas, while telling Carla to keep down. He saw no pursuer during the six-minute stop, so when they were back on the Sawmill, he gave Carla the all clear again.

She sat up. "I think I'm beginning to like it down there," she said. "I was almost asleep."

Stone continued up I-684 to I-84, after which they were on country roads. He stopped occasionally to check for a tail but saw only weekenders with New York plates, their cars stuffed with pumpkins and overpriced antiques, wending their way back to their very expensive cottages.

Finally, they arrived in Washington and drove down little streets choked with gold and red leaves to his own cottage. He pulled into the driveway and behind the hedge, now concealed from the road. "Stay here for just a minute while I check the house," he said.

"Oh, all right," she replied, "but very soon I'm going to want a drink."

"Very soon," he said, getting out of the car and unlocking the front door. The alarm system beeped at him, and he entered his code. Alarmingly, it continued to beep. He reentered the code, the only code he had ever had for this house, and without so much as taking another breath, a loud, electronic beep began screeching, and an even louder siren began to wail. He stepped outside the door and yelled to Carla. "It's all right; just wait a minute." He stepped back inside to hear the phone ringing and picked it up.

"Hello."

"This is Litchfield Security. To whom am I speaking?"

"This is Stone Barrington." He gave the man the cancellation code, and a moment later, the noise stopped. "My code didn't work," he said.

"What code are you using?"

Stone told him.

"I'm sorry, Mr. Barrington, but that is not the code programmed into your system."

"Then somebody has changed it, because I've never had another code for this system."

"No one here has changed your code, sir."

"Well, please change it back."

"What was the original code?"

Stone told him.

"You wish to use that?"

"Yes, please."

"May I have your social security number and your mother's maiden name for identification purposes?"

Stone gave them to him.

"One moment, please."

Stone stood waiting, tapping his foot.

"Mr. Barrington, your code has been reinstated. I'm sorry for the difficulty."

"But you have no idea how it got changed?"

"No, sir. It can be changed from your keypad, but that requires the original code."

"Thank you," Stone said, then hung up. He stepped outside the door. "Okay, Carla, we're all right now," he called. He opened the trunk with his key and brought their bags inside. "Here we are."

"It's lovely," she said. "Now can I have a drink? That bourbon you like, perhaps?"

Stone poured her a drink, then took their bags upstairs and returned to pour himself one.

Carla was sitting on the living room sofa. "It's very pretty, fresh flowers and all."

"The housekeeper," Stone said. "Do you mind if I make a quick phone call?"

"Of course not, as long as it's not for phone sex."

Stone laughed, sat down beside her, picked up the phone and called Bob Cantor.

"Cantor."

"Bob, I've just arrived at the Connecticut house, and my alarm code didn't work. Somehow, it had been changed. Do you have any idea how that could have happened? I mean, you installed the system, after all."

"A very sophisticated electronics nut could use a small instrument to read your code and change it," he said. "He would have to change the code to get past your system, then change it back before he left."

"He didn't change it back."

"Then one of two things happened: Either he forgot to change it back, or he wanted you to know he had been there."

"Why would he want that?"

"Just to annoy you, probably, and to make you feel unsafe in your own house."

"How can I prevent this happening again?"

"I have a modified circuit card that can be installed in your keypad that will make the alarm go off immediately if he should try it again. It won't even wait the usual thirty seconds."

"When can you install it?"

"How soon do you want it done?"

"As soon as possible."

"I can drive up there now, if you like, but you're going to have to buy me dinner and put me up for the night."

"There's a problem with that."

"I take it you are not traveling alone."

"Correct, but I'll put you up at the local inn and buy you dinner there."

"Oh, good, then I can bring company."

"Sure, you can." Stone looked at his watch. "We're going to dinner at seven-thirty; I suggest you arrive at the house shortly after that, do your work, then go check in at the Mayflower. I'll make your reservation."

"You are a prince, sir. Good-bye and God bless thee." Cantor hung up.

"That's pretty good service," Carla said.

"It's pretty expensive service, but it's worth it, so that we won't be disturbed."

"Do we have to do anything while we're here except make love?"

"Well, between times, when I should be resting, I have to go and see a client who lives a few miles from here. You might enjoy seeing his place."

"Well, all right, as long as I can spend most of my time enjoying you."

"You may certainly do that."

"After all, it's why we came, isn't it?"

"It's one of the reasons," he replied.

"What are the others?"

"You'll have to discover them one at a time."

"May I begin now, so that I will have something to freshen up from when we have dinner? Remember, you owe me one."

"I can arrange immediate repayment," he said, taking her hand and leading her upstairs.

32

Stone and Carla went to the Mayflower Inn for dinner, and as they entered, piano music was coming from the bar.

Carla perked up. "Who's playing?" she asked.

"David Grossman plays in the bar on weekends," Stone said. They stopped at the bar's entrance, the dining room still ahead of them.

"Can we eat in the bar?" Carla asked.

"Sure." Stone let the headwaiter know, and they found a snug table along the wall facing the bar and not too far from the pianist, who was playing standards twice as old as he with great fluency. They ordered drinks and menus.

"I like this inn," Carla said.

"Lots of people do. It was designed as a school by the same architect who did my cottage and the big house next door, called The Rocks, and it was redone at great expense by a retired stockbroker and his wife who recently sold it to somebody I don't know."

Their drinks arrived, and they began looking at menus. Stone looked up and saw Bob Cantor standing in the hall outside the dining room.

"Excuse me for a moment," Carla said. "Ladies' room."

Stone moved the table out for her and decided to go and speak to Cantor.

"Hey," Cantor said, as Stone approached. "Let me introduce you to Bonnie Pepper. Bonnie, this is my friend, Stone Barrington."

Bonnie Pepper was small, blonde and cute. "Hello, Bonnie, it's good to meet you. Bob, have you already been to the house?"

"Oh, yeah, it only took me ten minutes to change the circuit board and reprogram the system." He dug into a pocket and produced a card with a four-digit number written on the back.

Stone looked at the card. "These are the last four digits of my Social Security number," he said. "How did you know that?"

"There's nothing I don't know or can't find out about you, Stone," Cantor said.

"You want to join us for dinner in the bar?" Stone asked.

"I think we'll go to the dining room," Cantor said, winking.

Clearly Bob wanted to be alone with his girl.

"Was that your date who walked out ahead of you?"

"Yes," Stone replied.

"I know her," Cantor said.

"Lots of people do."

Someone tapped Stone on the shoulder from behind. He turned and found Harlan Deal standing there.

"Harlan!" Stone said, half in surprise, half in shock.

"Good evening, Mr. Barrington," Deal said. "What brings you to Connecticut?"

"I have a house here," Stone said.

"Would you like to join some friends and me for dinner?"

"Thank you, Harlan, but I've already eaten, and I want to turn in early. It's been a long week."

"Of course," Deal said.

Stone glanced over Deal's shoulder and saw Carla come out of the ladies' room. He hoped to God that she saw Harlan.

"I'm very grateful for the good work you did on the prenup," Deal said.

"I'm glad to have been of help. I hope you'll both be very happy."

Carla had not seen Deal. She was walking straight toward them. Then she stopped, started walking backward, and disappeared into the ladies' room again.

Stone tried to control his sigh of relief.

"Actually I've changed my mind and decided not to marry her," Deal said.

"A gentleman's prerogative as well as a lady's."

"I felt she was unfaithful."

"I'm sorry." God, he wanted to get away from this man, but he kept a smile frozen on his face. He was determined to let Deal break off the conversation first.

Cantor broke in. "Excuse us, Stone. Our table is ready," he said.

Stone gratefully turned toward him. "Bob, Bonnie, I hope you enjoy your dinner." He watched them walk into the dining room, then turned back, hoping to find Deal gone.

He was not gone. "Are you sure you won't join us, just for a drink?"

"Perhaps another time."

"I'm sure we'll have the opportunity," Deal said. "I've been house hunting all day, and I think I've found something."

"Congratulations, where is it?"

"It's called The Rocks, and it's only a quarter mile from here."

The Rocks was the big house next door to Stone's. "Oh? I hadn't heard it was on the market."

"It isn't, but my agent, Carolyn Klemm, showed it to me anyway. Anything is for sale, you know, at the right price."

"Well, Carolyn should know. She sold me my house, too. In fact, it was originally the gatehouse for The Rocks."

"Well, if I buy The Rocks, perhaps you'll sell me your place, and I can reunite the two."

"I don't think so, Harlan, but I'll be happy to have you for a neighbor." This was an outright lie, and Stone hoped it didn't show.

"We'll see," Deal said. "Well, I'd better join my friends. Good night." Deal shook his hand, turned and walked into the dining room.

Stone ducked into the bar and peeped into the hall, looking for Carla. She came out of the ladies' room and bolted for the front door.

Stone flagged down the bartender. "I have to go. Put the drinks on my account." He found Carla in the car, waiting for him.

"I don't believe it," she said. "That man is *everywhere*."

"He certainly is," Stone said, starting the car. "I think we'll dine elsewhere."

Stone and Carla sat on the bed, watching a DVD of *Singin' in the Rain* and eating a large, heavily laden pizza that Stone had picked up at the pizza parlor in the village.

"I love Gene Kelly," Carla said.

"So do I."

"I think he's the best dancer this country has ever produced."

"Better than Baryshnikov?"

"Baryshnikov was produced by Russia."

"Oh, right."

"I think he's a terrific singer, too."

"So do I, but he's not as good as you, and as far as I know, he didn't play piano, either."

Stone's cell phone vibrated on his belt. He looked at the calling number in the little window. Bob Cantor was calling. What the hell did he want? He ignored it and let it go to voice mail. He considered telling Carla of Harlan Deal's interest in The Rocks but thought better of it. That might put a damper on their sex life.

The following morning, Stone was contemplating getting out of bed when the phone rang. "Hello?"

"It's Dino."

"Good morning."

"It's almost afternoon."

"It's ten A.M.," Stone said. "What's up?"

"I got a call to come in this morning about another case, and I reran last night's GPS surveillance on Charlie Crow's car."

"Where did he go?"

"Just to one place: It was parked for a little under three hours at Abner Kramer's house."

"No kidding?"

"Well, he could have been next door or across the street, I guess. After all, the GPS unit is attached to his car, not to him, but that's where his car was parked."

"What was the time?"

"He arrived a little after eight and left a little before eleven."

"Sounds like dinner," Stone observed.

"Does Charlie Crow sound like the sort of guy an elegant fellow like Kramer would invite to dinner?"

"There's no accounting for taste," Stone reminded him. "Not even in dinner companions."

"Yeah, I guess. I just thought you'd like to know."

"Have you made up with Genevieve?"

"In a manner of speaking."

"What does that mean?"

"It means that she's talking to me but not sleeping with me."

"Have you found out what she was pissed off about?"

"Not a clue. I've wracked my brain."

"She'll get around to telling you, don't worry."

Carla stirred next to Stone.

"Gotta run," Stone said. He hung up and gave his full attention to Carla.

When they had showered and dressed, Carla suddenly said, "How about a picnic?"

"A picnic? What do you mean?"

"Well, you pack a lunch, put down a blanket in a pretty spot and eat."

"Oh, that kind of picnic."

"Is there any other kind?"

"I guess not."

"Do you know of such a spot?"

Stone thought about it for a moment. "Yes, I do," he said. "A clearing on a hilltop overlooking a fine landscape and a handsome house in the distance."

"That should do nicely," she said.

Stone found an old wicker basket with dishes and silver inside that he had discovered in a closet when he had bought the house. They drove down to the Village Market and bought a chicken, some salads and a cold bottle of wine, and Stone drove them to the hilltop road he had visited with Barton and Holly the week before. He parked the car, and they walked down a path to the little clearing.

"Oh," she said, regarding the vista, "this is perfect."

The weather was autumnal, but the sun warmed the clearing. Stone spread a blanket, and Carla busied herself arranging the lunch. "What are these for?" she asked, holding up Stone's binoculars, which he had placed in the basket.

"Oh, I don't know," he said. "Sometimes they make the view more interesting."

They sat cross-legged on the blanket, facing the distant house, ate their chicken and drank their wine. Stone lay back on an elbow and sighed. "This was a wonderful idea," he said.

"I know," she replied. "I have them all the time."

"Ideas?"

"Wonderful ideas."

"Well, so far I have no complaints about your ideas, only your ex-boyfriends."

"Harlan is a pig," she said.

"What did you ever see in him?"

"He's one of those men who can be perfectly charming when you first meet him, then, as time wears on, becomes first awfully boring, then finally just awful."

"I've known women like that."

"Really? I thought it was exclusively a male characteristic."

Stone sat up on the blanket and picked up the binoculars.

"What is it?" Carla asked.

"A truck," he replied.

"It is a very Harlanlike characteristic to find a truck more interesting than I," she said, archly.

"Oh, I don't find it nearly as interesting as you, but you're too close for binoculars," he replied, focusing more finely.

She pulled the binoculars away from his face and kissed him. "Does that help?"

"That was delightful, but they're unloading something from the truck, and I'd like to see what it is, if you'll give me just a moment, then you will have my undivided attention."

"Oh, all right," she said, handing him the binoculars.

Stone watched as four men removed a large crate from the back of the truck and began carrying it up the front steps of the house. The two men at the rear of the crate then hoisted it above their heads and climbed the steps.

"It's light," Stone said.

"Swell."

"And it's bigger at the bottom than at the top."

"Fascinating."

Someone opened the front doors wide, and the men carried in the crate.

"It's empty," Stone said.

"What?"

"Four men are carrying a large, empty crate into Ab Kramer's house."

"Ab Kramer? The financial guy?"

"One and the same. Now why would they take an empty crate into his house."

"Maybe they're going to pack something in the crate and take it away."

"Now that is an eminently sensible observation," he said, putting down the binoculars, taking her into his arms and pulling her down to the blanket. "And you have my undivided attention."

"I hope you're not thinking of undressing me," she said. "It's chilly out here."

"I was seeking only affection, not sex."

"Well, it's not as though we haven't been getting any sex, is it?"

He laughed. "I've no complaints in that department."

She sat up and looked toward the house, then picked up the binoculars. "They're bringing the crate out," she said.

"May I look?"

She handed him the binoculars.

Stone watched as the men reloaded the crate into the truck and was surprised that they coordinated their efforts and actually tossed the crate the last few feet. He could hear the noise when it fell into the bed of the truck. "There's still nothing in it."

"What?"

"They took an empty crate into the house, then brought it out again, still empty. Does that make any sense?"

"Not to me."

"Nor to me, either."

34

The sun passed behind the trees, bringing shade and chill to their clearing. Carla began collecting their debris and packing up.

"You have a domestic side, don't you?" Stone said admiringly.

"My domestic side begins and ends with picking up the phone and calling room service. Why do you think I live in a hotel?"

"Well, when required, you rise to the occasion."

"I could say the same of you," she said, handing him the basket and shaking out the blanket.

What am I going to do with this girl? Stone was thinking. If Harlan Deal so much as sees us together, he could yank his account from Woodman & Weld, and at least half my income would vanish in a puff of smoke. She's great, but is the relationship worth that risk? "I'd like you to meet someone," Stone said, an ulterior motive stirring deep down in his cerebral cortex.

"Who?"

"A client of mine. You'll like him."

"Does he live in the woods?"

"Yes, but not these woods. Next to a lake."

They drove down to Lake Waramaug and to Barton Cabot's

house. To Stone's surprise, Barton was standing outside the barn, waiting for them, his right hand in his trousers pocket.

"Good afternoon, Stone," Barton said as they got out of the car. He gave Carla a long look up and down. "And who's this?"

"Barton, this is Carla. Carla, this is Barton Cabot."

She offered him a hand. "How do you do?" she said.

"I do very well, but never better than now," Barton replied.

"You were expecting us?" Stone asked.

Barton shook his head. "Just something I ordered from a catalogue. It beeps in the house and barn when a car drives past the mailbox. Sort of a doorbell for automobiles." He led them into the house and the study and offered them drinks.

"I think I'd rather have tea, if you can manage it," Carla said.

"I'll have bourbon in my tea," Stone added.

Ten minutes later they were settled into comfortable furniture before a blazing fire.

"Carla, where do you live?" Barton asked.

"In New York City."

"Where in New York City?"

"At the Carlyle Hotel. I sing there, in the Bemelmens Bar, four nights a week. Play the piano, too."

"I'd love to hear you sometime."

"I'd love for you to hear me sometime."

"I have a piano."

"Is it in tune?"

"I'm afraid not."

"I'm afraid I don't play untuned pianos, and I sing only for money."

"I'll pay the Carlyle, then."

"Good."

Stone eased out of his chair, strolled to the other side of the study and inspected a set of leather-bound books. His ulterior motive realized, he was not needed on the other side of the room. He extracted a book, one of six in a leather-bound set. It was a signed first edition of Winston Churchill's history of the Second World War. He wondered, philistine that he was, what *that* was worth at auction. He moved to a wall hung with pictures, close together. The nearest to him was a Western scene by Albert Bierstadt. He spotted two very fine landscapes from the Hudson River School. This was the wall of either a multimillionaire or a very shrewd collector who had been at it for a long time. He went on exploring, listening in occasionally on the conversation going on behind him.

"You appear to be of Scandinavian extraction," Barton said.

"Half Swedish, half Sicilian."

"What an interesting combination."

"You have no idea."

The conversation fell into a gap, and Stone returned to his seat.

"Is there a powder room nearby?" Carla asked Barton.

"Through that door, first left," Barton replied.

Carla rose and left the room.

"Is she for me?" Barton asked.

"She is if you want her and she's agreeable."

"What have I done to deserve such a gift?"

"You'll be getting me off a hook. She recently left a former, very powerful boyfriend who is a legal client of mine, in a manner of speaking, and if he catches me in her company, it might reflect badly on the firm to which I am counsel."

"I'm happy to be of help," Barton replied with a small smile.

"Would you like to keep her for a couple of days, then return her to the city?"

"Yes, I would."

"Good. Now I have a puzzle for you."

"Shoot."

"Carla and I picnicked today at the spot where you and Holly and I watched Ab Kramer's house."

"Yes?"

"A truck arrived, and four men unloaded a large crate that, from the way they carried it, appeared to be empty."

"So Ab is packing up something?"

"I don't think so. A few minutes later the four men returned with the crate and practically tossed it back into the truck. I think it was still empty."

Barton's brow furrowed, then his eyebrows suddenly went up. "What were the dimensions of the crate?"

"I don't know exactly, but it appeared to be around seven or eight feet by four or five feet, and it was deeper at the bottom than at the top."

"Around the size it would take to hold a large mahogany secretary?"

Stone was about to reply when Carla came back into the room, and Barton signaled to stop their conversation.

"Somehow I sense you two have been talking about me," Carla said.

"Actually, we have," Stone said. "After running into our mutual acquaintance last night at the inn, I think it might be best if you didn't come back to the house with me."

"You mean you are abandoning me in the wilds of Connecticut?"

"Yes, I'm afraid so. Barton has agreed to shelter you for a bit, then return you to New York. I'll pack your things and leave them on my front stoop, and you and Barton can collect them when you go to the Mayflower Inn for dinner this evening."

"Why the Mayflower?" Barton asked.

"Because a former friend of Carla is staying there, and I think it would be a good idea if he saw the two of you together."

"Rather," Carla said, "than the two of us?"

"Yes. It would cause more grief than you can imagine if Harlan saw you and me together."

"If you say so," she replied.

Stone drained his teacup and stood up. "Will you two excuse me, then?"

"Of course," Barton said. "I'll walk you out. Be right back, Carla."

Stone and Barton shuffled through the leaves to where he had parked his car.

"That was deftly done," Barton said.

"It seemed the best solution to the problem for all concerned."

"I'm grateful for your solution."

"Barton, you were saying that the crate I saw at Ab's house was of a size and shape to hold a mahogany secretary?"

"Yes."

"But it was empty on both arrival and departure."

"There might be a very good reason for that."

"What would that be?"

"The crate was also of a size and shape that one could use to see if it would fit well in an empty space in Ab's study."

"Ah."

"Ah, indeed."

Stone got into the car. "We'll talk more about this."

"Good."

Stone started his car and drove away, relieved to have Carla off his hands, at least temporarily and maybe permanently.

Stone arrived at Elaine's that evening to find Dino parked at the usual table, but this time in the company of the lovely Genevieve. "Good evening," he said, sitting down. Somebody placed a glass of Knob Creek before him.

"How was the country?" Genevieve asked.

Stone noticed that she was wearing a small but lovely diamond bracelet that he hadn't seen before. "Like a picture postcard," he said. "The foliage is at its very peak. Why don't the two of you run up there for a couple of days and use the house?"

"What a nice idea," she said. "We'll have to coordinate our schedules, Dino, and see what we can arrange."

"I'm am at your beck and call," Dino said. Whatever his transgression against Genevieve might have been, he had apparently been absolved and had promised not to sin again.

Genevieve excused herself and went to the ladies'.

"Did you figure out what you did?" Stone asked Dino.

"Something to do with the relative placement of our shoes in the closet, I think. I'm still not sure exactly what."

"Never touch anything of hers, unless you're helping her remove it from her body," Stone said.

"Sage advice, for once."

"What do you mean, for once? I always give sage advice. Your life would be so much richer and fuller and happier if you would just take my sage advice. If you'll cast your thoughts back a few years, you'll recall that I advised you not to marry Mary Ann."

"Yeah, but you waited until she was pregnant to advise me."

"I didn't say my advice was always timely, just sage."

"It wasn't very timely with Genevieve, either."

"You had only to ask."

"You mean, I should call you up and ask you about the arrangement of her clothes in the closet?"

"Such a call might have saved you the purchase of a diamond bracelet."

Dino reddened slightly. "You noticed that, huh?"

"Noticed it? She was waving it back and forth under my nose. My eyes must have looked like I was watching a tennis match."

"Well, I know a guy in the diamond district; he gave me a price."

"I would not advise you on the purchase of diamond jewelry," Stone said. "I have always avoided anything to do with diamonds."

"That's because you don't know your women long enough to get around to gift giving, before they dump you."

"Once and a while, if I'm a little out of sync, a birthday pops up. Or Christmas."

Genevieve returned to the table and sat down. "Eliza is getting married to her doctor next Sunday afternoon," she said to Stone, not too casually.

Stone snorted. "I'll believe it when I see it," he said.

"You can see it next Sunday afternoon; she asked me to invite you. She's not sending out formal invitations."

Dino spoke up. "I think you should send her a wedding gift—something nice from Tiffany."

"If I did, she'd just have to return it when she calls off the wedding."

"You doubt her commitment?" Genevieve asked.

"Gen, less than a month ago, she was telling me she'd rather perform major abdominal surgery on herself than marry a doctor."

"Things change."

"Like wedding plans."

"This particular doctor is the most brilliant surgeon at the hospital."

"Good, then she won't have to perform surgery on herself."

"Half the celebrities and rich people in this city have gone under his knife."

Stone turned to Dino. "If I ever need surgery, put me in a different hospital."

"I'll just shoot you," Dino replied.

"Eliza has dangled this marriage possibility before me, looking for some response," Stone said.

"A response would be nice," Genevieve replied.

"She's expecting me to charge down the aisle when the minister gets to the part 'if any man can show cause why this woman should not marry this man'..."

"How romantic that would be," Genevieve said. "Shall I tell Eliza to expect you?"

"To charge down the aisle?"

"To come to the wedding."

"I suppose it would be churlish of me to decline."

"Very churlish."

"Well, okay. I'll send some sort of gift. What would be appropriate?"

Genevieve stared at the ceiling, as if deep in thought. "I don't think there is an appropriate wedding gift from a man who has disappointed a woman," she said finally.

"Disappointed? That assumes that I've appointed... uh, that I've made promises I didn't keep."

"Promises are often implied," Genevieve said.

"That's right," Dino said. "Promises are often implied." Genevieve patted his hand. Dino might finally get laid.

"You stay out of this," Stone said to him. He picked up a menu. "Let's order dinner." He waved his empty glass at a waiter.

Elaine came and sat down. "So, you going to the wedding?"

Stone didn't look up from the menu. "I'm a victim of a conspiracy," he said.

"We're just all concerned about you," Dino said, his voice dripping sarcasm.

Stone closed his menu. "Am I going to have to dine down the street somewhere?"

Elaine glared at him. "Not unless you want your legs broken," she said.

A waiter appeared with Stone's bourbon, then whipped out his pad. "What may I get for you?"

Stone ordered the green bean salad and the spaghetti carbonara and a bottle of the Mondavi Cabernet for the table.

"Elaine," Genevieve said, "after next Sunday, you're going to have to put crow on the menu for Stone's benefit."

Elaine laughed heartily. "Stone, you don't think she's gonna go through with it?"

"I have accepted her invitation to the wedding," Stone said, "and I will accept whatever she decides next Sunday."

Elaine laughed. "He doesn't think she's gonna go through with it."

"Of course not," Dino said.

Stone sipped his drink.

36

Stone got home late that night, having been somewhat overserved at Elaine's. He reset the alarm system and took the elevator upstairs to his bedroom.

He took off his jacket and reached to hang it up with his other jackets, but something was wrong. His suits hung where he ordinarily hung his jackets. He shook his head, disoriented, then looked around: His jackets hung on the opposite wall, where he kept his suits. He felt slightly nauseated, as if he were on a rolling ship.

He opened the top drawer of the built-in chest of drawers, where he normally kept socks and found shirts. He opened the third drawer, where he kept shirts, and found sweaters. He had begun to sweat. Stone went into the bathroom and threw up.

He blew his nose, splashed cold water on his face and reached for a towel on the ring beside the sink. He found his cotton bathrobe there. The hand towels were lined up on the edge of the bathtub. He did not throw up this time; instead, he got angry.

He went back into his bedroom and looked around. Four oil paintings by his mother, Matilda Stone, that normally hung to his left were on the opposite wall. The nonmatching lamps on either side of his bed had exchanged places. He reached into a bedside table drawer for tissues to mop his brow and found condoms. The bedspread had been reversed. The small rug beside his bed was now at the foot.

He went back to his dressing room and undressed, hanging his clothes on hooks, to be dealt with the next day, then, after trying half a dozen different drawers, he found a nightshirt and put it on. He got into his bed and discovered it had been short-sheeted. He remade the bed, got into it and fell asleep.

He had nightmares.

Stone met Bob Cantor for lunch the next day at P. J. Clarke's. "How was the Mayflower Inn?" he asked.

"Just lovely," Cantor said. "Bonnie and I had a fine night there. Good dinner, too. You're looking a little peaked, Stone. Drink too much last night?"

"Maybe," Stone said glumly. "You know that circuit board you changed in the Connecticut alarm system?"

"Yes."

"Change the one in my Turtle Bay house, too."

"Uh-oh, somebody get into the house?"

"Yes, and more."

"What?"

"Whoever got in rearranged my bedroom and dressing room. Helene is over there now, trying to straighten everything out. It's a mess."

"I've got a circuit board in the van," Cantor said. "I'll do it as soon as we leave here. You got any idea who's behind these two break-ins?"

"My best guess is Harlan Deal."

"The guy we met at the inn? Why would he do that?"

"It's about a woman."

"Carla?"

"Yes."

"I know her."

"I didn't know you were a music buff."

"It's not that. I installed a security system in her grandfather's house last year and met her there a couple of times."

"Her grandfather's house?"

"You remember, you sent me out there."

Stone was feeling nauseated again and asked the waiter for a beer. "Bob, I don't know what you're talking about."

"You recommended me to her grandfather."

Stone raised his beer. "Hair of the dog," he said, then drank deeply. "Who is her grandfather?"

"Eduardo."

"Eduardo who?"

"Your friend, Eduardo Bianchi."

"What?"

"Yeah, you sent me to him."

"Not that, the part about grandfather."

"Well, she's his granddaughter. You knew that, didn't you?"

"That's impossible; she's Swedish."

"Half," Cantor said. "Her father was Eduardo's son."

"He has a son?"

"Had. He caught a number of bullets when Carla was about to start music school at Juilliard. She stopped using her last name after that."

"How do you know all this stuff?"

"My old man knew the family, and so did I. Eduardo's son, Alberto—Carla's father—was a couple of years ahead of me in school. I knew him to speak to, that's all. My old man didn't want me making friends with mafiosi."

"Who was her mother?"

"Her, I didn't know. Somebody Alberto met in the city, I heard. Swedish immigrant, apparently."

Stone spent a few sips of his beer trying to reorient himself. His world seemed to have been shaken and stirred.

"How do you know Carla?" Cantor asked.

Stone told him the story.

"So now this Harlan Deal is on your case?"

"Apparently."

"How much on your case?"

"Enough to be annoying."

"Enough to hurt you?"

"I don't think so. He may have his suspicions, but he can't put me together with Carla. And I handed her off to the Colonel yesterday."

"To the Colonel?"

"I was feeling crowded by Deal, and I feel even more so now. She's spending a couple of nights with him, and he's bringing her back to the city."

"Well, that's good, I guess. The Colonel always liked the ladies."

"Yeah, I noticed that; it's what gave me the idea."

"You're well rid of her, if it gets Deal off your back."

"Who might he have sent to break into both my houses?"

"A pro, I can tell you that much."

"Somebody like you?"

"Yeah, I guess." Cantor smirked. "Somebody with a sense of humor."

Stone ignored that. "Somebody you might know?"

"Well, there isn't exactly an American Association of Semilegal Techs that meets every Tuesday for lunch, but I know a few guys. You want me to check around?"

Stone thought about that. "No, forget it; what good would it do? As soon as Harlan Deal finds out Carla is seeing the Colonel, he'll get off my back."

"And onto the Colonel's back?"

Stone frowned. "I hadn't thought about that, but no, I don't think so. Deal is pissed off at me, because I did the prenup job for him, and he paid me well. He figures I've betrayed him in some way, which I haven't. Carla's a big girl, and she makes her own decisions. This will blow over."

"I hope you're right," Cantor said.

"Listen, on another subject, Dino's guys put a GPS tracker on Charlie Crow's Rolls-Royce, and it was parked outside Ab Kramer's house for three hours the other night."

"Well, that's interesting. You think they were sitting cross-legged on the floor, addressing invitations to our little upcoming reunion?"

"Not for three hours. You remember that time you tapped a phone for me through the phone company?"

"Yeah, I've still got my guy on the inside."

"I want you to tap Charlie Crow's phone. See what we can come up with."

"Okay, but it'll cost you a grand up front plus five hundred a day for as long as the tap runs. My guy puts his pension at risk."

"All right, I'll buy that for three or four days. How about his cell phone?"

"I've got a scanner that will pick that up, but I'd have to follow him around; the range is short."

"Let's keep that in reserve."

"Okay. Can we order lunch, now?"

Stone ordered the soup; it was all he felt like eating.

37

As Stone was leaving Clarke's his cell phone vibrated, and he flipped it open. "Yes?"

"It's Eggers. Where are you?"

"Just leaving P. J. Clarke's."

"Come see me." Eggers hung up.

Stone walked over to the Seagram Building and took the elevator upstairs. The receptionist was on the phone, apparently with a girlfriend. She thumbed him toward the corner office.

Stone walked through Bill Eggers's open door and tossed his coat on a chair. "What?" he demanded.

"You're in a shitty mood," Eggers said.

"Somebody is fucking with me, probably Harlan Deal."

Eggers looked over Stone's shoulder. "Hello, Harlan," he said. "Come in."

Harlan Deal walked around Stone and sat down. Eggers waved Stone to a chair.

"Now," Eggers said, "what's going on with you two?"

"He stole my girl," Deal said.

"He had my house, ah, houses broken into."

"You stole his girl?"

"Certainly not. If he lost her, that was her decision, not mine."

Eggers turned to Deal. "You had his houses broken into?"

"I've nothing to say on that subject," Deal said.

Stone opened his mouth, but Eggers held up a hand. "Stone, did you have anything to do with Harlan's girl leaving him?"

"I did not," Stone said. "I saw her when I was in Connecticut, though."

"Aha!" Deal shouted, pointing a finger at Stone.

"She was at the home of a friend of mine, Barton Cabot."

"The antiques dealer?" Eggers asked.

"You know him?"

"My wife and I have bought a few pieces from him over the years. We're collectors of American furniture."

Deal spoke up. "Are you saying that Carla left me for an *antiques* dealer?"

"Not that kind of antiques dealer."

"What kind, then?"

"One who likes women more than antiques."

"I don't believe it," Deal said.

"Well, she was there when I arrived at Colonel Cabot's house yesterday afternoon, and she was there when I left. My impression was that she was staying over."

"*Colonel* Cabot?" Eggers asked.

"He was a career officer in the Marines before he was an antiques dealer."

Deal looked at Stone as if he were insane. "A former Marine is an antiques dealer? That doesn't make any sense at all."

"I don't care if it makes any sense," Stone said. "It's true."

"Then you didn't steal my girl?"

Stone reminded himself that it had been Carla's idea to sleep with him. "I did not."

Eggers spoke up. "Harlan, it appears that you've been misinformed."

Deal blinked, literally and figuratively. "Then I must apologize to Mr. Barrington."

Stone waited for him to do so. "All right, apologize."

"I apologize."

"For having my homes broken into?"

"I know nothing about that."

Eggers looked at him sharply. "Harlan?"

Deal threw up his hands. "My people just had a look around."

"They rearranged my bedroom and dressing room," Stone said.

"That was not part of my instructions," Deal said. "My man has . . . a whimsical nature."

"Well, you tell him that if I catch him being whimsical in any residence of mine again I will make a point of curing his whimsy."

"Now, Stone," Eggers said. "Clearly, there's been a misunderstanding all around, and Harlan has apologized. Will the two of you now shake hands and forget this?"

Stone and Deal stared at each other. Finally, Stone extended a hand, and Deal shook it.

"I have to get back to my office," Deal said, rising. "I'm sorry for the misunderstanding." He walked out.

Eggers got up and closed the door behind Deal, then looked at Stone. "You fucked his girlfriend?"

"Bill, didn't you hear anything I just said?"

"Stone, I know you."

"Tell you what, pick up the phone and dial this number." Stone read from the jotter in his jacket pocket.

Eggers dialed.

"Ask to speak to Carla."

"What's her last name?"

"She doesn't have one."

"Oh, come on, Stone."

"She's Eduardo Bianchi's granddaughter, and she doesn't like using his name."

Eggers put down the phone in haste. "You fucked a woman who is both Harlan Deal's fiancée and Eduardo Bianchi's granddaughter? I don't know why you're not somewhere in a shallow grave."

"She isn't Deal's fiancée anymore, and she wasn't when I fucked her, and Eduardo and I get along just fine, thank you."

"Does Eduardo know you're fucking his granddaughter?"

"I am *not* fucking his granddaughter...anymore. Barton Cabot may be, but I'm not."

"How the hell do you know Barton Cabot, anyway?"

"We both have houses in the same town; why shouldn't I know him?"

"It's just bizarre," Eggers said.

"What's bizarre about it?"

"Well, I'll bet he's the only former Marine colonel you know and the only antiques dealer, too. Am I wrong?"

"Well...no."

"Then it's bizarre."

"If you say so."

"Listen," Eggers said, "as long as you know Cabot, maybe you could run down a rumor for me."

"What sort of rumor?"

"Word around town is Cabot has got hold of a very fine eighteenth-century mahogany secretary."

"Where the hell did you hear that?"

"If the rumor is true, I'd be interested."

"Bill, please tell me where you heard that rumor."

"Stone, the number of people in New York who would be interested in a piece of that caliber is very small. We talk to each other."

"Tell me the name of the person who told you this."

"I'm afraid I can't do that."

"Is there anything else, Bill?"

"No."

"Then I bid you good day." Stone got up and headed for the door.

"Let me know if you hear anything about that secretary," Eggers called after him.

38

When Stone arrived at home his housekeeper, Helene, was picking up her paycheck from Joan. "I got your bedroom back like it was," Helene said.

"Thank you, Helene."

"Except for those things in the bedside drawers," she sniffed.

"I'll deal with that, thank you."

"You must have had some weekend upstairs, to get it like that."

"Helene, I was in Connecticut this weekend. Somebody got into the house and did that as a joke."

Helene muttered something Stone didn't quite hear, then left for home.

"She was really pissed off," Joan said.

"I was pretty pissed off, myself. The guy who had this done just apologized to me in Bill Eggers's office, though."

"This was about a girl, wasn't it, Stone?"

"Don't go there, Joan. It was Harlan Deal's mistake; let's leave it at that."

"He didn't stop payment on his check, did he? Because I've already paid the bills."

"No, he didn't, and if he does..."

"Sorry I brought it up," she said.

Stone went into his office and checked his desk for messages. None. He sat down and concentrated on making his anger go away. It took time, but he got there.

Stone was about to leave his desk for the day when Bob Cantor called. "I got news," he said.

"What?"

"Something interesting on Charlie Crow's phone."

"Already?"

"The tap had been in for less than an hour when this call was made: Listen."

Stone heard electronic noise, then a woman's voice. "This is the office of Mr. Charles Crow. He's sending a van to pick up a piece of furniture from his storage unit tomorrow morning at eight A.M. It's locker three-two-zero."

"Yes, ma'am," a man's voice said. "I'll put it on the list."

The call ended.

"I can't believe we got that lucky," Stone said. "But wait a minute. We don't know where she called."

"Yes, we do. The number is listed for Sutton Moving and Storage. It's downtown, near the South Street Seaport."

"Then let's get there first."

"Okay," Cantor said. "The place is open twenty-four/seven, but let's wait until this evening, when the workday is over. Can the two of us handle it?"

"I'll get Dino to come with us. You want to pick us up?"

"Okay. Seven-thirty."

"See you then."

"I'll bring some coveralls, so you guys won't look like who you are."

"Good idea." Stone hung up and called Dino. "I think we found the secretary," he said.

"Where?"

"In a storage facility downtown. Cantor and I are going to pick it up, and we need your help."

"So now I'm a furniture mover?"

"I'll buy dinner. Be here at seven-thirty sharp."

"Oh, what the hell, okay."

Stone and Dino were standing on the curb at seven-thirty, when Bob Cantor pulled up in his van. He tossed them both coveralls, and they put them on and got in.

"How long is this going to take?" Dino asked as they drove downtown."

"I don't know. An hour, maybe," Stone replied.

"So we'll have dinner after?"

"Dino, we've got to deliver the piece to Barton Cantor in Connecticut."

"Oh."

"You don't have to come along; we just need your help getting the thing in the van. Barton will help us get it out."

"I'll go; I hate eating alone."

"Maybe we'll have dinner up there."

They arrived at Sutton Moving & Storage, and presented themselves at the night desk on the loading dock.

"We're here to pick up something from Mr. Charles Crow's locker," Cantor said. "Number three-twenty. His secretary called."

The man consulted a list. "Nothing on here for tonight."

"Sure there is," Cantor said.

"Oh, here it is. It's scheduled for eight A.M."

"Nah, she told you eight P.M."

"She didn't tell me nothing; I just came on half an hour ago."

"Well, whoever took the call screwed up and put down A.M. instead of P.M. You going to make a big deal out of this and piss off Mr. Crow?"

"Nah, what do I care? Go on up. You know where it is?"

"Third floor?"

"Yeah, turn left out of the elevator. There's a couple of hand trucks over there, if you need them." He pointed.

Stone and Dino got hand trucks, and Cantor led the way. They took the elevator upstairs and found the locker, a big one, and it was padlocked. Cantor took a small leather case from his pocket, unzipped it and took out a set of lock picks. After a minute with the picks, the lock snapped open, and Cantor swung the doors wide.

It stood there alone in the locker, in two pieces, wrapped in movers' blankets and secured with duct tape.

Stone pulled off some tape and looked at the piece underneath. "This is it!" Stone said. "Now be careful with the thing; we don't want to damage it."

They got each piece loaded onto a hand truck and relocked the locker. They took the two pieces downstairs in the big elevator and loaded them into Cantor's van.

"That was slick," Stone said as they drove away.

"You going to tell Barton we're coming?" Dino asked.

"Yeah." Stone got out his cell phone and called Barton's house.

"Hello?"

"Barton, it's Stone Barrington. Are you going to be home this evening?"

"Carla and I are just on our way out to dinner."

"Well, be home in an hour and forty-five minutes, because I'm bringing you a present." He hung up before Barton could ask any questions. "We'll surprise him," he said to Dino and Cantor.

Near the appointed time they turned into Cabot's driveway and found him waiting for them outside the barn. He unlocked the door, and the four of them carried the two pieces inside.

"Let's get these blankets off," Barton said, tugging at the duct tape that secured them.

They stripped off the blankets and set the bookcase on top of the base.

Barton walked around the secretary, looking at it closely, running a hand over the varnish. "Very nice," he said, "but it's not mine."

Stone stared at the secretary. He turned and looked at Barton.

"What do you mean, it isn't yours?"

"I thought I was pretty clear," Barton said.

"This is the secretary that was locked in Charlie Crow's storage locker. It was the only thing in there."

"I'm not arguing with you," Barton said. "It's quite beautiful, but it just isn't mine. This piece is a copy of the Newport secretary. It was manufactured in Charleston, South Carolina, sometime between eighteen ninety and nineteen ten. The quality of the mahogany isn't anything like that of my secretary, and the company built more than three hundred copies over the twenty-year period, more than half of which survive. I could take it down to my shop and get seventy, seventy-five thousand dollars for it. Anybody who paid more would be an idiot."

"How do you know all that?" Dino asked.

Barton crooked a finger, led them behind the piece and pointed at a brass plate that gave the name and address of the manufacturer and a number, 241.

Dino directed a withering glance at Stone. "So, under your sterling leadership, we stole the wrong secretary."

"That's not fair, Dino," Cantor said. "After all, we didn't even take all the wrapping off."

"Stone wouldn't have known the difference if we had," Dino said.

"Did I ever say I was an expert on eighteenth-century American furniture?" Stone asked.

"Look, fellas," Barton said, "just rewrap the bloody thing and get it out of here, will you?"

The three of them went to work, taping the blankets around the piece, while Barton watched impatiently, then they loaded it back into the van and left.

"Why don't we get some dinner and take the thing back tomorrow?" Dino asked.

"Because," Stone said, "Charlie Crow is sending somebody to pick it up tomorrow morning at eight."

"Oh."

Stone looked at his watch. "We might make it to Elaine's by midnight."

"Yeah," Dino said, "if we don't get arrested for grand theft secretary."

At the Sutton warehouse, they woke up the night man, who was snoring away, his feet on his desk.

"What?" he said, snapping his eyes open.

"We're taking this piece to Mr. Crow's locker," Cantor said.

"Didn't you just take it out?"

"We got our orders," Cantor replied.

"Okay, go ahead," the man said.

They trundled the two pieces up to the locker, which Cantor opened with his lock picks, and, when the pieces had been returned to their original spot, snapped the lock shut again.

Stone and Dino walked into Elaine's at half past midnight, while Cantor parked the van. The joint was jumping. Gianni, one of the two headwaiters, approached them. "Why didn't you let me know you were coming? I'd have kept a table for you."

Stone looked at his regular table and saw four people he didn't know sitting there. "Who's that?"

"A guy named Charlie Crow, big deal in real estate."

Dino began to laugh.

"Oh, shut up," Stone said.

"All I've got is something in the next room," Gianni said.

"I've never even been in the next room," Stone said, "except for a party."

"Come on," Gianni said. "I'll bring you a cake with a candle on it."

Dino was still laughing when they sat down.

"Gianni," Stone said, "head off Bob Cantor when he comes in, and bring him in here. Don't let Mr. Crow see him, if you can help it. And bring whiskey, quickly."

Cantor was at the table by the time the drinks came. "Jesus, I just saw Charlie Crow in the other room, sitting at your table."

"Yeah, I got that," Stone said.

Dino began to laugh again. "Shall we send Mr. Crow's party some drinks?"

The three of them ordered dinner.

Dino," Stone said when they had finished eating, "can you put a couple of guys on the warehouse tomorrow morning? I want to know where Crow has the secretary delivered."

"Yeah, I guess," Dino said, getting out his phone.

Stone was having breakfast the next morning when the phone rang. "Hello?"

"It's Dino."

"Where'd they take it?"

"I don't know."

"What do you mean, you don't know?"

"My guys watched them load the secretary into a dark green furniture van with the name Van Hooten on the side, then they followed the van. It got onto the West Side Highway and headed north. They followed it up the Sawmill River Parkway as far as Yonkers, then they called me, and I told them to come back to the precinct."

"You couldn't let them follow it all the way?"

"All the way to where? Montreal? You don't know where the fuck they're taking the thing."

Stone thanked Dino and hung up. "Maybe I do," he said aloud to himself. He picked up the phone and called Barton Cabot.

"Hello?"

"It's Stone, Barton. I'm sorry about last night. I thought we had found your secretary."

"No harm done," Barton replied.

"I hope you had a good dinner with Carla."

"I had a good everything with Carla. She's quite a girl. I'm taking her back to the city this morning."

"Dino put a couple of detectives on the warehouse, and a van with the name Van Hooten picked it up and drove north. They followed it as far as Yonkers, then broke off the tail."

"Van Hooten is a respected dealer in furniture," Barton said.

"I wonder if you'd do something for me before you leave for New York?"

"What?"

"Could you drive up to the clearing that overlooks Ab Kramer's house and see if the van turns up there? It's dark green, and it should be arriving in about an hour, if it's coming."

"All right, I guess I could do that. You think maybe Ab bought the piece from Charlie Crow?"

"Let me ask you this: If Ab saw the piece we had last night, could he distinguish it from the real thing?"

"He could, if he read the brass plate on the back."

"What if Charlie was smart enough to remove the plate?"

"Ab has a good eye, but he doesn't have any real depth of knowledge about that period. It's a handsome piece; it might fool him. You think Charlie is ripping off Ab?"

"It's a possibility," Stone said. "It's not hard to fool somebody who already believes he's getting the real thing."

"How very interesting," Barton said. "I'll call you when I know more."

Stone was about to go to lunch when Joan buzzed him. "Barton Cabot on line one for you."

Stone punched the button. "Barton?"

"Yes. Carla and I are on the way to Manhattan."

"What happened at Ab's house?"

"The Van Hooten van arrived, and they unloaded two pieces, wrapped the way the ones last night were wrapped."

"So, Ab bought the Charleston secretary from Charlie Crow."

"It would appear so. Next time I see Ab, he'll tell me about it, if he thinks he has the real thing."

"I especially want to know if Ab thinks he has the real thing."

"If he thinks so, he might ask me to authenticate it."

"He might, if he had no part in Charlie's stealing the original."

"We don't know if Charlie stole the original," Barton pointed out. "He may just be selling Ab a copy, identified as such."

"I guess I still have more work to do on the original theft, then."

"I guess you do." Barton hung up.

Joan buzzed again. "Dino on line one."

"Good morning."

"Yeah, I guess so. Charlie Crow is on the move today."

"Where?"

"He's in Bristol, Rhode Island, right now. Drove up this morning."

"You have an address?"

"It's Water Street, which is only a block long, but I don't have eyes on him, so I don't know which house or building."

"I wish we had somebody up there," Stone said.

"Wait a minute," Dino said. "I know a retired police captain in Providence who will do anything for two hundred bucks. He's not that far away. Let's see if he'll drive down there."

"Call me back."

Dino hung up, and Stone ordered in a sandwich; he didn't want to miss this call.

Nearly two hours passed before Dino called back. "Hey. My guy knows somebody in Bristol, and he went down there. We'll give them a hundred each, okay?"

"Okay. What do we know?"

"Crow's Rolls was parked in front of number eleven Water Street, and he left half an hour ago. He answered to the description of Crow. Hang on, call on the other line." Dino put Stone on hold.

Stone worked on the *Times* crossword for three minutes.

"I'm back. You there?"

"I'm here. What's a four-letter word for a Siouxan tribe?"

"Otoe."

"Right." Stone wrote that in. "What did he find out?"

"Our guy made some calls. The owner of the house is a Mrs. Caleb Strong, first name, Mildred. She's a widow in her nineties, a prominent member of Rhode Island society for many decades. Her late husband was the last of a New England shipping family that goes back more than two hundred and fifty years."

"Listen, give this guy a hundred and fifty; he does good work."

"Does all this mean anything to you?"

"Not a fucking thing."

"So why do I have to give him an extra fifty?"

"Because he's thorough."

"As long as it's your fifty."

"I'm good for it. Don't let Charlie fall off your computer screen," Stone said. "I want to know where he goes next."

"We'll know until the batteries run out on the GPS unit," Dino said. "He seems to be headed back to New York now."

"Maybe you'd better send a man to change the batteries."

"I'll do that as soon as Charlie gets back to town."

"By the way, what's the name of the doctor that Eliza is marrying?"

"Edgar Kelman."

"Thanks."

"See you at the wedding?"

"Oh, shut up." Stone buzzed Joan. "You've got a Tiffany catalogue, haven't you?"

"Sure. A girl never knows when a friend will suddenly get remarried."

"Can I borrow it for a minute?"

"I'll bring it in." Joan came in with the catalogue. "Anything else?"

"Hang on a minute." Stone leafed through the catalogue. "Order this silver bowl, and have the initials EK engraved on it," he said. "Then send it to Eliza at the hospital."

"Eliza is getting married to a K?"

"She is."

"I thought she was pretty much your girl."

"She was, pretty much, until she decided to marry a doctor."

"You might leave off the initials, in case she changes her mind."

"That's why I want the initials on it," Stone said. "So she won't be able to return it to Tiffany."

"That's mean," Joan said.

"It is not. It just means that I fully accept her decision to marry a bloody doctor, something she said she'd never do."

"And they talk about a *woman* scorned," Joan said as she left Stone's office.

Stone phoned Bill Eggers.

"Hello?"

"Bill, I might have something for you on that mahogany secretary you're interested in."

"Tell me."

"Do you know a guy named Charlie Crow?"

"Yeah, I'm doing some work on a deal between Crow and Harlan Deal."

"He may have what you're looking for."

"Okay, I'll call him."

"Bye-bye." Stone hung up. He would be very interested to know the result of Eggers's call to Crow.

41

Stone and Dino were having dinner at Elaine's when Barton Cabot walked in. Stone pushed back a chair for him.

"I thought I might find you here," Barton said.

Stone gave him a menu and waved at a waiter. Barton ordered a drink and some dinner.

"Why were you looking for me?" Stone asked.

"I need a bed, and I wondered if you could put me up for the night."

"Sure, but what happened to Carla's bed?"

"The girl wore me out, and I don't think I could have survived another night with her right away, so I told her I'm driving back to Connecticut tonight. I'm too tired for that, though." His drink arrived and he sipped it gratefully.

"More news from today's events," Stone said.

"What?"

"Charlie Crow drove up to Bristol, Rhode Island, and visited the home of a woman named Mrs. Caleb Strong."

"Mildred? I know her."

"Why on earth would Charlie Crow be visiting a woman in her nineties in Bristol, Rhode Island?"

"Well, let me tell you about Mildred. She is the grande dame of Rhode Island society, at the very top of the ladder, but she's penniless, for all practical purposes. Lots of assets, no cash to speak of, just the dividends on some bank stock she owns. She also has a house full of authentic and gorgeous things that have been handed down in the Strong family for more than two hundred years. We're talking about pieces that have been in the same house for that long, and they're worth, probably, many millions of dollars. Dealers have been circling her home for years, like vultures, waiting for her to die, but she seems to be in rude good health, and she won't even talk to them let alone sell anything."

"Doesn't she have any children or grandchildren?"

"No, old Caleb was the last of the Strong line, and she's outlived all the members of her own family. Nobody even knows who her heirs are. Museums have been kowtowing to her for decades, hoping to pull in her collection when she goes, but she won't tell them anything."

"The question now arises," Stone said, "why is she talking to Charlie Crow? He spent a good two hours in her house today. What could he possibly have to offer her?"

"Now, that's a very interesting question," Barton said, sipping his drink. "What could a jerk like Charlie Crow have to offer Mildred Strong?"

Dino spoke up. "Money? You said she was penniless."

"Yes, sort of, but she's not without assets besides her furniture. Her husband was a founding investor in a thriving local bank up there, and she's never sold any of his stock. Rumor has it that she has fifty-one percent, but nobody knows for sure. The bank has no choice but to carry her. If she writes a check, they pay it, and she must have a very big overdraft by now."

"How do they explain that to the bank examiners?" Stone asked.

"I suppose the bank's board members must be putting their own funds in her account to keep her in the black. They certainly don't want to piss her off, because she holds all that stock. She could sell it to one of the big banking conglomerates in a heartbeat, and the board would suddenly find themselves out of their cushy seats and into the street. So they pay her checks."

"I wish I had that kind of a relationship with a bank," Dino said.

"Don't we all?" Barton replied.

They were all quiet for a few minutes, eating their dinner.

"I can think of something Crow could offer her," Stone said.

"What?" Barton asked.

"An annuity."

"I don't follow."

"Suppose our Charlie approaches her—he gets an introduction through some mutual acquaintance—and Charlie says, 'Look, Mildred, you've got some beautiful things here, and I never want you to be separated from any of them. I understand that you need funds, though, so I'm prepared to offer you an annual income for the rest of your life, if you'll make me the heir to the things in your house.' "

Barton nodded. "Either that or he just offers her ten or twenty million now, and she keeps her lifetime ownership. After all, how much longer can she last?"

"My impression is that Charlie doesn't have that kind of cash on hand," Stone said. "He seems to have been sailing pretty close to the wind. For a long time. I don't even know if he could raise the annuity."

"An annuity is an interesting idea," Barton said. "I wish I'd thought of it."

"Is it too late?" Stone asked.

Barton shrugged. "Maybe not. Mildred likes me, and I think she might talk to me. If she does, that would give me a chance to find out exactly what she's got in that house, too."

"How long since you've spoken to her?" Stone asked.

"I saw her at a dinner party at Marble House in Newport last year, and she seemed very pleased to see me. We chatted for nearly an hour over coffee, and I was careful never to bring up anything about her possessions."

Dino broke in. "All this is very interesting, but let's get back to Charlie Crow. Why the hell would he be interested in antique furniture?"

"Money," Stone said. "Charlie is very interested in money."

"I'll grant you that," Dino said, "but why furniture? Why does he even know anything about it? I saw a picture of his apartment in a magazine a few weeks ago, and it was full of a lot of awful gilded tables and chairs and huge chandeliers. Why would a guy like that know about or have any interest in eighteenth-century American furniture? If he were buying it, how would he know what to pay for it? And I find it hard to believe that Charlie and this Mildred would have *any* mutual acquaintances."

"Good point," Barton said. "It's a mystery."

"Barton," Stone said, "do you have Mrs. Strong's phone number?"

"Yes, I do."

"Why don't you call her tomorrow morning and tell her you'll be passing through Bristol tomorrow and that you'd like to stop in and see her?"

"I could do that."

"And maybe, if Crow has made her some kind of offer, you could top it."

"That would depend on what he's offered her," Barton said.

"You might find a way to slip something into your conversation that would give her doubts about dealing with Crow."

"I'd be doing her a favor," Barton said. "Charlie is the kind of guy who'd screw her out of everything she's got, if he could find a way, and he's good at finding a way."

Stone nodded. "Think of it as a rescue mission," he said.

42

Stone was having breakfast in the kitchen the following morning when Barton came down.

"Good morning," Stone said.

"Yes, good morning," Barton replied. He seemed preoccupied.

"What would you like for breakfast?"

"Oh, just toast and coffee."

"You sure you wouldn't like some eggs? Helene does wonderful scrambled eggs."

"Perhaps just a plain omelette and orange juice."

"Yes, sir," Helene said, then went to work.

"I've been thinking about our conversation last night," Barton said.

"And what have you concluded?"

"I think it's worth a shot, assuming she doesn't live forever."

"How old is she, exactly?" Stone asked.

"At that dinner party where I last saw Mildred, another woman there told me she was ninety-six, and that was last year."

"Well, if she's ninety-seven and still healthy, she might live another ten years, maybe more."

"Not unless she's a freak of nature," Barton said.

"You could assume that as a downside. How long could you afford to go on paying her?"

"If you can get my stolen secretary back, I could afford to pay her for a long time."

"Decisions, decisions," Stone said.

Barton dug into his omelette. "Delicious," he said to Helene. "Stone, would you draw up a contract for me?"

"What kind of contract?"

"I'd like to say something like this: 'I, Mildred Strong, agree to sell all the items listed on the attached list to Barton Cabot for the sum of blank, to be paid at the rate of blank annually until my death, at which time the residue would become payable to my estate, and Mr. Cabot would take possession of all the listed items. Until my death all the items would remain in my possession in my home. I instruct my executor to honor this contract within ten days of my death, upon receipt of the residue of funds from Mr. Cabot.' "

"That's a pretty good contract right there," Stone said. "Best to keep it simple, to one page, if possible, and you'd want at least one witness. You'd need to catalogue the goods, of course, and get her to sign the list, as well. How long would an inventory take?"

"To do a thorough job, probably a day or two. I'd want to get any documents she might have to provide provenance."

"Is she likely to have eighteenth-century receipts?"

"That depends on whether Caleb Strong's ancestors were sticklers for keeping records. Some of those old New England families never threw anything away."

"Finish your breakfast and come into my office. I'll draw up something for you."

Barton read the document and set it on Stone's desk. "Perfect," he said.

Stone tapped a few computer keys, printed out some copies and put them into an envelope. "Here you are," he said, handing over the envelope. I've put in some blank pages for the inventory which, I suppose, you'll have to do by hand."

"I suppose," Barton said. "May I use your phone?"

"Of course," Stone replied. "There's one on the coffee table in front of the sofa. Would you like some privacy?"

"No, that's all right." Barton took an address book from his pocket, walked to the sofa and dialed a number. "May I speak to Mrs. Strong, please? This is Barton Cabot calling."

Stone's phone buzzed, and he picked it up. "Yes?"

"A woman who says her name is Carla is on line one for you."

"Tell her I'm with a client, and I'll call her back in a few minutes." He hung up.

"Hello, Mildred?" Barton was saying. "How are you? Yes, it's been a few years. I hope you're well. I'm very well, thank you. I'm in New York, at the moment, but I'll be driving to Newport in a few minutes, and I thought that, if you're amenable, I might drop by Bristol and call on you." Barton consulted his watch. "Lunch would be delightful. Would it be all right if I brought a friend?" He pointed at Stone and mouthed YOU.

Stone shrugged and nodded.

"You're sure we won't be putting you out? Fine, I'll see you at one o'clock. Good-bye." He hung up the phone, smiling. "That was easier than I expected," he said. "She sounded very happy to hear from me."

"You're off to a good start, then."

"I suppose I am. We better get moving, I guess."

"I'll open the garage door for you," Stone said. He got up and pressed the button, then opened the inside door to the garage. "Just let me speak to Joan for a moment, then I'll be right with you." He walked into Joan's office. "Please give me Carla's number." She did. "I'm going to drive up to Rhode Island with Barton. I should be back tonight."

"Have a nice trip," Joan said.

Stone went back to the garage. "I'd better follow you in my car," he said to Barton. "You don't want to have to drive me back to New York."

"Good idea," Barton said.

Stone hung his jacket in the backseat and got his car started. A moment later, they were headed to the East River Drive and thence to I-95.

When they were well under way, Stone called Carla.

"Hello?" Her voice was low and sexy. Stone repressed his thoughts.

"Hi, it's Stone. I'm sorry; I was in a meeting when you called."

"Are you out of your meeting, now? Would you like to come at... to lunch?"

Stone chuckled. "Love to, but I'm on the road. I have to drive up to Rhode Island for a meeting with a client."

"Oh, shit," she said.

"It's just as well; Harlan Deal could still be having you watched. We had a meeting yesterday, and I think I threw him off the track, but you never know."

"You mean we can't get together at all?"

"Let's give him time to lose interest," Stone replied. "How did you and Barton get on?"

"Exactly how you thought we would," she said with a little petulance.

"My congratulations to you both," Stone said.

"Oh, go fuck yourself," she said.

"That seems to be my only alternative."

"Call me next week." She hung up.

Stone tried redirecting his thoughts to eighteenth-century American furniture but did not entirely succeed.

43

Stone followed Barton up I-95, all the way through Providence, then they left the interstate and drove down the Bristol Peninsula to the town of Bristol.

Eleven Water Street turned out to be a large brick and limestone house in the Federal style, perhaps even the period. The door was answered by a middle-aged woman in a black housemaid's uniform. They gave their names and were escorted into a spacious ground-floor drawing room.

"Mrs. Strong will be down directly," the woman said, then left them.

Stone had expected the house to be something elegant but seedy, but there was no peeling paint or worn upholstery. The room was immaculate and beautifully furnished. Stone took a chair and watched Barton roam the room like a panther, looking closely at a piece here, a piece there.

Barton then joined Stone, taking the sofa next to him. "It's a treasure trove," he half whispered. "There's at least ten million dollars at auction in this room."

A door opened, and a tall, slender, beautifully dressed woman swept into the room, moving like someone half her age. She was perfectly coiffed and made up, and Stone wouldn't have thought she was a day over seventy. He and Barton were immediately on their feet.

"Mildred! How good to see you!" Barton said.

She allowed herself to be kissed on both cheeks. "Barton, you look well."

"May I present my friend, Stone Barrington?"

She extended a hand. "How do you do, Mr. Barrington."

"I'm very pleased to meet you," Stone replied, receiving a firm handshake.

"Would you like a glass of sherry, or shall we go straight in to lunch?" she asked.

"Whatever is convenient," Barton said.

"Let's have lunch," Mildred said, leading the way toward the rear of the house, outside through French doors and down a staircase into a garden, looking south over Narragansett Bay, where a table had been set for three.

Barton held her chair for her, and they sat.

"Mr. Barrington, would you pour the wine?" Mildred asked.

"Certainly," he replied, "and please call me Stone."

"And I'm Mildred."

Stone took the bottle from the ice bucket next to him and glanced at the label. It read Montrachet 1955. Good God! he thought. He poured a little for Mildred Strong.

She tasted it. "Oh, very nice," she said. "Caleb was an avid collector of wine. I've hardly been able to put a dent in his cellar since he died, twenty-five years ago."

Stone sipped the wine. It was a deep golden color and tasted of honey and pears. "This is perfectly wonderful, Mildred."

"Are you a collector of wines, Stone?"

"I have a very nice cellar in my house in New York, but only a few good cases, I'm afraid."

"It is so nice not to have to shop for wine," she said. "Caleb has already done it for me."

The maid appeared with bowls of chilled asparagus soup.

"So, Barton," Mildred said, "what brings you to Rhode Island?"

"It occurred to me that I haven't done the shops in Newport for a couple of years, and I thought I'd see what I could pick up for my own place."

"From what I hear, you don't spend much time in your shop," she said.

"That's perfectly true; I have a woman who runs it for me, while I scour the countryside for good pieces."

"And that's why you've come to see me, isn't it?"

"My first impulse was to see you, Mildred, but it is a treat to see your beautiful house."

"Yes, it is beautiful, isn't it? In the daylight hours all I have to do with myself is to keep it that way, and the garden, too, and to write thank-you notes to my hostesses."

"Do you still buy things?"

"Never. I haven't bought a piece in thirty years. Caleb's family collected so much over the centuries, that I haven't had to shop. If I'm redoing a room and need something, I have no farther to look than my attic. There are dealers about who would pay a pretty penny for what I have in that attic."

"Have you ever sold anything?" Barton asked.

"Not a th... well, nothing until... recently."

Charlie Crow, Stone thought.

"Have you decided to finally begin selling?"

"Oh, no, there was just this one... thing."

"May I ask what you sold?"

"Oh, I don't want to talk about that. Did you come to buy my things?"

"I came to make you a proposition," Barton said.

"I'll just *bet* you did."

"But I don't want to take a single piece from your house...not anytime soon, at least."

"What, exactly, do you mean by, 'anytime soon'?"

"Not for as long as you live."

Mildred chuckled. "I intend to make it to a hundred and fifty," she said.

Stone believed she could do it.

"I hope you do," Barton said, "but I'm prepared to make you what I hope you'll think is a proposition worth considering."

"Make your proposition, and I'll consider it," Mildred replied, "but probably not for very long."

"I understand your attachment to your beautiful things and your reluctance to part with any of them," Barton said, "and I will not ask you to do so. What I will do is this: I will make you an offer for a large group of specific pieces. Since I am not a very rich man, I will pay you a substantial part of my offer each year for the rest of your life. Upon your death, I will remit the unpaid balance to your executor, then take possession of the pieces."

"And then you will auction everything and quadruple your money?"

"No, I would not like to auction such a collection and have it dispersed. What I had in mind is to interest a major museum in taking everything and, perhaps, re-creating some of your rooms to house a permanent collection."

"Now *that* is an interesting idea, Barton," Mildred said, looking thoughtful. "But why shouldn't I just leave it all to a museum?"

"Because then you would realize nothing from the transfer of your possessions. You would lose a large annual income. Also, you would find yourself haggling with half a dozen museums over where the collection would go and how it would be displayed."

Mildred frowned. "God knows I would hate doing that," she said.

Stone watched as she sat perfectly still, soup spoon in midair for so long that he thought she had had a stroke and become catatonic. Then, suddenly, she spoke. "All right, Barton, I'll do it," she said, "in principle, contingent upon the details of your offer. You may have the run of the house this afternoon, or for as long as it takes, to put together your proposal."

Barton nearly choked on his soup.

Stone had trouble not laughing out loud.

44

When they had finished their Dover sole and drunk their wine, Mildred went upstairs for a nap while Stone sat in a living room chair and wrote down descriptions of pieces and prices as Barton dictated them.

Three hours later, Mildred appeared, just as they were finishing the living room list. "Would you like to see my attic now?" she asked.

"Oh, yes," Barton said.

She led them to an elevator in the hall, they rode it to the top floor of the house, then walked up a flight of stairs. Mildred unlocked the attic door with a very old key, and they stepped inside. "Have a good time," she said. "Drinks are at six-thirty, dinner at seven. You'll be staying the night." It wasn't a question. She left them.

Barton switched on all the lights, and he and Stone looked around. The attic was as well arranged as a gallery in a museum, except the pieces were closer together. Everything was dusted and polished, and there was none of the clutter one associated with attics. "Stone, I don't know if you realize this, but you are witnessing something that may never be seen again: the first cataloguing of what is, without doubt, the most important collection of American furniture in existence outside a museum, and only one or two museums might match it."

"I understand," Stone replied. He also understood that Barton was beginning the process of making himself the richest antiques dealer in the country.

Barton began moving slowly about the room, dictating to Stone. They were not interrupted until six o'clock, when the maid came into the attic.

"Drinks are in half an hour," she said. "May I show you to your rooms?"

Barton retrieved his bag from his car, and Stone the small bag containing a couple of fresh shirts, underwear, socks and toiletries that he kept in the trunk of his car for unexpected occasions. They were taken to the third floor of the house and installed in bedrooms.

Stone's room contained a mahogany secretary that, although smaller than Barton's piece, seemed just as beautiful, and his bath was a wonderland of Edwardian plumbing. He took a quick shower and changed, then joined Barton downstairs.

Mildred Strong appeared moments later. "Well, gentlemen, how did your afternoon go?"

"Mildred," Barton said, "you were right about your attic; it's very impressive."

"Tomorrow you can do the study, the library and the bedrooms."

"I look forward to it," Barton said.

"So do I," Stone added. "This has been an education for me."

They dined on cold lobster salad, followed by an expertly prepared chicken breast in a tarragon cream sauce, with *haricots verts* and *pomme soufflé*. The wines were a 1959 Puligny-Montrachet Clos des Perrières and a 1945 Lafite Rothschild, something Stone never thought he would taste. He decanted it for Mildred, and there was an inch or so of sediment left in the bottle. It was in perfect condition.

The conversation never touched on Mildred's possessions but

ranged over Newport gossip, sports (Mildred was a big Red Sox fan) and jazz. Stone had little to say; he preferred listening on this occasion.

They talked over coffee until ten o'clock, when Mildred excused herself and retired.

"You must be very happy," Stone said to Barton when she had gone.

"I'm stunned, frankly," Barton replied. "I have been since I walked into this house. I'm going to have to sell or mortgage everything I own to make this deal work; that's if I can sell my banker on a long-term investment."

"She may outlive you, Barton."

"That has occurred to me, I assure you."

"You haven't asked her about Charlie Crow. That transaction she mentioned must have been with him."

"I'm afraid to bring it up," Barton replied. "But after tomorrow, she'll be protected from his like."

"She doesn't seem to need much in the way of protection," Stone pointed out. "She's very much in command of herself."

"She certainly is," Barton agreed.

They finished their brandy and went upstairs to bed.

The following morning they breakfasted at seven and went to work at seven-thirty, doing the library and the study. They broke for lunch, then went to work on the bedrooms.

At four o'clock they had finished their work and were summoned to tea.

"Well, Barton," Mildred said, "make me your offer."

Barton handed her his list and waited while she read it. When she had finished, he said, "Mildred, I will offer you eighteen million dollars for everything on the list, and payments of eight hundred thousand dollars a year."

Without hesitating, Mildred said, "Make it twenty million and a million a year; I'm fond of round numbers. Shall I call my lawyer?"

"Done, Mildred. Call him."

The man, apparently alerted, appeared ten minutes later, and Mildred introduced him as Creighton Adams. Stone gave him a copy of the proposed contract, with the blanks filled in, and Barton gave him the list.

"Mrs. Strong," the man said when he had read everything, "I see no problems with the contract. Are you satisfied with the numbers in it?"

"I am," she said. "Oh, I know Barton will make a lot of money on the deal—eventually—but I admire his patience and his fortitude to take such a leap. Type it up."

"I'll have everything done by nine tomorrow morning," he said, "including a codicil to your will, acknowledging the arrangement and instructing your executors."

Mildred saw him to the door and returned. "I have a dinner invitation this evening," she said. "Would you two like me to have something prepared for you here, or would you prefer to go out?"

"Thank you, Mildred. I think we'll go out," Barton said.

"Then I'll see you at nine tomorrow morning. I will probably sleep through breakfast." She excused herself and went upstairs.

"I'll take you to dinner, Stone," Barton said. "We'll celebrate."

They dined at the Black Pearl, in Newport, ordering steaks and, eventually, two bottles of Veuve Clicquot La Grande Dame.

"This," Stone said, tapping the bottle, "is Carla's favorite, if you don't already know."

"I'm happy to have that information," Barton said. "By the way, bill me for your time at your usual hourly rate; I know this work hasn't been in your regular line, but you did it well."

"It was instructive," Stone said.

At nine o'clock the following morning Creighton Adams arrived with a notary and two associates for witnesses to the codicil. Both Mildred and Barton read the contract and the list, and both signed.

Barton took a checkbook from his pocket and wrote a check for a million dollars. "And another on this date each year," he said, handing it to Mildred.

"Thank you, Barton, you have made this experience very pleasant."

Her lawyer and his entourage rose to go, but Mildred waved them back to their seats. "Stay," she said, "there's something else I'd like to discuss with you."

Barton and Stone made their good-byes.

"You've been very kind to us," Stone said, shaking her hand.

"I would like very much to see you again, Stone," Mildred replied. "You were excellent company."

As Stone drove back to New York, he reflected that he had never spoken so little in two days. He reckoned that was what had made him such good company.

But, he remembered, he and Barton still did not know why Charlie Crow had visited Mildred Strong and what had transpired at their meeting.

45

Stone was halfway home before he thought of it. He called Bob Cantor.

"Hello?"

"Hi, it's Stone. Can you still get into people's bank accounts?"

"Most of the time; depends on which bank it is."

"I don't know its name, but it's an independently owned bank in Bristol, Rhode Island."

"That shouldn't be a problem. Hang on while I look it up." Cantor clicked some computer keys. "I've got the Bristol Trust, the only independent in town. What's the name on the account?"

"Last name Strong; first name either Mildred or Mrs. Caleb."

"What do you want to know?"

"I want to know if any deposits were made yesterday or today."

"Here we go. Only one deposit has been made this month, and that was yesterday, a check in the amount of half a million dollars. Nice deposit, but it's still uncollected."

"How long does it take a bank to collect on a deposit?"

"Depends on how hard they're trying, I guess. I'd allow a week."

"Any information on the account that the check was drawn on?"

"An account number at the Central Manhattan Bank."

"Can you see who the account belongs to?"

"Hang on. I'll have to bust into that bank's accounts." More typing. "Well, well, it's drawn on the account of one Charles Crow."

"Can you get into that account? I'd like to know of any large deposits this month and where they came from."

"Gee, you want a lot, don't you?"

"Always."

More typing. "Here we are. Charlie deposited half a million bucks yesterday, and... Wow!"

"What?"

"Six and a half million dollars today."

"From where?"

Much typing. Stone paid attention to not running into the huge truck ahead of him.

"It's not from a bank; it's wired from an account in a brokerage firm, Swensen-Styne, a big Internet firm."

"In whose name?"

"That's odd. The account name is encoded; all I can see is two series of asterisks with a space in between."

"How many asterisks?"

"Five in the first group, six in the second."

"Can you decode it?"

"The short answer is maybe, but it could take days or even longer. You want to pay for that kind of time?"

"No, I don't," Stone said. "I'd rather guess."

"What's your best guess?"

"Abner Kramer."

"That fits the asterisks, but so would a lot of other names."

"That's the only name I care about, at the moment."

"Whatever you say, Stone."

"Bye-bye, Bob."

"See ya." Cantor hung up.

So did Stone. He checked his watch. Barton Cabot would still be on the road home. He called his cell phone.

"Hello?"

"It's Stone."

"Hi. You home already?"

"No. I'm still half an hour away."

"What's up?"

"I ran a check on Mildred's bank account, and yesterday she deposited a check for half a million dollars from Charlie Crow."

There was a long silence. "Interesting," Barton said, finally.

"It gets even more interesting. I checked on Charlie's account, too. Yesterday he deposited a check in his own account for half a million dollars, and—get this—today he received a wire transfer of six and a half million dollars."

Barton was silent again.

"Are you thinking what I'm thinking?"

"I don't know, Stone. What are you thinking?"

"I'm thinking that Charlie Crow bought the mahogany secretary that I temporarily stole and delivered to your house from Mildred Strong, then sold it to Ab Kramer for seven million dollars, representing it as the real thing."

"What about the brass plate on the back of the piece?" Barton asked. "Ab wouldn't pay seven million dollars for a piece clearly identified as a copy."

"Charlie would have told Ab that he, himself, put the plate on the piece to disguise the real maker."

"And why would Ab want it disguised?"

"Because he thinks the secretary is the one Charlie stole from you."

"Let me get this straight," Barton said. "You think Charlie stole the secretary from me, then sold Ab a copy, telling him that it was mine, right?"

"Right."

"That brings to mind two questions: One, if Charlie had my secretary, what has he done with it, and two, what did he buy from Mildred?"

"He bought the Charleston piece from Mildred."

"And paid her over four hundred thousand dollars more than it was worth? I thought we agreed that Charlie wasn't stupid."

"If he's getting seven million for it, what does he care if Mildred holds him up for an extra three hundred thousand? We already know she's a shrewd lady."

"That's possible, I guess. What's your answer to my first question?"

"I forgot the question."

"If all you guess is true, what has Charlie done with my secretary?"

"That remains to be seen. Maybe he has another buyer, one who's less gullible than Ab Kramer."

"I would not describe Ab as gullible."

"Then maybe the secretary that Charlie had delivered to Ab yesterday is your piece, not the one I delivered to you."

"Then that would still mean that Charlie paid Mildred four hundred thousand dollars too much for the Charleston copy. It's possible but certainly not plausible. What would he want with a copy anyway, if not to fool Ab? If I'm to put any credence in your theory, I'd have to accept that either Charlie or Ab is a fool, and I can tell you that, from my knowledge of both of them, neither is a fool."

"Let me think about this some more," Stone said. He hung up and continued driving home, baffled.

46

Late Sunday morning Stone woke up with a feeling of unease. He was in the shower before he figured out why: The wedding was at two o'clock. Unease turned to dread. Why, he asked himself, had he promised to go to the wretched event? Because, he replied to himself, he didn't think it would actually happen.

He grabbed a towel and stepped out of the shower. She might not show, he pointed out to himself; there was still time. He felt better.

He made himself a large brunch: a bagel, cream cheese and Irish smoked salmon, orange juice and coffee, enough to last him until dinner. The phone rang, and he picked it up.

"Hello?"

"It's Dino."

"Hey."

"You want a ride to the church?" Dino sounded as if he were suppressing laughter.

"Oh, shut up. I'll take a cab."

"I just want to be sure you show up; you promised Genevieve, remember?"

"I remember."

"If you don't show up, she'll blame me."

"Why would she blame you?"

"For not seeing that you got to the church on time."

"I'll manage."

"I'll pick you up at one-thirty."

"Okay." Stone hung up and looked at the kitchen clock. He had only forty-five minutes. He finished eating, went upstairs and got into a suit and tie and some well-polished black shoes. He was standing outside the house when Dino's car, driven by his rookie detective, pulled up. Stone got into the backseat with Dino and Genevieve.

"I'm so glad you're going to the wedding," Genevieve said.

"I told you I would, didn't I?"

"Dino said he didn't think you would."

Stone leaned forward and glared at Dino, who was sitting on the other side of Genevieve. "Dino was just covering his ass in case I didn't show," he said, then leaned back again.

"Did you send a gift?" Dino asked.

"I sent a very nice silver bowl from Tiffany," he replied acidly.

"Did you have it engraved?" Genevieve asked.

"Of course."

"With Eliza's initials or his?"

"With one of each."

"That's mean."

"How do you figure that?"

"Now she can't take it back."

"So what?"

"Suppose she decides not to go through with it?"

"Then she'll still have a very nice silver bowl and a reminder of her former fiancé."

"You're hoping she won't go through with it, aren't you?"

"I'm hoping no such thing. She's a free woman, and she can do whatever she wants. She *will* do whatever she wants."

"No, she won't."

"What do you mean?"

"She wants you, not Edgar."

"She told you that?"

"She didn't have to."

"You divined it, then?"

"I know her very well."

"I thought I did, too. I thought she'd never marry a doctor."

"She may not."

"You're kidding, aren't you?"

"I kid you not," Genevieve said. "I don't think she'll go through with it."

"Well, she's leaving changing her mind kind of late, isn't she?"

"She won't make a decision until she has to."

"And when do you think that moment will come?"

"You'll have an opportunity to stop it, Stone."

"Genevieve, are you telling me that you expect me—that Eliza expects me—to leap to my feet when they get to the line in the ceremony about... Well, you know the line."

"I don't expect you to, but I think Eliza does."

"So I'm supposed to kidnap her from the church and drive her away in my little red sports car while Simon and Garfunkel sing the sound track?"

"That would be nice."

"It would be insane."

"Dino," Genevieve said, "help me out here."

Dino leaned forward and looked at Stone. "Kidnap her and drive her away in your little red sports car. If Simon and Garfunkel don't show up, *I'll* sing." He leaned back.

"I don't want to discuss this any more," Stone said. No one spoke for the rest of the ride.

The church was at Madison and Seventy-first, next door to the Ralph Lauren store. Stone and Dino walked halfway down the church and took seats on opposites sides of the aisle, while Genevieve went into an anteroom to assist the bride.

Stone looked around. It was as motley a collection of people as he had ever seen. Half of them were wearing scrubs, as if they had left the hospital in the middle of surgeries; others were dressed in jeans and parkas; and a few were dressed quite elegantly—Edgar's friends, he supposed. Somebody was playing jazz tunes on an electric piano, while a couple of other musicians played bass and guitar. Stone wondered what the Episcopal priest thought about that. Then he felt himself dozing off.

A slamming door snapped him out of it. The priest was entering, and he gave the audience an apologetic shrug for the noise. He was joined at the altar by Dr. Edgar Kelman, the renowned surgeon, then the trio swung into some uptempo Mendelssohn, and Stone heard footsteps behind him. He looked back to see Eliza coming down the aisle, with Genevieve right behind her. Eliza looked lovely, and for a moment Stone's heart began to melt, but when he made brief eye contact with her he spun his head around, eyes front. The ceremony began.

Stone sat rigid, his jaw clamped shut, as the priest recited the ceremony. Then he came to that awful line, "If any person here knows any reason why this man and this woman should not be joined in holy matrimony, let him speak now or forever hold his peace." Stone held his breath.

He was sure the dead silence in the church lasted at least two minutes, but then realized that it was probably more like five seconds. The priest continued, and Stone exhaled in a rush. Half the audience, including Genevieve, turned and looked at him questioningly. Then the priest pronounced them man and wife, and everybody clapped.

The happy couple strode quickly down the aisle, and as they passed, Eliza tossed her bouquet into Stone's lap, getting a big laugh from everybody.

Stone tried not to turn red.

47

Stone arrived home, still angry and depressed, to find a creamy envelope under the front door knocker, apparently delivered by hand, since it was Sunday. Inside, he ripped it open and read an engraved dinner invitation for that evening from Harlan Deal. RSVP was crossed out. "Just come" was scrawled next to it.

Why the hell would Harlan Deal want him at his dinner party at the last minute? He tossed the invitation onto the front hall table, went into the library and made himself a drink. He did not often drink this early in the day, but it was the only thing he could think of that would change his mood.

He switched on the library TV, settled into a chair and began surfing the channels, looking for something to take his mind off his day. A shopping channel was selling wedding dresses; an Asian evangelist was marrying four hundred identically dressed and unsuspecting couples in a football stadium; Martha Stewart was teaching her viewers how to plan the perfect wedding.

He switched off the TV and turned on the local classical music radio station. Fucking Mendelssohn again. He switched to the jazz station. Ella Fitzgerald was singing "Making Whoopee." "Another bride, another groom," etc. He switched off the radio.

He took his drink upstairs, stripped off his suit and lay on the bed. Drinking horizontally was hard. He pressed the button on the remote that raised the head and foot of the bed. Easier. He drained his glass, set it down and dozed off.

He woke, befuddled and hazy about date and time. A glance at the clock on the wall told him it was half an hour before the dinner party. He splashed some water on his face, got into his evening clothes and left the house, taking the invitation with him. What the hell.

Harlan Deal lived in a Fifth Avenue penthouse in an elegant old co-op building with a spectacular view of Central Park. He would, wouldn't he? A uniformed maid took his coat and an actual tails-wearing English butler showed him into a huge living room hung with a collection of mostly large abstract paintings and occupied by a larger group of people than he had expected to see, at least fifty.

He spotted a Motherwell, a Pollock, a Rothko, two Hockneys and a Frankenthaler without even trying. All Harlan Deal needed was an eighteenth-century mahogany secretary from Newport, but it wouldn't have looked so good among the classic modern furniture, all Mies and Breuer. He spotted no one he knew until Harlan Deal broke out of the crowd and greeted him, hand out.

"Good evening, Mr. Barrington," he said. "I'm sorry for the short notice, but I'm very glad you could make it."

"Thank you for asking me, Mr. Deal."

"Harlan, please."

"And I'm Stone."

A waiter appeared, took his drink order and was back in a flash with a Knob Creek on the rocks. Harlan excused himself to greet other arriving guests.

Stone wandered around the room, looking at the art, then walked out onto a large terrace that had been glassed in for the winter. Central Park, lamplit, stretched out before him, and across the park the lights of the tall apartment buildings on Central Park West glittered in the distance. He was alone on the terrace, except for a woman who stood at the north end, looking out toward the reservoir.

She held a martini glass in her left hand, displaying a bare third finger. Stone moved closer, and she turned to face him. He froze for a moment and took her in. She was the most beautiful woman he had ever seen: tall, slender, raven hair perfectly coiffed, nails perfectly polished, perfectly dressed in a longish thing that Stone reckoned was Armani. He exhaled.

"Come closer," she said. "I can't hear you, if you stand way over there."

He did as she commanded.

"Good evening," she said, holding out a hand with long fingers and a large emerald ring. "I'm Tatiana Orlovsky."

Stone took the hand, cool and soft. "I'm Stone Barrington," he managed to say.

"Why are you and I the only people on this lovely terrace?" she asked.

"Because God meant us to be alone together." There was some laughter a few footfalls behind him. "But not for very long."

She laughed, a very nice sound.

"Your name has a heavy Russian accent," he said, "but your voice does not."

"My name has been in this country since my grandfather stole a lot of very good jewelry from a titled Moscow family during the revolution in 1917 and stowed away on a ship bound for New York," she said. "I, on the other hand, have been here for only thirty-four years, and English is my only language."

"I hope you still have the jewelry," he said.

"Oddly enough, we do.... At least, my mother does. My grandfather was clever: He borrowed money on the jewelry, invested it in the stock market, redeemed the jewels and spent the rest of his life building a business and a lifestyle in which the jewelry would not look out of place."

"Is the very beautiful necklace you're wearing part of the collection?"

"No. It's a string of cubic zirconia that cost less than two thousand dollars at Bergdorf's. The design is a copy of a Harry Winston necklace, though."

"You make it look like real diamonds."

She laughed that laugh again. "My husband never notices."

Stone's heart sank.

She must have seen the look on his face. "Oh, no. I don't... I mean, I'm not... I'm in the process of being divorced, at the moment. I've stopped wearing my wedding ring."

Stone's heart soared again. "I'm relieved to hear it," he said, "because I'm opposed to adultery. I'm afraid that, in your case, I might have gone against my principles."

"I'm flattered that you would think of abandoning your principles," she said, "but I'm glad you don't have to."

"So am I," he replied.

"And what, may I ask, do you do?"

"I'm an attorney."

"With a firm?"

"I'm of counsel to Woodman and Weld."

"Oh, I know the firm, but what does 'of counsel' mean?"

"It means that I handle the cases that they would rather not be seen to be associated with."

"That sounds a lot more interesting than drawing wills and managing estates."

"Believe me, it is, and it suits me perfectly. Before I was an attorney I was a police detective, and that experience has come in handy when dealing with people like Harlan Deal."

"I should imagine so. Do you deal with Mr. Deal?"

"I have in one instance, but, I'm happy to say, it won't be a regular thing."

A silver bell rang somewhere.

She glanced inside. "Why don't we go inside and eat some of our host's very expensive food?"

Stone offered her his arm, and they wandered in to join the buffet line.

48

They found seats on the sweeping staircase that led to Harlan Deal's no doubt very elegant bedrooms, and were kept in Dom Perignon by revolving waiters.

"Who are these people?" Tatiana asked, looking around at the crowd.

"The crumbs of the upper crust, as Charlie McCarthy used to say."

"Who?"

"A woodenheaded young gentleman who used to sit on the knee of a man named Bergen."

"Oh, of course. What are the qualifications for being crumbs of the upper crust?"

"Well, they used to be money and breeding, but now it's just money. Consider our host. How do you know him, by the way?"

"A friend of a friend," she replied. "I think she had some matchmaking in mind, but after meeting Mr. Deal..." She didn't finish the sentence; she didn't have to.

"You have such good taste."

"I know what I don't like when I see it. You're right. His only qualification is money."

"Apart from a nearly-ex husband, do you have other means of support? A career, I mean."

"I'm an illustrator."

"Of what?"

"Of anything anyone will hire me to illustrate: advertisements, book jackets, fashion layouts for magazines. I was going to say album covers, but they're too small these days to be much fun, and matchbooks, but since nobody smokes anymore, they hardly exist."

"Have you actually illustrated a matchbook?"

"I did several tiny drawings for ones you used to see on restaurant tables. They're gone, mostly . . . the restaurants, I mean."

"Where do you live?" He asked.

"In Turtle Bay on the north side."

"You are conveniently located. I live in Turtle Bay on the south side."

"In that case, you must lead me up the garden path some time."

"I would be delighted to lead you up the garden path."

She laughed. "Oh. I didn't mean it that way."

"Didn't you?"

"Well, not yet."

"Where will you live when you're divorced? Or have you thought that far ahead?"

"I'm determined to keep the house," she said. "I'll have to buy his half with some of my settlement."

"Is the divorce amicable?"

"Not by any stretch of the imagination. He's very angry."

"Are there children?"

"Only a cat, and she is a premarital asset, so I expect to retain custody."

"It sounds as though you have the settlement all worked out."

"Oh, no. We may end up in court, though I'm trying to avoid that."

"Don't try too hard to avoid it; you'll damage your negotiating position. You must appear willing to sue, if necessary."

"That's good advice. Do you always give good advice?"

"As I was telling a friend the other day, yes. If I don't know what I'm talking about, I try and shut up."

"That's more than I can say for most people."

Stone looked up and saw Barton Cabot and Carla approaching. "My word," he said.

"What?" Tatiana asked.

Stone got to his feet. "I'll explain later." He shook Barton's hand and was allowed to peck Carla on the cheek. "May I introduce Tatiana Orlovsky?" he said. "Tatiana, this is Barton Cabot and Carla. Just Carla, before you ask."

Tatiana shook their hands.

"I must say," Stone said, "I'm even more surprised to find you two here than I am to find me here."

"An invitation was delivered this morning," Barton said, "as we were leaving the house."

"I took it as a sort of peace offering," Carla said, "since both our names were on the envelope."

"We spent most of the day in Bristol, photographing Mildred Strong's house and all her pieces," Barton said. "Carla turns out to be an excellent photographer."

"Did you remember to inquire about her acquaintance with our friend, Crow?"

"I did. She admitted to selling him something, but she wouldn't say what. Not something on our list, though."

"Did you ask how they met?"

"Through a friend, she said, but when I asked who, she changed the subject."

"I hope you were able to warn her about Crow."

"I tried. I hope it registered."

"So do I. Tatiana, forgive us for discussing business. We'll stop now."

"You are kind. I think I'll seek out the powder room."

"May I join you?" Carla asked.

"Of course." The ladies left them.

Stone turned to Barton. "How did Mr. Deal react at seeing you together?"

"Graciously," Barton replied. "Having invited us, how else could he behave?"

"I don't know," Stone said. "He's an odd one. He sent people into my houses in Washington and in the city. Messed with my dressing room."

"What?"

Stone told him about the incident. "You may arrive home and find your living room rearranged."

"I don't think *odd* is a strong enough word for this fellow," Barton said, gazing across the room at his host.

"I was about to say," Stone said, "that I think I'll avoid his company in the future, but then, look what I found by seeking his company tonight." He nodded toward Tatiana, who was coming back from the ladies', followed by Carla. They stopped to speak to someone.

"There's something I should tell you about Carla," Stone said.

"What's that?"

"Oh, I know that, by now, you must know her better than I, but it's about her last name."

"What is her last name? She wouldn't tell me."

"It's Bianchi. Her grandfather is a friend of mine, Eduardo Bianchi."

"How odd," Barton said. "I sold him a pair of tables a few years ago."

"You do get around, Barton. So you know who he is?"

"You mean the Mafia connection? I've heard about that."

"Some of the women in the family can be a little screwy," Stone said, reflecting on his experience with Dolce, Eduardo's daughter. "You might keep that in mind."

49

Stone and Tatiana left the party, having said good night to their host, and they got into a cab. "Would you like to take the scenic route home?" Stone asked.

"Why not?" Tatiana replied.

Stone gave the cab driver his address, and when they arrived, he let them into the house and pressed the switch that turned on lights in every room.

"Oh, it's bigger than my house," Tatiana said. "And beautifully furnished."

"I inherited the house from a great aunt several years ago and did most of the renovations myself. Much of the furniture and all of the cabinet work were built by my father, who had a reputation in that field. Most of my decoration was just updating upholstery and fabrics on the original furniture and adding some pieces." He showed her the library and kitchen. "My offices are on the ground floor, where there used to be a dentist's office. Would you like to see the master suite?" he asked.

She gave him a little smile. "Perhaps another time," she said, glancing at her watch. "It's late, and I'm tired."

"Then let me lead you up the garden path," he said, opening the kitchen door to the garden.

"Sooner than I had expected," she said, stepping outside. "Your garden looks very nice."

"Oh, I have someone who looks after it."

"You're not a gardener?"

"I don't bend over unnecessarily." He opened the gate at the end of his plot, and they stepped into the common garden. The moon was big and high, and it illuminated the trees and plants.

"It's such a beautiful place, isn't it?" she said.

"The jewel of the city, as far as I'm concerned."

She led him into her garden and to the kitchen door. "If you don't mind I'll give you the tour of my house after the housekeeper comes." They exchanged cards.

"I'll look forward to it." They kissed lightly, and Stone left her and returned to his own house.

The following morning, Stone had just reached his desk when Joan stuck her head into his office. "I think you'd better come and tell me what to do with all this," she said, and was gone before he could ask.

He followed her out the front door to the street, where a number of wooden crates were being unloaded at the curb. "What is this?" he asked.

"You tell me," Joan replied. "It seems to be wine. I hope to God you haven't bought a lot of wine. Right now, you can't afford wines that come in wooden crates."

Stone took a closer look at the crates. Château Palmer, 1961; Beaune, Clos de Roi, 1959; La Tache, Domaine de Romanée-Conti, 1959; Le Montrachet, 1955. "Good God," he said.

"How much did all this cost?" Joan demanded.

The truck driver handed him an envelope. "There's a note," he said. "Where do you want all this put?"

Stone opened the envelope and extracted a sheet of very fine stationery.

My dear Stone,

I hope you will do me the favor of taking some of Caleb's wine off my hands. There is so much, I'll never be able to finish it before . . . well, before I kick off, as they say. It should be drunk by someone who loves and appreciates it as much as you. Enjoy it in good health!

Mildred Strong

"Don't worry, Joan; it's a gift," Stone said. "Show them where the cellar is, please, and just have them stack it up. Don't take it out of the crates." He counted as they moved the crates: There were eight of them, each among the twentieth century's finest vintages.

Stone sat down to write to Mildred. Joan returned a few minutes later. She came into Stone's office. "I know the names of some of those wines," she said. "Shall I call Christie's or Sotheby's about auctioning it?"

"Don't you dare," Stone said. "I plan to drink every bottle of it."

"You should live so long,"

"I should," he said, handing her his note. "Would you mail this, please?"

"Sure, I will, but if you're ever broke again, and you will be, if I know you, then you'll have a way to raise money."

"I don't want to think about that," Stone said. He picked up the phone and called Tatiana.

"Hello?"

"I hope it's not too early to be calling," he said.

"Are you kidding? I've been up since five."

"Well, be sure to take a nap this afternoon, so you'll be fresh when I come to take you to dinner."

"Oh, that would be nice. What time?"

"Pick you up at seven-thirty?"

"Perfect. Where are we going, so I'll know how to dress."

"How about La Goulue?"

"I love it there. See you at seven-thirty. Will you come through the back door?"

"That's the most convenient way."

"I'll leave the kitchen door open for you."

"See you then." He hung up. The phone rang, and Joan picked it up.

She buzzed him. "There's a man on the phone named Creighton Adams, says you've met. He's a lawyer in Rhode Island?"

"Oh, yes. I'll talk to him." Stone punched the button. "Good morning, Creighton."

"Good morning, Stone. I'm afraid I have sad news."

"What's wrong?"

"Mildred Strong died last night."

Stone was stunned. "She seemed so well when we met. What happened?"

"It was an embolism. Her doctor had found it in a scan some weeks ago. It was operable, but she refused the surgery. Said she didn't want to be that sick at this time of her life. So she just carried on until it burst as she was leaving a dinner party last night."

"She was such a remarkable woman," Stone said, genuinely sad. "She sent me some wines from her cellar. They arrived only a few minutes ago. I had already written her a note."

"That was like her: She was given to bursts of generosity, especially after she knew she might die at any moment."

"Thank you for letting me know, Creighton. I'd like to attend her funeral or memorial service. Will you let me know when that is?"

"Of course. Now to business. I've written you a letter that will be delivered tomorrow, but I'll give you a day's head start. Please inform your client, Mr. Cabot, that he has ten days to pay the remaining nineteen million dollars called for in his contract with Mrs. Strong. Please tell him that we must be strict about the deadline."

"Certainly, I'll tell him," Stone said. "And thank you again for calling me." He hung up and sat there a while, thinking of Mildred Strong and her amazing generosity. He was glad to have had the experience of knowing her.

Then something else occurred to him. He hoped Charlie Crow hadn't heard about her death, yet. It would be like him to stop payment on his half-million-dollar check.

50

Stone dialed Barton Cabot's cell number, since he didn't know if he was back in Connecticut yet.

"Hello?"

"Barton, it's Stone."

"Good morning, Stone."

"Not so good; I have sad news."

"What?"

"Mildred Strong died last night. Creighton Adams called me a couple of minutes ago."

Silence.

"Barton?"

"I'm here; I'm just stunned."

"So am I. She seemed so healthy, but Creighton said she'd known for some weeks that she had an embolism, and she elected not to have the surgery."

"So she knew she was going to die."

"Yes, but she didn't know when."

"That's why she did the deal with me."

"Someone once said that the foreknowledge of death concentrates the mind. I guess she wanted to get her affairs in order."

"I last saw her at five o'clock yesterday, after we'd finished photographing everything. She seemed just fine."

"She sent me eight cases of her best wine. It arrived this morning."

"That was sweet of her."

"It certainly was. There was a note saying that she didn't think she could drink it before she 'kicked off,' as she put it."

Barton laughed.

"Creighton also gave us verbal notice of the need for you to complete the contract. You have ten days from when we receive written notice, which will be tomorrow."

"Good God! I hadn't thought about that! I'm going to have to see my banker while I'm in New York. It's a good thing we took the photographs; I'm going to have to put together a prospectus to send to a number of museums."

"Do you anticipate any problem borrowing nineteen million dollars?"

"The furniture will be its own collateral, but I'll have to borrow twenty million: I'll have to send a specialist moving outfit to pack and store everything, and it will have to be insured."

"Well, I'll leave you to get started, then."

"Will you call Creighton Adams and tell him the house should be put under guard immediately? I don't want people taking things out of there."

"Yes, I'll do that."

"Talk to you later." Barton hung up.

Stone buzzed Joan. "Please get me Creighton Adams." He sat and waited for her to make the call, then he thought of something.

"Creighton Adams."

"Creighton, it's Stone Barrington."

"Yes, Stone?"

"I've spoken to Barton, and he asked that you put the house under guard immediately and for twenty-four hours a day."

"And who's going to pay for that?"

"Until the deal is closed, it's the estate's responsibility, and you're the executor, aren't you?"

"Well, yes."

"There's at least twenty million dollars of very fine antique furniture in that house, and you don't want any of it lost, and I doubt very much if it's insured for its full value. You'd better get it insured for the next ten days, and I'd use a value of forty million dollars."

"That's going to cost a fortune."

"You can pay it out of the nineteen million you're getting from Barton. Anyway, it's only for ten days."

"I suppose you're right. I'll take care of it."

"Something else, Creighton. Last week Mrs. Strong did some business with a man named Charlie Crow. Are you aware of that?"

"No," Adams said. "I've never heard of him."

"He's a New York real estate developer and not the straightest arrow in that particular quiver."

"Why would such a person have business with Mildred? That doesn't make any sense."

"She sold him something; she wouldn't say what."

"Wait a minute, she asked me to send a notary over there to witness a document. Can you hang on for a minute?"

"Sure." Stone sat and waited. Two minutes passed.

Adams came back on the line. "Stone?"

"I'm here."

"I've spoken with the notary who witnessed the signatures, Mildred's and Crow's, on two documents: a bill of sale and a letter, both handwritten by Mildred."

"The amount of the sale?"

"Half a million dollars. That explains the balance in her bank account."

"What did Mildred sell Crow?"

"The notary was unable to see that; half the document was covered by Crow."

"Creighton, have you made a public announcement of Mildred's death?"

"No, but of course word is already all over Newport, because of the people at the dinner party."

"I would advise you to withhold the public announcement until you're sure Mr. Crow's check has cleared."

"You think he might try to stop payment?"

"I do. Did your notary say that Crow took anything with him when he left?"

"He didn't."

"So Mildred may not have delivered the item she sold him."

"Not unless it was something he could put in his briefcase."

"Just be sure the check has cleared before you make an announcement. There's no rush, is there?"

"No, I guess not."

"I think Charlie Crow, all by himself, is a good reason for having the property guarded."

"I'll take care of that right now, and I'll call our insurance agent, too. Chubb will handle this very quickly, I'm sure; they hold the policy on the house."

"Good-bye, then." Stone hung up and called Barton.

"Hello?"

"I've spoken with Creighton, and he's agreed to put guards on the house immediately and to have Mildred's things insured."

"That's good."

"I told him he should insure for forty million, and I think you should do that, too."

"More than that," Barton said.

"I also asked him about Mildred's transaction with Charlie Crow. He said he sent a notary over there who witnessed two documents:

a bill of sale for half a million dollars and a letter, both in Mildred's handwriting. The notary couldn't tell what was sold, but Charlie didn't take anything with him, and we were there for the next two days, and he didn't pick up anything then."

"I don't understand. What could she have sold him?"

"Maybe something that would fit in a briefcase. Jewelry, perhaps? Did she have any valuable jewelry?"

"Yes, she often wore fine pieces to dinner parties, but Mildred wouldn't sell her jewelry."

"Then I'm baffled," Stone said.

"So am I."

51

Stone was about to leave his office for the day when a FedEx envelope arrived. Inside was a dinner invitation from Abner Kramer for the coming Saturday night at his house in Connecticut. That was fortunate, he thought, because there was something he wanted to investigate in Kramer's house.

He walked through the garden and appeared at Tatiana's kitchen door on time. She was on the phone in the kitchen, and she waved him inside.

Stone walked to the kitchen counter, took a stool and watched her. She was wearing tan slacks and a black cashmere turtleneck sweater that called attention to her breasts. She looked smashing, he thought.

"Henry," she was saying into the phone, "you're going to have to get used to the idea of a property settlement. I'm sure your lawyer has explained to you that New York State law requires an equitable division of property. There are two ways we can do this: We can decide between us, with legal advice, or we can go to court and add legal fees to the total costs. I don't much care, since you'll end up paying my legal fees anyway." She gave Stone a big shrug, pointed at the phone and drew a finger across her neck.

"No, I won't wait six months," she said. "If we don't have an agreed settlement by the end of the week, I'm filing suit, and I'm also going to ask the judge for a hundred thousand dollars a month in temporary support while we're waiting for a trial date."

There was an unintelligible squawk from the other telephone, followed by some sort of tirade. Tatiana softly replaced the receiver and smiled at Stone, who was applauding.

"Very good," he said. "I couldn't have done better myself."

"He's probably still yelling," she said, "thinking I'm still on the phone. Would you like a drink, or shall we go?"

Stone winced and slapped his forehead. "I forgot to book at La Goulue, and they'll be full by now. Shall we go to Elaine's instead?"

"Oh, yes! I've heard a lot about it, but I've never been there."

Stone glanced at his watch. "We're a little early for Elaine's. It will be empty, so let's have that drink."

She waved him through the kitchen, then the dining room, then into a lovely living room. "What, sir, is your pleasure?"

Stone smiled. "Well... for the moment, just that drink—bourbon, if you have it."

She opened a liquor cabinet and checked. "I have four bourbons," she said.

"The one in the rectangular bottle, there," he said, pointing.

"What would you like in it?"

"Ice," he replied.

She poured the drink, then a Scotch for herself, and they settled into the sofa.

"You are the first date I've had since Henry and I separated," she said.

"I'm glad I got here first," he replied. "After Harlan Deal's party there would have been a line."

She laughed. “He called me today.”

“Harlan?”

“Yes. Apparently, he was miffed that I left with you.”

“Oh, good. I'm happy to miff him. He's a very annoying man.”

“I thought so, too.”

“Great minds . . . et cetera, et cetera.”

“Indeed. Henry, my husband, is in commercial real estate, and he sucks up to Deal at every opportunity.”

“Does your husband know a real estate guy named Charlie Crow?”

Tatiana rolled her eyes. “God, yes! I've had to suffer through two dinner parties with that man, one in his apartment and one here. Did you know his wife used to be a stripper?”

“I didn't, but I'm not shocked. I've had occasion to learn a little about him recently, and I'm glad I don't have to do business with him.”

“Henry was happy to do business with him. He invested his firm's money in two Charlie Crow projects, and I'm sure he's never going to see a dime of it again. Crow is in some sort of financial difficulty, Henry said, and he's frantic that he's been had by Crow.”

“You remember Barton Cabot, from last evening?”

“Of course.”

“Well, Barton was Crow's commanding officer when they were in the Marines, and he has just as low an opinion of him as you do.”

“Barton was in the Marines?”

“Yes, a career officer, until he ran afoul of a superior.”

“He looks more like a slightly faded movie star,” she said.

“That's a good description. You'd probably think his younger brother looks like the current item.”

“*Mmmm,* I think I'd like to meet the younger brother.”

“No, you wouldn't; he's a spy and, as such, completely untrustworthy. Well, nearly completely. You can trust Lance to make the right decision if it's in his own best interest.”

Tatiana laughed aloud. "That sounds very much like Henry!" She furrowed her brow. "You know, I think he may be having me followed."

"Then we'll leave through the garden," Stone said. He looked at his watch. "I think we can go now, if you like." He took out his cell phone, speed-dialed Elaine's and made a reservation.

They walked into the garden, then to Stone's house and out the front door. Ten minutes later, they were at Elaine's. They had not been there more than five minutes when Tatiana suddenly held up her menu to hide her face.

"You're not going to believe this," she said, "but my husband just walked in."

Stone looked up. "The one with the blonde?"

"Yes, with the blonde."

"I know her. She's an actress of sorts. She doesn't work much, but she always seems to have money. There are many rumors about her."

"Trust Henry to choose somebody like that," she said.

"Actually, this is good. You should let him see you."

She looked horrified. "Why?"

"Because New York is not a no-fault state where divorce is concerned. If he were here alone, he might think about accusing you of adultery, seeing you with me. As it is, you've both canceled out that option. If he sues you, claiming adultery, you can do the same to him. I'll be your witness, and your lawyer could dig up enough dirt on her to make Henry's life miserable."

Tatiana put down her menu, caught her husband's eye and waved gaily. Henry did an about-face and hustled his date out of the restaurant.

"I think you've just improved your chances for a negotiated settlement," Stone said.

52

Stone let them into his house and locked the door behind him. He didn't turn on a light but kissed her in the dark. She leaned into him and gave him her lips and tongue.

"I think I'd like to see the master suite," she breathed in his ear.

"Right this way," he replied, steering her into the elevator. He continued kissing her on the way up. They reached the third floor and left the elevator.

"It's very nice," she said, looking around. "Where is the bathroom?"

He pointed to the door, then undressed, turned off the bedside light and got into bed. The moonlight flooded the room, as it had the garden the night before, and when she came out of the bathroom, naked, her body in that light might have been marble. She slid into bed beside him and snuggled close.

"Let's not rush," she said. "We have time."

"We certainly do," he replied, kissing her ear.

They kissed for the longest time he could remember since high school, until he pulled her leg over his and felt the wet on his thigh. He worked his way down her body, kissing and biting her nipples and feeling a satisfying response to each nip. He spent some time on her belly and navel, then she pushed his head farther down.

He used his lips and tongue for a very long time, until he brought her fully to climax. He waited until her last shudder, then asked, "Again?"

"Again," she said, "but this time I want you inside me."

He rolled on top of her and waited while she took him in her hand and guided him inside, then he moved slowly, while she became fully aroused again. He took her all the way before allowing himself to follow her, then let their passion cool before he moved beside her and took her in his arms. "More, later," he whispered.

"*Mmmmmm*," she said, burying her face in the hollow of his neck. In a moment she was breathing deeply.

Stone didn't know how long he had been asleep when he was awakened by the sound of breaking glass and a soft *pop.* He laid Tatiana gently onto her pillow, got out of bed and listened. A flicker caught his eye, and he looked out the window into the garden. Inside Tatiana's kitchen window he saw a flame.

Stone picked up the phone and dialed 911. "There's a fire at the rear of a house in Turtle Bay," he said, then he gave the address and hung up. He woke Tatiana gently. "I'm afraid there's trouble," he said.

She opened her eyes. "How could there be trouble?" she asked, raising herself on one elbow.

"Look," he said, pointing out the window. They could hear the fire truck's siren approaching.

They stood in front of her house, watching the firemen carry out the hose. When the men were out, a captain approached them.

"You were lucky," he said. "Come with me." He led them through the living and dining rooms into the kitchen, which was a mess. The captain pointed to a blackened spot on the floor. "Someone dropped a bottle of an accelerant, probably gasoline, and tossed a match into it. Fortunately, it was in an open area, and there wasn't much to consume. It was a small bottle, too, probably no bigger than a Coke bottle. You'll have a lot of cleaning to do, from the smoke, but there's remarkably little actual fire damage."

"I heard the bottle pop," Stone said, "and I could see the flames from the rear window of my house, across the way."

"A quick nine-one-one call always helps," the captain said. "If there's nothing else we can do for you, I'll say good night." He gave Tatiana a little salute and left.

"It was Henry," Tatiana said.

"It's always the husband," Stone replied. He glanced at his watch. "You're sleeping at my house tonight."

"I certainly am," she said.

The following morning, after breakfast, when Tatiana had gone home, Stone called Bob Cantor.

"Yeah?"

"I've got some work for you," he said.

"Always good news."

"The name is Henry Kennerly, real estate guy. It's a bad divorce."

"And you're a friend of the wife," Cantor said.

"Right. He set a fire in her house last night. Luckily, there wasn't much damage. I want phone, bank and credit card records. He has an expensive girlfriend, and I want to know how much she's costing him." He gave Cantor the address. "And I want you to replace all the locks with better locks."

"Right. How's the mahogany-secretary thing going?" Cantor asked.

"Still simmering but not on the boil yet. I'll bring you up to date on developments when I see you. Anything interesting on Charlie's phone?"

"There have been a couple of short, cryptic phone calls to a cell phone. Just a few words exchanged."

"What sort of words?"

"They're like 'It's done. Good. Details later. Good.' "

"Whose cell phone?"

"I don't know; I can't trace it. Probably a prepaid job from Radio Shack or a supermarket."

"I don't like it when the guy I'm on to gets that smart," Stone said.

"Neither do I."

"If he's going to be that cryptic, is there any point in paying your guy at the phone company five bills a day?"

"Probably not."

"End it, then."

"Will do. I'll e-mail you Mr. Kennerly's printouts later today."

"That's fast."

"We aim to please." Cantor hung up.

Stone hung up, too. He was going to give Tatiana all the ammo she needed to nail her husband's hide to the barn door.

53

Barton Cabot visited the Madison Avenue branch of his bank and asked for James Foster, an important senior vice president who was in charge of all Manhattan branches. He was shown directly in.

"Good morning, Barton," Foster said, waving him to a seat.

"Good morning, James. I have some new business for you."

"Always good news. Tell me about it."

Barton removed a stack of eight-by-ten prints of the photographs he had taken in Bristol and handed them over.

Foster leafed through them rapidly. "This is all very nice, but what am I looking at?"

"You're looking at the largest and finest collection of eighteenth-century American furniture in private hands," Barton said.

"In whose hands?"

"Mine."

"Congratulations. It must have taken a long time to put together that collection."

"It took me two days," Barton said.

"I don't understand."

Barton sighed. The man was a banker. "All these pieces have been, since they were made, in one house, that of a Mrs. Caleb Strong of Bristol, Rhode Island, who passed away Sunday night at the age of ninety-seven."

"And you inherited all these?"

"No, a few days before her sudden death, when she appeared to be in excellent health, I contracted with her to buy the collection for twenty million dollars, to be paid at the rate of a million dollars a year for the rest of her life, the remainder upon her death."

"Which was Sunday night?"

"That's correct."

"So now you owe her estate twenty million dollars?" The banker's eyes were wide.

"Correct again."

"Do you *have* twenty million dollars?"

"Of course not. Why do you think I'm here?"

"You want to borrow twenty million dollars from *us*?"

"What's the matter, James, don't you have twenty million dollars?"

"Of course we do, but... what sort of collateral can you offer?"

"The collection itself. I put its value at between forty and fifty million dollars."

"Have you had an independent appraisal?"

"That would take weeks, perhaps months. I know as much about these pieces as anyone in the country; I am certain of their value, and I must close this deal in ten days."

"Barton, do you know what you're asking?"

"Of course I do. I would only need the loan for a short period, perhaps as little as three months."

"It's not the term of the loan that worries me, Barton; it's the ten days before you must have the money."

"I know this is unusual, James, but it's also the greatest opportunity of my lifetime, one that will make me very wealthy."

"How would you realize the value of the collection? Auction it?"

"It would take at least a year to pull off an auction this big," Barton said. "I have a different plan."

"I'd like to hear about that," Foster said.

"It's my intention to offer the collection to some of the biggest museums in the country," Barton said, "intact. They would pay for the collection by soliciting large donors, and they would display it, permanently, in replicas of some of the rooms of the Strong house."

"It sounds as though you're talking about building a wing onto a museum. That would take a lot longer than an auction."

"No, there are several museums that could make room for the collection in their present space."

"Barton, I really think it would be better to auction the collection piece by piece. You'd get huge publicity for such a sale, wouldn't you?"

"Certainly," Barton said, "but I don't think you'd realize as much money from such an auction."

"You expect to get more from a *museum*?"

"The whole of the collection is worth more than the sum of the parts," Barton explained, "and only a museum could raise sufficient funds to buy it intact. You have to understand that the availability of this collection is an historic event, one that will never occur again."

"Well, I suppose you have a point there, Barton, but you're talking with a *bank* here. The loan committee could not approve such a large loan; it would have to go to the board, and it couldn't even be presented to them until the whole collection had been appraised by an established authority, like an auction house, perhaps more than one. There are also questions of security and insurance that would have to be satisfied."

"I understand that this is an unusual request, James, but I've been a client here for a long time, and I have put much more than twenty million dollars in cash flow through this bank during those years."

Foster consulted his calendar. "Barton, the next scheduled meeting of the board is five weeks from today, and I'm not sure we could get the appraisals done by that time. They're certainly not going to call a special board meeting for this purpose, and, anyway, I happen to know that three of the board members, including the chairman, are abroad. Couldn't you ask for more time to close the deal?"

"The executors of Mrs. Strong's estate have made it clear that they will be strict about the terms of the contract. For all I know, they may have an auction house waiting in the wings to pull this collection to pieces and scatter it all over the world."

Foster spread his hands wide. "Barton, I appreciate everything you've said, and I'm sure the collection is as important and worth as much as you say it is, but I'm afraid that, given the time pressure, the deal is just not doable for us. And I'm afraid that you'd get the same answer from any other bank."

Barton hauled himself to his feet. "Thank you for your candor, James."

Foster walked him to the door. "A better bet might be to approach a very wealthy individual who might buy the collection and present it to a museum."

"Then I would lose any control I might have over where and how the collection would be displayed."

"It's an imperfect world, Barton."

The two men shook hands, and Barton left. He went to a Kinko's, where copies of his prospectus had been run off and bound. He messengered copies to Carla and Stone, then FedExed others to eight museum directors with a covering letter, then he drove back to Connecticut, feeling dejected and numb.

When Barton reached home, he got the mail from his mailbox and let himself into the house. He made a fire in the study, poured himself a drink and sat down to warm up. In his mind he riffled through his client list, most of them wealthy people, but he could not come up with one who would have both the cash and the commitment to collecting that would be required to bring the deal off. Harlan Deal, for instance, certainly had the money, but not the taste or sophistication to appreciate the value of the collection, let alone the commitment to a museum.

He began opening his mail. Halfway through the stack he came across an engraved envelope; inside was a dinner invitation for Saturday night from Ab Kramer.

Perhaps, he thought, he might know the right man after all.

54

Stone sat at his desk, going over the bank statements, brokerage statements and credit card statements of Henry Kennerly, jotting down notes and amounts as he went. It took him more than two hours to complete the job and total the amounts and categories. When he was done, he called Tatiana.

"Hello?"

"It's Stone. How is the cleanup going?"

"I've got a professional crew, and they've promised to stay until it's done, even if it's midnight."

"Good. Be sure and call your insurance company; they'll pay for it."

"I have already done that; their adjuster just left. I had to file a police report, though."

"Good. That's one more bargaining chip. And speaking of bargaining chips, do you have a pencil and paper?"

"I'll get one," she said and put down the phone. A moment later she was back. "Go ahead."

"First of all, how long ago did you and Henry separate?"

"About five weeks ago."

"Good. All of the following expenditures were made since that time."

"Expenditures? Henry's?"

"Yes."

"How would you have access to his expenditures?"

"You're not to ask me that; just listen."

"All right."

"During the past thirty days, Henry has spent more than eight thousand dollars in restaurants. I can tell you from experience that he would have to order a lot of expensive wines to get that figure so high. He has also spent more than two thousand dollars with a florist, and about twelve thousand dollars with three jewelers. Has he taken you to dinner, sent you flowers or given you jewelry during the past thirty days?"

"Certainly not."

"Then here's what you do: You instruct your attorney to get a subpoena for all of Henry's financial records and to look for these expenditures, but don't mention the exact amounts or tell him that I gave you this information. Remember, he has spent all this money from marital funds, so you're entitled to half in cash."

"That's wonderful, Stone! How on earth..."

"No, no, no," Stone interrupted. "Don't ask."

"Oh, all right."

"And don't tell your attorney that you've learned all this; just tell him you've become suspicious of Henry's spending habits since you parted."

"All right."

"Now to more pleasant things. I have a little house in Washington, Connecticut, and I've been invited to a very nice dinner party on Saturday night. Will you come up there with me for the weekend?"

"Oh, I'd love to!" she said. "I've been stuck in the city for too long."

"Good. We'll drive up Saturday morning and come back Sunday or Monday, whichever you prefer."

"It sounds wonderful. Now I have to get back to work."

"Talk to you later." Stone hung up, and Joan came in with an envelope.

"This arrived by messenger," she said.

Stone opened the envelope and found Barton's prospectus. He leafed through it slowly, marveling at the pieces, and suddenly he came to a stop. He found himself staring at a photograph of Barton's mahogany secretary. He read the accompanying caption:

> A very fine example of a secretary, in two pieces, from the firm of Goddard-Townsend, of Newport, commissioned by Josiah Strong in 1760 and housed in the family home since that time. It is, very possibly, one of only two pieces still in private hands. A sister piece sold for $12.1 million at Christie's in June of 1989.

Stone remembered that he had walked through the entire house with Barton, cataloguing each piece, and there had been no Goddard-Townsend secretary in any of the rooms or the attic. It seemed that Barton had thought of a way to give the remaining piece still in his possession an instant provenance. Stone also recalled that Barton had said he could not remember whether the stolen piece was the original or his copy and no one could tell the difference.

Joan buzzed. "Barton Cabot on line one."

Stone picked up the phone. "Barton?"

"Yes, Stone. Did you get the prospectus?"

"Yes, I was just reading it."

"I saw my banker earlier today, and my loan request was denied."

"I'm astonished," Stone said. "Isn't the collection its own collateral?"

"That was only part of it. He said that such a large personal loan would have to be approved by the board of directors of the bank, which doesn't meet again for another five weeks."

"That's bad news," Stone said. "What is your next move?"

"It appears that my only move is to find a person who is wealthy enough and motivated enough to come up with the money. The drawback is I'll have no control over how it's sold. The pieces might have to be auctioned, piecemeal, to recover the investment, and even if a museum buys it, I'll have no control over how the collection is displayed."

"Have you sent the prospectus to any museums?"

"Yes, I've sent it to the eight directors most likely to want it, afford it and house it."

"Well, maybe one of them will be able to come up with the money in time to close the sale with Mildred's executors."

"That will never happen. Even if they're dying for it, they'd have to go first to their boards, then to their richest donors for the money. That could take months to resolve."

"I wish I could help in some way," Stone said, "but I don't see what I can do."

"No," Barton said wearily, "I'll have to find a way out of this myself, which means I have to come up with nineteen million dollars by Tuesday."

"If anyone can do it, Barton, you can."

"Tell me, Stone, did you, by any chance, receive an invitation to a dinner party at Ab Kramer's on Saturday night?"

"Yes, and Tatiana is coming up to Washington with me."

"Oh, good. Carla's coming up, too. Her engagement at the Carlyle has ended. Could you give her a lift?"

"Of course. Are you thinking of going to Ab for the money?" Stone asked.

"Ab would never make me that kind of loan."

"You could sell him your secretary."

"He already has one, remember?"

"Well, I'll see you at the party," Stone said. "It should be fun."

"It may be more fun than you think," Barton said. Then he hung up.

55

Before Stone left the house that evening, he called Tatiana. "How's the cleanup going?" he asked.

"Pretty well, actually," she replied.

"Would you like to join me for dinner, then?"

"Oh, I think I'm going to be very tired when we're done. Will you forgive me, if I don't?"

"Of course. I'll be at Elaine's with some friends, so if you feel like it, join us."

"If I'm up to it," she said.

Stone took a cab up to Elaine's and found Dino and Genevieve sitting with Elaine. He joined them and ordered a drink.

"So, how's it going?" Dino asked.

"So-so, I guess."

"Any progress in finding our missing piece of furniture?"

"I'm afraid not."

"So we're going to miss the payoff, then?"

"Looks that way."

"You don't seem too upset about it."

Stone shrugged. "You win some; you lose some."

"Speaking of which," Genevieve said, nodding toward the door, "here comes one of your losses."

Stone looked toward the door and saw Eliza and Edgar arriving. Genevieve was waving them over.

"Hello, Stone," Eliza said, permitting him to peck her on the cheek.

"Hello, Eliza, Edgar." He shook Edgar's hand.

"Stone, Eliza and I must thank you for the lovely wedding gift," Edgar said.

"Yes, Stone," Eliza chimed in, "it's just beautiful."

"I'm glad you like it," Stone said.

They all got up to allow the waiters to put a bigger top on the table, and more chairs were found.

Stone realized that this was the first time Eliza had crossed his mind since he had met Tatiana, and he was feeling pretty good about that. Still, he was uncomfortable, and he had a strong suspicion that Genevieve had staged all this.

"So," Dino said to Eliza and Edgar, "when are you two going to have a honeymoon?"

"Oh," Eliza said, "Edgar is fully scheduled for surgery for the next month."

"Yes," Edgar said. "I've stopped taking new elective cases, so that we can have a decent enough gap to be able to go away for a bit."

Swell, Stone thought. This is really what I want to talk about.

"And I have a lot of thank-you notes to write," Eliza said, "so it's just as well we can't get away immediately."

Stone wanted to scream.

Menus arrived, and everybody chose something. Then Genevieve and Eliza began dominating the conversation, as if they hadn't spent the whole day together in the emergency room.

Genevieve turned toward Stone. "Oh, Stone, there's a new nurse in the ER I'd like to fix you up with. She's very pretty and she's bright, too."

"Thank you, Genevieve, but I'm seeing somebody," he said with some satisfaction. He saw a flash of disbelief in her eyes.

"Oh, how nice for you. Who is the lady?"

"No one you know," Stone replied.

"Oh, come on. Tell us her name."

"Oh, all right. It's Tatiana Orlovsky."

"What a charming name!" Genevieve said, as if she didn't believe a word of it. "What does she do?"

"She's an illustrator."

"Oh, good! Does she specialize in anything?"

"She's more of a generalist."

"Well, isn't it convenient that she's come along just at this moment in your life."

Stone was embarrassed that this was going on in the presence of Eliza. "Dino," he said, in a desperate attempt to change the subject, "what's new in the world of crime?"

"Same old, same old," Dino said. "You know how it goes." He gave a little shrug, as if to say you're on your own, pal.

"Excuse me," Stone said, getting up. He went into the men's room, though he didn't need to, and splashed some water on his face, taking his time. They'd have to talk about something else, since he wasn't there, and he could rejoin the conversation when the new subject was established. He dried his face and went back to the table.

"Stone," Genevieve was saying, "while you were gone, Eliza and I were talking about having a little dinner party at Dino's and my house. Saturday night? We'd all love to meet... what was her name?"

"Tatiana," Stone said through clenched teeth.

"Can you come Saturday?"

"I'm sorry, but we've accepted an invitation to dinner in Connecticut that night, so we're going up for the weekend."

Genevieve smiled sweetly. "What a pity. I was sure it would be something like that."

Dino turned to his girlfriend. "Genevieve," he said softly but with an edge, "put a sock in it."

She swiveled toward Dino but was met with a steely gaze. "I'm sorry, Stone," she said, a little sheepishly.

At that moment the heavens opened for Stone along with the door to the restaurant, and Tatiana walked in, looking fresh and ready for the evening. Stone, vastly relieved, stood up and kissed her on the lips. "Tatiana Orlovsy, this is Dino, Genevieve, Eliza, Edgar and Elaine."

"I'm so pleased to meet all of you," Tatiana said, taking an offered chair next to Stone. She turned to him. "The men finished half an hour ago, and you'd never know anything had happened in the kitchen."

"I'm *really* glad you could make it," Stone said. He turned to the others. "Tatiana had a small fire in her kitchen last night, but there was no serious damage."

"No," Tatiana said, "just smoke and water, and it cleaned up nicely." A waiter brought her a menu, and she ordered.

Stone watched and listened as, for the rest of the evening, Tatiana charmed and amused everybody except, maybe, Genevieve.

In the cab home, Stone kissed Tatiana. "I can't tell you how glad I was to see you this evening."

"Just what every girl wants to hear," she replied, kissing him back.

"I used to go out with Eliza before she and Edgar were married, and Genevieve has been giving me a hard time about it."

"Well," Tatiana said, "she won't do that while *I'm* around. You're now under my protection. Oh, I talked to my lawyer, and he's applied for a subpoena for Henry's financial records."

"Good."

"I still wonder how you know about those expenses."

"Trade secret," Stone said, then changed the subject.

56

When Stone got to his desk the following morning there was a message from Bill Eggers on his desk. It read: "Get your ass over here."

Stone buzzed Joan. "Is this note on my desk your interpretation of what Eggers said?"

"No. That's what he said verbatim."

"Thanks." Stone hung up and got into his jacket.

Stone reached Bill Eggers's office seconds ahead of Harlan Deal.

"Sit down, gentlemen," Eggers said.

They sat.

"Stone," Eggers said, "it grieves me to hear that you are, once again, the principal suspect—in fact, the *only* suspect—in the tampering with yet another female friend of Harlan."

"Frankly, Bill," Stone said, "I'm getting a little tired of this."

"So is Harlan," Eggers replied, "which is my point. Do you deny this?"

"Let me lay this out for you both as clearly as I can," Stone said. "I was invited to dinner at Harlan's home last Sunday evening—at the last possible moment, I might add—and I believe I caught sight of you, Bill, across a crowded room. I also encountered the lovely Carla there, in the company of Barton Cabot, so I naturally assumed that Harlan's purpose in asking me there was to observe me in her company, which I thought was a petty thing to do."

Deal came to life. "Now wait a minute—"

"When I'm finished, Harlan," Stone said. "While in Harlan's apartment I encountered another woman, who explained to me, in due course, that she was an unattached female and was amenable to seeing me socially. We spent the rest of the evening together and all our free time since then, and if Harlan doesn't like it, he can go—"

"Stone!" Eggers interjected at the last possible moment. "Let's try to maintain a sense of decorum."

"I don't see the need for that any more than I see the need for Harlan to concern himself with whom I take out," Stone replied. "He's not my client, and I owe him nothing, certainly not any explanation."

"Harlan," Eggers said in a fatherly tone, "I believe Stone has a point, too. You're both grown men, and if you insist on competing for the same women, one of you is going to win and the other is going to lose. 'It's the law of the jungle,' as someone once said in an old movie, 'and the way the cookie crumbles.' "

Deal sat and stared at Eggers but said nothing.

"Furthermore, Harlan," Eggers continued, "I am not grateful for the opportunity to involve myself in yours and Stone's petty differences, and I would appreciate it if it did not become necessary for me to do so again. This is a business relationship, and I'd like to keep it that way."

Deal finally got a word in. "You're quite right, Bill, and I apologize for having brought you into this. You and your firm have served me well, and I don't want you to think that I'm not grateful."

"Thank you, Harlan," Eggers began but was cut off.

"But if you ever again let this person," he waved in the general direction of Stone, "near any piece of business related to me, I will yank my account from this firm in short order. I hope we understand each other."

"We do, Harlan," Eggers said.

"I bid you good day," Deal said, then departed the room.

Stone started to get up but was pushed back into his chair by Eggers's voice.

"You," Eggers said, "had better take what he just said as gospel, because Harlan and Charlie Crow have put together a new real estate company; they're going to take it public, and this firm is handling all the legal work, including the IPO, and you will not fuck it up by so slavishly following your dick anywhere near it. Do I make myself clear?"

"Bill," Stone said, "I did not invite myself to this party. You brought me in, so it is incumbent upon you to keep me out of it. I would like never to see that man again under *any* circumstances." He stood up. "I will go now."

"No objections," Eggers said, then he leaned forward in his chair. "Who's the lady?"

"Her name is Tatiana Orlovsky, and she's dynamite!" Stone said, then walked out. All the way down the hall he could hear Eggers laughing.

Stone returned to his office, and as he walked in, a strange man sitting in the waiting area stood up.

"Mr. Barrington?"

"Yes?"

The man handed him a sealed envelope. "You've been served," he said, then walked out.

Joan was behind her desk. "I tried to warn you," she said, "but you wouldn't look at me."

Stone ripped open the envelope and read the subpoena. "Alienation of affection?" he said incredulously. "What is this, Victorian England?"

"You've been named a corespondent in a divorce, haven't you?" Joan said, sounding amused. "It *had* to happen."

"Oh, shut up," Stone said and went into his office. He tossed his coat across the room, sat down and called Tatiana.

"Hello?"

"Good morning," he said.

"Oh, it's so nice to hear your voice."

"And yours, as well. Your divorce has taken a turn," he said. "I've been named corespondent. The assertion is that I have alienated your affection."

"I'm so sorry, Stone, but you're guilty, after the fact."

"I'm so glad you said, 'after the fact.' Now what you should do is call your attorney and ask him to name Darlene Harris a corespondent. That's who Henry was with the other night at Elaine's, and he should see that she is served today. She lives at 682 Park Avenue."

"And how is it that you know her exact address?" Tatiana asked, with mock suspicion.

"I looked it up before I called you," he lied. "Serving her will even the score until you get his financial records, then it will be game, set and match. And, by the way, you shouldn't be surprised if this turns up in some gossip column or other. They have people at the courts who tip them off about these things."

"Oh, no," she said.

"The price of freedom, my dear."

"Well, then, I'll shut up and pay it. What kind of clothes will I need in Connecticut this weekend?"

"Country stuff like tweeds for the daytime and, I don't know, maybe an LBD for the dinner party. It's black tie."

"Is black tie the norm up there?"

"No. It's very odd. I sense some sort of special occasion, but I don't know what it is. You'll enjoy seeing the house, though; it's very beautiful."

"That's not all I'm going to enjoy," she said, then hung up.

"That's great."

"Yes, it is. Now, here's what I want you to do: First of all, I want you to be at Mildred's house tomorrow morning at ten-thirty."

"All right, I can do that if I leave early enough."

"And on the way, I want you to call... What's Mildred's lawyer's name?"

"Creighton Adams."

"I want you to call him and have him tell the guards on the property to let us in the house at ten-thirty."

"I can do that, and I'm sure he won't have any objections. Why do you want me there?"

"Because Peter is bringing his witness, and I want one, too, so that I can hold him to account for anything he says tomorrow. Also, I would not be surprised if, after he has satisfied himself about the quality of the collection, he will have something for me to sign, and if so, I want you there to read it."

"All right."

"I'll see you tomorrow morning at ten-thirty, and don't be late."

"I'll be there," Stone said. "But Barton, there's something you'd better be prepared for."

"What's that?"

"I noticed that you included a photograph of your remaining mahogany secretary in your prospectus, but it's not listed in the inventory we prepared and that you and Mildred signed."

"Don't be concerned about that. If it comes up, just follow my lead."

"I do have a very important concern, Barton."

"What's that?"

"You've told me that you don't know whether the stolen secretary is the original or the copy. I am not going to be a party to defrauding the Metropolitan Museum, so you must do nothing to put me in that position. If you do, I'll have to do whatever is necessary to protect myself."

57

Late that night, as Stone was returning home from dinner, the phone rang.

"Hello?"

"Stone, it's Barton Cabot."

"Good evening, Barton."

"I'm sorry to call you so late, but something has come up."

"What's wrong?"

"Nothing. Quite the contrary."

"Okay, what's right?"

"I've just had a call from Peter Cavanaugh, the director of the Metropolitan Museum of Art."

"Oh?"

"Yes. He wants to see Mildred's collection tomorrow morning at eleven, and he's bringing along his chief curator of American furniture."

"That's great."

"Greater than you know. This means two things: One, he's moving fast in order to get in ahead of the other museums, and two, he's already got the money, or most of it, promised by some benefactor or benefactors."

"I understand, and you need not be concerned. If I sell the Met the secretary, it will be the original, I assure you. By the time this is over, you will understand fully."

"Thank you, Barton. I'll see you at ten-thirty tomorrow morning."

"Good-bye." Barton hung up.

Stone was up early the following morning and on the road by eight-thirty. On the way he called Creighton Adams and arranged for them to be let into the house.

He arrived in Bristol five minutes early and found Barton already in the house. He gave the guard his name and walked in.

Barton was pacing around the living room with the housekeeper, making minute adjustments to the positions of things in the room while she was putting coffee and cups on the sideboard. When he was finished there, he visited both the library and the dining room, then went upstairs to the bedrooms while Stone had coffee.

Barton came down looking happy, and the housekeeper returned to her work. "We're ready," he said, then he was immediately on his feet, looking out the window. "They're here early."

The housekeeper answered the door and brought the two men into the living room, accompanied by a photographer and his assistant, who was laden with equipment.

Barton introduced Stone, and Cavanaugh introduced Julian Whately, his curator of American furniture. The two men were craning and turning their heads like a pair of exotic birds as they took in the room's contents; they were clearly excited.

"Would you like some coffee?" Barton asked.

"Perhaps later," Cavanaugh said. "Let's get started."

"Stone and I will sit quietly while you and Julian examine the pieces," Barton said. "When you're done here, I'll take you through the other rooms."

Armed with their copy of Barton's prospectus, the two men began their tour of the living room, piece by piece, while the photographer started taking pictures of the room and the individual pieces.

Barton drank coffee while Stone read the *Times.* He was about to start on the crossword when Cavanaugh finally spoke to them.

"May we see the library and the dining room now, please?" he said.

"Of course," Barton replied. "Right this way." He led them out of the living room, and Stone started on the crossword. Half an hour later the three men came out of the library and took the elevator upstairs.

Stone had finished the crossword and was looking idly about the living room when they returned.

"Now I'd like some coffee," Cavanaugh said.

Barton filled their cups from the heated urn, and they all sat down.

"First of all, Barton," Cavanaugh said, "there is a piece missing: the Goddard-Townsend secretary."

"Ah, yes, the secretary. I have already removed that to my home in Connecticut."

Stone tensed at this, feeling they might suddenly be in deeper water.

"I'm still not certain whether I will offer the secretary as part of the collection," Barton said. "I may retain it and sell it at a later date."

"Barton," Cavanaugh said, "I would regard the collection as incomplete without the secretary."

"I can understand how you might feel that way, Peter," Barton replied. "I'm prepared to consider including it in the sale, but that will depend on your willingness to address its proven value."

"I came here willing, upon a careful inspection of the collection, to offer you forty-five million dollars."

Barton shrugged. "That is a figure nearly high enough for the collection, without the secretary."

"The proven value of the secretary is twelve million dollars."

"That was in 1989," Barton said, "and the number at that time was twelve point one million. Need I point out that fine American pieces are bringing a great deal more now than they did then and, moreover, that a private collector bought the last Goddard-Townsend secretary? There are a great many more billionaire private collectors around now than then. I should think a well-publicized auction might result in a bidding frenzy that could well bring double the last price for such a piece."

Cavanaugh and Whately exchanged a long glance. Whately gave a tiny shrug.

"All right, Barton, tell me what you want for the lot, including the secretary."

"If you require me to name a number, Peter, that will be the price, without further negotiation. You will have to take it or leave it."

"What is the number?"

"First of all there are conditions beyond the price."

"What are they?"

"I want the pieces in the living room, library and dining room to be permanently displayed at the Metropolitan in replicas of the original rooms. If you wish, you may alternate pieces from the bedrooms and the attic in replicas of other rooms, as space allows. I want the collection to be called the Caleb and Mildred Strong Collection, and I want my name under theirs as originating curator. After that, you may list the name or names of benefactors."

Cavanaugh looked at Whately and got a small nod, then he turned back to Barton. "The name or names of benefactors may have to be listed in such a way as to be equal to those of the Strongs."

Barton nodded his agreement.

"Are there any other conditions?"

"The collection must remain in my possession, housed in a suitable, secured facility for one year, after which the sale will close."

"You're thinking of the capital gains tax?" Cavanaugh asked.

"Of course."

"It will take us at least that long to arrange space and build the rooms, anyway, so that is acceptable."

"And you will pay for insurance and security."

"In that case, we would have to house the collection in the museum's storage areas. We could say that you're loaning the collection to us for a year, in order to satisfy your tax requirement. Perhaps we could display a few of the more important pieces, like the secretary, with our current collection."

Barton looked at Stone questioningly. "Would lending them the collection for a year satisfy the capital gains requirement?"

"I'm not an accountant or tax lawyer, but I believe so."

"Also, Barton," Cavanaugh said, "such an arrangement would dictate that we pay the full price of the collection at the time of closing. That way, you would not have to pay the full income tax on a down payment."

Barton thought about this for a long moment.

Stone knew he was thinking about the nineteen million dollars he needed to close the deal, and that he didn't have.

"Barton," he said, "perhaps you should ask for a down payment and accept the tax consequences." He was sure Barton knew exactly what he meant.

"No, Stone. Peter is right. We'll close on the full amount in a year."

Stone nodded, but he had to wonder where Barton was going to come up with the nineteen million by Tuesday.

"Now, Barton," Cavanaugh said, "the number?"

"Seventy million dollars, *but* I will make a donation to the Metropolitan of five million, upon close of the sale. And in any publicity, interviews or conversations about the sale, you will state that the secretary accounted for twenty-five million of the seventy million dollars you paid."

Cavanaugh looked at Barton appraisingly for a long moment, then he said, "Agreed, upon the condition of inspection of the secretary by Julian and me."

"When?"

"Julian and I are both coming to a dinner party at Abner Kramer's house on Saturday night. I understand that you live nearby?"

"Yes."

"Then we could inspect the piece that afternoon?"

"Yes, that's agreeable. Stone and I will be at that dinner, too, and I would be very pleased if you and Julian and your wives or companions, if they are coming, would be my guests overnight or for the weekend, if you like."

"Thank you, Barton, that would be most agreeable."

"Then, Peter," Barton said, "let's fill in the blanks in that agreement in your pocket and get it signed."

And they did so.

58

Stone and Barton stood on the sidewalk outside Mildred Strong's house and watched the two men from the Met drive away.

"That was quite a performance," Stone said.

"The performance of my life," Barton said, mopping his brow. "I'm still sweating."

"You can retire after this one," Stone said.

"Oh, no. I'm going to copy a few of Mildred's pieces while I still own them, and selling them should keep me busy for a few years."

"Have you figured out what sort of deal Charlie Crow and Mildred made?"

"I think so, but we'll know for sure on Saturday night."

"Why is Ab Kramer collecting you, Cavanaugh and Whately at the same dinner party?"

"I think because he has something he wants to show us," Barton said.

Before Stone could ask what, or how he was going to come up with nineteen million dollars, Barton shook his hand and drove away.

Stone arrived home, garaged his car and entered his office the back way. Joan immediately came into the office.

"There's a Mr. Henry Kennerly to see you," she said.

"Oh?"

"I believe that's the gentleman who is accusing you of adultery with his wife?"

"I believe you're right," Stone said. "Wait until I buzz you, then show him in and stick around while I talk to him. I want a witness."

"Whatever you say," Joan replied, then went back to her desk.

Stone took off his jacket and tie and hung them up, then he opened his desk drawer and took out two rolls of quarters, putting a roll in each of the front pockets of his trousers. He buzzed Joan. She opened the door to Stone's office and showed the man in, then stood next to the door.

Henry Kennerly was even bigger than Stone remembered from his sighting at Elaine's. He was at least two inches taller than Stone and forty pounds heavier, and it wasn't all fat. He had a longer reach, too, Stone observed. He had known people like Kennerly before, starting in the schoolyard: bigger than everybody else and meaner, and accustomed to pushing people around.

"Good morning, Mr. Kennerly," Stone said. "Now kindly leave my offices at once. You are unwelcome here."

Kennerly moved his right hand. There was a click, and a steel police baton telescoped to its full length.

Stone stood up, put his hands in his pockets and walked around his desk. "You'd better make your first swing count," Stone said, "because you're not going to get a second one. After that, I'm going to punish you for invading my offices and refusing to leave when asked, while my secretary calls the police."

"I don't care if she does," Kennerly said. "I'm going to beat you to a pulp."

"Thank you for that warning. Did you hear that, Joan?"

"Yes," she replied.

"As soon as this is over call nine-one-one. And, Mr. Kennerly, if you don't mind a little free legal advice, possession by a civilian of the baton you're holding is a felony in New York City. You'll be charged with aggravated assault."

"It'll be worth it," Kennerly said, advancing. He was big, but not very fast, and his body language telegraphed his move. He swung the baton in a wide arc at Stone's head.

Stone removed his hands from his pockets, stepped into the move and ducked as the thing whistled past him. With a roll of quarters in each hand, he swung twice, first straight into the man's solar plexus. With Kennerly's weight moving toward him, that brought him to his knees. Then Stone walked behind him and punched him in the back of the neck, and the big man fell forward onto his face, stunned.

Joan left the room.

Stone went to his desk, put the quarters in a drawer and took out his old NYPD handcuffs. He walked over to Kennerly, put a knee on his back to pin him in place and cuffed him.

Joan walked back into the office. "I saw it all," she said. "The police are on their way."

"Thank you, Joan," Stone said. He sat down at his desk and called Dino.

"Bacchetti."

"It's Stone."

"Hi."

"You remember that gorgeous woman you met at dinner?"

"How could I forget? Oh, I'm sorry about Genevieve's behavior. That's been straightened out."

"Thanks. Speaking of straightening out, the lady's soon-to-be ex-husband, one Henry Kennerly, is lying on the floor of my office. He came in here, threatened to beat me to a pulp and assaulted me with a perfectly illegal police baton, which I think qualifies nicely as a deadly weapon. I disarmed him and cuffed him, and Joan has called nine-one-one, having witnessed the whole business. I just wanted you to know that he'll be at the precinct soon, and I'll come in later and sign the complaint."

"I'll fill it out for you. You want me to forge your signature?"

"Sure, why not, and I wouldn't mind if it took a while to process him. See if you can house him with one or more persons he won't feel very comfortable with; I want this to be an unforgettable experience for him."

"Sure thing."

"I know his lawyer's name, because he had me served yesterday." Stone gave him the name. "Call him when Mr. Kennerly feels well enough to ask for his attorney."

"Will do."

"See you at dinner?"

"I'll be there."

Stone hung up. Kennerly was stirring now, and swearing. A moment later Joan led two police officers into the room.

"This our guy?" one of them asked.

"That's the assailant," Stone replied. "I'd appreciate it if you'd use your cuffs and give me mine back." He gave them an account of the incident, Joan backed it up, then the two cops recuffed Kennerly, stood him up and frog-marched him out of the room.

"I'll get you for this!" Kennerly screamed on his way out.

"Please make note of that threat," Stone called to the cops and got a thumbs-up in return.

Stone went back to his desk and called Tatiana.

"Hello?"

"Hi, it's Stone. Good news: Henry just came over here and took a swing at me with a club."

"Oh, Stone, I'm so sorry. Are you badly hurt?"

"Not at all. I said it was good news. He's on the way to the police station now, and I imagine it will be some hours before his attorney can bail him out. Call your lawyer and tell him to add assault with a deadly weapon to Henry's list of misdeeds."

"I will do so immediately."

"I think your settlement problems will all be over before the weekend, to which I am greatly looking forward."

"And I as well."

"Pick you up Saturday morning at ten?"

"See you then."

Stone hung up, feeling he had done a good day's work.

59

On Saturday morning Stone collected first Tatiana from her home and then Carla from the Carlyle, and they headed north to Litchfield County.

The two women chatted amiably, which was good, as long as they weren't chatting about him. He hated the thought of the two of them in the ladies' room together.

"How much longer are you singing at the Carlyle?" Tatiana asked.

"I've just finished three months in the Bemelmens Bar," Carla said, "and, after a few weeks' rest and preparation, I'm moving into the Café Carlyle, across the hall, with a bigger backup group, and we'll be there through New Year's Eve."

"That sounds like a wonderful step up," Tatiana said.

"It certainly is a promotion, and the money's better, too. And I'll like having a six-piece group backing me, instead of just a bass player. The arrangements are being written now."

They drove on, and the conversation fell away in favor of exclamations about the increasingly beautiful fall foliage as they headed north. Finally, they arrived at Barton's house, and he came out the kitchen door to greet them.

"Stone, Peter Cavanaugh and Julian Whately will be staying over tonight—no women or companions along this time—so will you and Tatiana come over around six for a drink?"

"Of course."

"Good. Peter will have the final contract ready for our signatures, and we'll have plenty of witnesses. "I'd also like your help in showing them the mahogany secretary."

"I'll be glad to help." Stone got Carla's bags from the car, then he and Tatiana continued to his house.

"So," Tatiana asked, "who will be at dinner tonight?"

"The four of us, plus Peter Cavanaugh, director of the Metropolitan Museum, and his furniture expert, Julian Whately," Stone said. "Then there'll be our hosts, Abner Kramer and his wife, and, I suspect, Mr. and Mrs. Charlie Crow."

"Oh, God," Tatiana said. "I have to deal with them again?"

"I think they're going to have very little to say this evening. The subject is going to be furniture, which is a little out of Charlie's line."

"Do we have time for a, ah, nap before cocktails?"

"Oh, yes, plenty of time."

They arrived at the house; he gave her a quick tour, then took their luggage upstairs. In a moment, they were in each other's arms.

Darkness came early, since they were back on standard time, and the night was chilly but bright, with many stars and a waning but still bright moon. The moonlight glittered on the lake as they drove along its shores to Barton's little peninsula.

Everyone else had gathered in the study for drinks by the time they arrived, and a roaring fire had taken the chill from the air. They were given drinks and fell to talking, mostly about furniture.

"Barton," Peter Cavanaugh asked, "what do you think Ab Kramer has in mind for this evening?"

"I think he plans to impress us, especially you and Julian."

"Has he bought something new?"

"He has a Goddard-Townsend mahogany desk and bookcase," Barton replied, "one almost as nice as your new one."

"Oh? Two popping up at once?"

"Well, not exactly, since Ab's secretary is a fake."

"How do you know that?" Cavanaugh asked.

"Because I made it myself, in my workshop."

"Really? Does Ab know it's a fake?"

"Well, since he didn't buy it from me, I don't know what provenance the seller offered him. He'll be looking for approval from you and Julian, so please, don't puncture his balloon and his ego. I think he'll be happy, if you're just noncommittal."

"As you wish, Barton. Now, are you ready to show us the real thing?"

"Of course. Let's go out to the barn, and bring your drinks." Barton lead them out through the kitchen door to the barn, unlocked its massive door and showed everyone inside.

"This is quite a barn," Cavanaugh said, looking around.

"Yes, we've done a lot of good work here. Stone, will you give me a hand, please?"

Barton and Stone unlocked the large cabinet, removed the false back wall and rolled out the Goddard-Townsend secretary on its dolly into a carefully designed pool of light, then stepped away.

Cavanaugh and Whately circled the piece slowly, taking it all in, then Cavanaugh stood back while Whately circled it again with a pocket flashlight and a small magnifying glass.

Stone stood next to Carla, who was watching everything with interest. "I believe I know your secret," Stone said to her.

She looked at him appraisingly. "Secret?"

"I thought Peter Cavanaugh came up with seventy million dollars awfully quickly."

"I wouldn't know about that," Carla said.

"Of course you would, since you got Eduardo to put up the money."

"*Shhhh,*" she whispered. "How did you know?"

"I've known Eduardo for some years, as you well know, and I know that he's on the board of the Metropolitan and one of its most generous contributors for special projects."

"Don't you tell Barton," she hissed.

"I won't, if you'll tell me how much Eduardo committed to."

"Eighty million," she whispered, "and don't you tell Barton that, either."

"I promise," Stone said.

Finally, Whately came and stood beside Cavanaugh, and Stone found himself holding his breath.

"Magnificent," Whately said, "and in absolutely outstanding condition, the result, no doubt, of having been in one house since it was made."

Cavanaugh clapped Whately on the back. "My judgment, precisely," he said. He turned to the others and raised his glass. "A toast," he said, "to the good eye and prescient judgment of the Met's friend, Barton Cabot, not to mention his perfect timing in acquiring Mildred Strong's collection. May we always be friends and colleagues."

Stone took a large swig of his drink, greatly relieved. They went back into the house, Stone read the contract, and it was duly signed and witnessed.

They trooped over to Ab Kramer's place, Cavanaugh and Whately in Stone's car, since Barton was driving his usual van. This was the first time Stone had approached the house through the front gate, and the landscaping and well-lighted exterior made the place all the more impressive.

They were received on the front steps by Abner Kramer and his beautiful wife, and hands were shaken all around. They were led inside to an entrance hall, where Charlie Crow and his blonde bombshell awaited them. A butler took their coats, and they were led into the living room for cocktails.

The butler and a maid served them champagne or poured drinks, while another maid circled with a silver bowl of beluga caviar on a tray, with small buckwheat pancakes and condiments. Stone reckoned there was two thousand dollars' worth of caviar in that bowl, and he dug in enthusiastically.

After a couple of drinks they were called to dinner, and Stone was happy to be seated between Tatiana and Mrs. Kramer, whose conversation was of art and the needs of the Metropolitan. It seemed likely Ab Kramer expected to be hit up for a donation before the evening was out.

After dessert, Peter Cavanaugh stood with his glass. "Ab, Charlotte, if you will permit me, I'd like to make an announcement. This won't be made public for a few weeks, so I would be grateful for your discretion." There were murmurs of agreement, then Cavanaugh continued. "I'd like you all to be the first to know that the Metropolitan Museum of Art has today, with the brilliant participation of our friend, Barton Cabot, acquired the largest and most perfect collection of eighteenth-century American furniture in the United States: the collection of Mildred Strong of Bristol, Rhode Island."

There was glad applause from everyone, then Cavanaugh continued. "I wish I could take you there and show it all to you tonight, but that will have to wait for a year or so, while the Metropolitan clears gallery space and constructs replicas of the principal rooms of Mrs. Strong's house, where the collection will be housed and displayed. I assure you, you will all be invited to the opening. Thank you."

Cavanaugh sat down, and Ab Kramer stood and gave a brief but charming response. Then his wife invited the ladies to join her for coffee, in the manner of an English country house, while the gentlemen retired to Mr. Kramer's study for half an hour of brandy and cigars.

As the butler opened the double doors, the men filed into the room to find, perfectly lit, the second Goddard-Townsend secretary some of them had seen that evening.

Everyone politely examined the secretary, and Julian Whately and Peter Cavanaugh gave it particularly close scrutiny. Finally, they pulled back, gazed at the piece and simultaneously nodded.

"An exceptional piece, very fine," Whately said.

"Absolutely," Cavanaugh concurred.

Stone made his own cursory inspection, feeling behind the piece for the brass plate. It was not there. He opened a couple of drawers and looked at the dovetailing, then joined the others as the cigars and brandy were passed.

Stone, who despised cigars, sat next to Barton, who didn't smoke. "Since it's practically indistinguishable from the other secretary," he whispered, "why didn't they think it was the genuine article?"

"Because," Barton said, "if you ask an expert to authenticate a piece, presenting it as genuine, he will look for evidence that it's a fake. But, if you tell him it's a fake, he will not contradict you."

Peter Cavanaugh turned to Abner Kramer. “Ab, do you mind if Julian and I have a look at some of your pieces in the living room?”

Kramer stood up. “Not at all. I’ll give you the tour.”

Cavanaugh held up a hand. “No, no, we’d just like to wander. You attend to your other guests.”

“As you wish,” Kramer said, sitting down.

Cavanaugh gave Barton a wink as he and Whately left the room, leaving Stone and Barton alone with Kramer and Crow.

Barton spoke first. “Ab, I assume you have provenance for your piece.”

“Of course,” Kramer replied, “would you like to see it? I’d appreciate your opinion on its authenticity.”

“Thank you, yes.”

Kramer walked across the room to his desk, opened a drawer, removed an unsealed envelope and brought it to Barton.

Barton opened the envelope and read the two sheets of paper inside. He shook his head. “Ab, I’m very sorry to tell you this, but I’m very much afraid you’ve been defrauded.”

"Impossible," Kramer said. "That bill of sale and letter are on Mildred Strong's own letterhead, in her own handwriting, which I've had authenticated by an expert."

"Oh, it's Mildred's stationery and handwriting," Barton said, "but it's a fraudulent bill of sale."

Kramer looked a little concerned now. "Why would you say that, Barton?"

Barton turned to Crow. "Charlie, when did you remove the secretary from Mrs. Strong's house?"

"Why, the following afternoon," Crow replied, but there was a sheen of sweat on his forehead.

"That's impossible, Ab," Barton said. "You see, Stone and I were in the house that afternoon and for all of the next day, making an inventory of Mildred's collection, and Charlie was never in the house."

"That's a lie!" Crow said angrily.

"And how much did you pay Mildred for her secretary, Charlie?"

"A very high price, I assure you."

"Ab, you know that to be a lie, because you paid Charlie seven million dollars for the piece." Barton held up a hand. "Please don't deny it. I sold the Met Mildred's secretary today for twenty-five million dollars. Peter will confirm that, if you like. And her piece is safely locked away in a secure location."

Kramer turned and looked at Crow. "Charlie?"

"Don't bother asking Charlie," Barton said. "He'll just keep lying to you. Charlie didn't buy any piece of furniture from Mildred. What he bought was this." He held up the envelope containing Mildred's letter. "It cost her nothing to write it, and she gained half a million dollars. She would never allow Charlie to walk away with the centerpiece of her beloved collection."

"Then how did you get the whole collection?" Kramer demanded.

"I offered her a million dollars a year for the rest of her life, and the balance of the agreed sum to her estate upon her death."

"I'm sorry, Barton," Kramer said, collecting himself. "But you can't prove any of this. It's your word against Charlie's, and I choose to believe him."

"Ab, Charlie and some friends of his beat me up and stole that secretary from me, and I can prove it. If you will go to the piece and remove the left-hand drawer, you will find my initials burned into the back side of it."

Kramer stared at Barton for a moment, then went to the secretary and removed the drawer. He looked at it, then turned to Crow. "The initials are there. Charlie, how could Barton's initials be there, unless he had had possession of the secretary before you did?"

"Come on, Ab. You didn't care where I got it," Crow said.

Barton spoke again. "Ab, I know you are in a difficult position, but I want to offer you a way out of it. You have three choices, really: One, Stone and I can load the piece into my van and return it to my home; two, you can write me a check for twenty million dollars and right now; three... well, that choice would involve the police and the newspapers, and I could write a very interesting article for *Antiques* magazine. But Peter and Julian will tell you that twenty million is a cheap price for a Goddard-Townsend secretary. They paid twenty-five million dollars for theirs, thus establishing a market."

Stone now knew why Barton had specified a value for the piece in the contract with the Metropolitan.

"But I've already paid Charlie seven million dollars for it," Kramer said.

"That, I'm afraid, is between you and Charlie," Barton said. "I'm sure you'll find a way to extract it from him."

Charlie had gone very quiet and was staring at the floor.

Kramer thought about it for a minute, then went back to his desk, removed a large alligator-bound checkbook from a drawer, wrote a check and took it to Barton. "I'll need Monday to move the money from my brokerage account," he said.

"Of course," Barton said, accepting the check. "You may have until three o'clock Monday afternoon to move the money, and at that time I'll provide you with a genuine provenance for the piece. I'm sure you no longer wish to be associated with Charlie's fraudulent one." He tucked the documents Mildred had sold Crow into his pocket, along with Kramer's check.

Cavanaugh and Whately returned to the study. "Beautiful things, Ab," Cavanaugh said. "I hope you'll think of giving the museum some of them at some future date."

"I'll consider that, Peter," Kramer said. He seemed to have recovered from the shock of writing the check.

The women rejoined them, and they chatted for another hour, then the guests took their leave.

Back in Barton's study, Stone took his host aside. "So the secretary you said was made in Charleston was yours all along."

"Yes," Barton replied, "it was. I thought I could get more from Ab for the piece by exposing Charlie than by auctioning it."

"And, of course, you would save the million dollars you promised me for finding it."

Barton looked stricken. "I really must apologize for that, Stone. I never intended to withhold your reward."

"Then you won't mind writing me a check now, will you?"

Barton swallowed hard. "Of course not," he sighed. He went to his desk, wrote the check and handed it to Stone. "I wouldn't want you to think I was trying to avoid paying you."

"Oh, I was certain you wouldn't do that," Stone said. He reached into his pocket and removed a small leather pouch and dangled it from its string. "Otherwise, I'd be minting my own very rare twenty-dollar gold pieces." He dropped the pouch into Barton's hand. "I found it in a drawer of Ab's secretary when I was examining it."

Barton smiled and slipped the die into his own pocket. "Then I think our business is concluded, and now we can concentrate on being friends."

"I'd like that, Barton," Stone said, tucking the check away.

EPILOGUE

On Monday morning in New York, after a good breakfast at Stone's house, Tatiana called her attorney and spoke briefly with him, then hung up the phone. "Henry has agreed to my settlement terms," she said, smiling. "I think his night in jail made him more reasonable."

"I'm delighted to hear it," Stone said, kissing her. "You'll soon be a free woman."

"I'm looking forward to that," Tatiana said. "Now, I must go home and get some things done."

"Dinner tonight?" Stone asked.

"Of course," she replied. "I'm going to be taking up most of your dinner hours from now on."

"I wouldn't have it any other way," Stone replied. He walked her over to her house through the garden and set her luggage in the kitchen, then returned to his own house and went into his office. He read slowly through the *Times* and stopped at the business section. A headline on the first page caught his eye.

KRAMER COMPANY JOINS DEAL & CROW IN REAL ESTATE VENTURE

Abner Kramer, in a fax to this newspaper on Sunday afternoon, announced that he had paid Charles Crow of the new firm of Deal & Crow seven million dollars for two hundred thousand of Mr. Crow's personal shares in the new company, which will have a public offering next month. Observers were surprised at the transaction, since Mr. Crow might have profited by retaining his shares for the IPO.

The rest of the piece didn't matter. Ab Kramer had extracted his pound of flesh from Charlie Crow's carcass.

Joan came in with the mail, and Stone handed her Barton Cabot's check. "Please deposit this," he said. "Then write Dino a check for two hundred thousand and one to Bob Cantor for fifty thousand. Then give the IRS their share."

"Good," Joan said. "What's left will just about cover the bill on top of your mail." She went back to her office.

Stone opened the envelope and found the invoice for the conversion of his airplane to a turboprop. Joan was right; what was left of Barton's money would just about cover it.

ACKNOWLEDGMENTS

The Goddard-Townsend desk and bookcase is real, and the one sold at Christie's in June 1989 actually brought $12.1 million, at that time the highest price ever paid for a piece of American furniture. I am told that it was bought by a member of a Texas oil family and, indeed, now stands in a house that rests upon the San Andreas Fault in California.

I am grateful to my friend Nick Brown, who sold the desk at Christie's, for sending me to Dean Failey, the gentleman who was in charge of arranging the sale. Mr. Failey was extraordinarily helpful to me in learning about the piece and its sale.

Before selling the secretary, Nick Brown had a replica built by a very fine cabinetmaker for a rumored price of $38,000. I tried very hard to learn the name and address of the maker, but neither Nick nor Mr. Failey nor Christie's nor Google was able to help me. Mr. Failey did, however, tell me of the maker's search in Central or South America for the perfect mahogany tree and of its delivery to the United States disguised as a shipping crate, and I have shamelessly adapted that story to my own ends in this book. Whoever and wherever the gentleman is, I thank him.

I am, once again, grateful to my agent, Morton Janklow, of

Janklow & Nesbit, and especially to his principal associate, Anne Sibbald, and to all the other folks at J&N for their hard work on my behalf over the past twenty-seven years.

I am grateful, too, to my publisher, Ivan Held; to Michael Barson, head of publicity at Putnam, and his hardworking staff (Michael also works hard); and, especially, to my editor, the incredibly light-fingered Rachel Kahan, for her support and guidance.

AUTHOR'S NOTE

I am happy to hear from readers, but you should know that if you write to me in care of my publisher, three to six months will pass before I receive your letter, and when it finally arrives it will be one among many, and I will not be able to reply.

However, if you have access to the Internet, you may visit my website at www.stuartwoods.com, where there is a button for sending me e-mail. So far, I have been able to reply to all of my e-mail, and I will continue to try to do so.

If you send me an e-mail and do not receive a reply, it is because you are among an alarming number of people who have entered their e-mail address incorrectly in their mail software. I have many of my replies returned as undeliverable.

Remember: e-mail, reply; snail mail, no reply.

When you e-mail, please do not send attachments, as I *never* open these. They can take twenty minutes to download, and they often contain viruses.

Please do not place me on your mailing lists for funny stories, prayers, political causes, charitable fund-raising, petitions or sentimental claptrap. I get enough of that from people I already know.

Generally speaking, when I get e-mail addressed to a large number of people, I immediately delete it without reading it.

Please do not send me your ideas for a book, as I have a policy of writing only what I myself invent. If you send me story ideas, I will immediately delete them without reading them. If you have a good idea for a book, write it yourself, but I will not be able to advise you on how to get it published. Buy a copy of *Writer's Market* at any bookstore; that will tell you how.

Anyone with a request concerning events or appearances may e-mail it to me or send it to: Publicity Department, Penguin Group (USA) Inc., 375 Hudson Street, New York, NY 10014.

Those ambitious folk who wish to buy film, dramatic or television rights to my books should contact Matthew Snyder, Creative Artists Agency, 9830 Wilshire Boulevard, Beverly Hills, CA 90212–1825.

Those who wish to make offers for rights of a literary nature should contact Anne Sibbald, Janklow & Nesbit, 445 Park Avenue, New York, NY 10022. (Note: This is not an invitation for you to send her your manuscript or to solicit her to be your agent.)

If you want to know if I will be signing books in your city, please visit my website, www.stuartwoods.com, where the tour schedule will be published a month or so in advance. If you wish me to do a book signing in your locality, ask your favorite bookseller to contact his Penguin representative or the Penguin publicity department with the request.

If you find typographical or editorial errors in my book and feel an irresistible urge to tell someone, please write to Rachel Kahan at Penguin's address above. Do not e-mail your discoveries to me, as I will already have learned about them from others.

A list of my published works appears in the front of this book and on my website. All the novels are still in print in paperback and can be found at or ordered from any bookstore. If you wish to obtain hardcover copies of earlier novels or of the two nonfiction books, a good used-book store or one of the online bookstores can help you find them. Otherwise, you will have to go to a great many garage sales.